the
LIFE
of the
WORLD
to
COME

the
LIFE
of the
WORLD
to
COME

DAN CLUCHEY

ST. MARTIN'S PRESS

NEW YORK

THE LIFE OF THE WORLD TO COME. Copyright © 2016 by Daniel Cluchey. All rights reserved. Printed in the United States of America. For information, address St. Martin's Press, 175 Fifth Avenue, New York, N.Y. 10010.

www.stmartins.com

Designed by Philip Mazzone

Library of Congress Cataloging-in-Publication Data

Names: Cluchey, Dan, author.
Title: The life of the world to come : a novel / Dan Cluchey.
Description: First edition. | New York : St. Martin's Press, 2016.
Identifiers: LCCN 2016000024| ISBN 9781250077165 (hardcover) |
    ISBN 9781466889019 (e-book)
Classification: LCC PS3603.L83 L54 2016 | DDC 813'.6—dc23
LC record available at http://lccn.loc.gov/2016000024

Our books may be purchased in bulk for promotional, educational, or business use. Please contact your local bookseller or the Macmillan Corporate and Premium Sales Department at 1-800-221-7945, extension 5442, or by e-mail at MacmillanSpecialMarkets@macmillan.com.

First Edition: June 2016

10 9 8 7 6 5 4 3 2 1

For Miriam, who turned my worst facts into fictions

"I am the last president of the United States!"

—JAMES BUCHANAN

the
LIFE
of the
WORLD
to
COME

ONE

"I HAVE A THEORY ABOUT THE UNIVERSE that, if true, will just blow the lid off of everything," Fiona whispered to me from her side of the hospital bed.

"Go on."

"You're not listening if you're playing with the chart," she said, but what she didn't understand—what she *couldn't* understand—was that I could play with the chart and listen at the same time. I relented, although, again, I could have read the chart—actually just a frayed clipboard gripping salmon and citrine forms, and not at all the chart you think of when you think of the many graphs that describe how you are living—I knew that I could have clap-clap-clapped at the chart while listening and done well.

"Okay. So would you agree that time is infinite in both directions? I mean infinite into the past and the future."

"This sounds pretty heavy, Fiona dear."

"Do you agree or not?" she inquired roughly, turning suddenly so close that I was sure I could feel the breath of her "not" winnow through the wires of my unripe beard.

"I need to know first where this is going, because it sounds pretty heavy," I said, chart-free but now snapping at the hair elastic she kept stationed always around her stalky wrist.

"Don't be a brat. This is groundbreaking new knowledge, alright? This could be Descartes—I'm essentially the new Descartes right now, or Kierkegaard. I mean I could be, if I'm right. Do you agree about time?"

"Do I agree that it's infinite? I mean, there was a point in the past where no life existed, right?"

"I don't mean life; I mean time. Even if there's no life, there's time and some sort of existence. It's not nothingness. What I mean is . . . there's a venue, even if there are no planets or stars or anything."

"Got it. Yes, I have no reason to believe that there isn't an eternal venue that spans out infinitely into the past and the future."

Fiona's imagination was a tempest, and this sort of conversation—which I believed that nobody ever had, anywhere—was for us nothing short of typical, and this was simply because half of us was her. With two lazy fingernails, I traced her skin from its point of exposure just above her left elbow and just below the amorphous opening of her pale green gown diagonally down to the wrist for another snap. Again: elbow, wrist, snap.

"Okay," she continued, "so if time is infinite, then everything that could possibly happen in the universe—say, for example, the formation of Earth—has to happen, not just once, but an infinite number of times."

"You're talking infinite Earths?"

"I'm saying the Earth we live on, let's say it gets destroyed in a billion years. Hundreds of trillions of years go by, and more planets are formed, but they're all different. If time is infinite, though, then trillions of trillions of years later—or before!—eventually the exact circumstances have to come together again to form another planet exactly like Earth, even if it takes billions of planets similar to Earth but not *exactly* like it. You dig?"

"I dig," I said, even though I only maybe half-dug.

"Okay, and, again, time is infinite, so maybe it takes billions of these exact Earth replicas, but eventually one comes along that not only is exactly like Earth, but it develops human life. And maybe every billion or so of those, an exact version of you or me comes along. This would take forever, but that's okay, because, you know, infinity."

"This is a conversation that happens after you wake up, Fiona, after we've filled you full of the drugs."

"Come on, just play along for a minute. Just do this. We've got this Earth now, okay? *At last*, we've got this Earth that has one of us perfectly re-created—our minds, bodies, souls, even. Everything. One-in-a-kajillion odds—"

"But that's okay, because kajillions of years and planets have gone by at this point."

"Exactly! Yes. So eventually, untold eons into the future, there has to be an Earth that has not just you, not just me, but both of us, and at the same time and place."

"This is very cute," I whispered into her neck.

"This is serious, though. This is extremely important in case I don't wake up."

Here Fiona sighed quietly, and looked away from me for effect. How was it that an actress so gifted could at once be so reliably transparent in her emotional life off-screen? In a moment, somebody was bound to draw back the pigeon-blue curtain separating us from the world. In a moment—but not yet.

"Nobody dies during wisdom tooth removal surgery," I reminded her gently.

"You don't know that. You don't know that."

"No one dies from this."

"Fine, but the point is that death isn't important anyway— not anymore, not after this groundbreaking new theory I've developed. Even if I accidentally get quadruple anesthesia and I die, doesn't matter: we'll have another life together at some point in the future, actually we'll have infinite lives, and also in the past. So this isn't the first time we've been together, you know?"

"This isn't the first time we've had this conversation," I offered.

"Exactly!"

"We've had it, I suppose, infinity number of times? And we will have it infinity times again, right?"

"Right."

"Even if we only have it once every billion lives we spend together, each of which is only one of every billion of our own, solo lives, each of which is only one of every billion Earths, each of which is only one of every billion Earth-like planets?"

I snapped at her hair elastic, too hard this time. Fiona gathered her frantic, splayed curls into a loose rope on the pillow, and looked up.

"Infinity is forever. This isn't ridiculous."

· · ·

Scientists claim that the universe was created thirteen-point-seven-five billion years ago, a fact that—and I'm sorry, science—but a fact that is absurd to insist we can ever really know. The point is, an extremely long time ago this happened, and things percolated for a bit, and four-point-five-four billion years ago collected remnants of the solar nebula fused together to form the Earth, a massive sphere covered mainly by vast expanses of salt water. It took less than a billion years after that before self-reproducing ribonucleic molecules became life (not sure how), followed thereafter by the invention of photosynthesis, complex cellular organisms, fish, seeds, plants, bugs, and, about two hundred million years ago, mammals. There was an ice age, and there were monstrous, hulking dinosaurs, and then humans emerged a couple of hundred thousand years back. They learned to walk, to catch the fish, sow the seeds, eat the plants you can eat, squash the bugs, and in 2012 I graduated from law school nearly one-hundred-and-fifteen-thousand dollars in debt.

Ernest Hemingway once wrote that all stories, if you follow them far enough into the future, end in death, and that nobody who claims to be a true storyteller ought to keep that information from you. Of course, he was almost certainly drunk at the time. He forgot to say where all stories begin if you follow them far enough into the past, but the creation of the universe seems as reasonable a guess as any. I like Hemingway, and I'd like to be true. So it is: like every story, this story begins with the creation of the universe and ends in death. And if it doesn't, that's only because this story is not, in truth, over. At the very least, this is how I remember it; a friend recently told me to make my life sincere, and I have sworn to try.

The last time I saw Fiona Fox-Renard I was twenty-six,

the universe was thirteen-point-seven-five billion and twenty-six, and Fiona still went by her real last name: Haeberle. She and I had met in college just four years earlier, at the terrible party of a mutual friend of a friend, six weeks before graduation. Said party was one of your standard red-plastic ordeals—strident bass in a dark dorm, the windows overlooking the quad slick with condensation, the children overlooking each other slick with sweat, what air there was in the room nearly tropical despite this being Massachusetts and despite this being April. I had handed in my senior history thesis that morning—*States of Confusion: A Political-Psychobiographical Analysis of the James Buchanan Presidency*—and my roommates, bless their twisted little hearts, had forced me to attend under threat of being *c'mon, dude*-d all the way to the grave.

She was the only person at the party who belonged there less than I did—that much I knew right away—but where I sipped drippy in the corner with a lone boot sole pressed tightly to the wall, she bounded briskly to the thumph thumph thumph of a song I believe-it-or-not remember but won't mention here out of respect for the seriousness of the situation to come. This was not a very good song. I surveyed the room listlessly, monitoring the graceless, exuberant hordes from my perch, and waited for her to stop dancing before I approached. Saying that I waited for her to stop dancing before I approached is a bit like saying that the astronaut waited to return to Earth before taking off his or her space helmet, which is to say I am not a strong dancer. Ten minutes later, loafing behind her in line for the restroom, I calculated what to say, how to look, how to be, when to—

"Hi."

"Heh—hey. Hey-lo. Hello. How's . . . it going?"

Nailed it!

"I'm Fiona. *You* look like you're having absolutely no fun."

"That's . . . you're dead on. I'm emphatically not having fun, although I'm committed to turning things around. Keeping a positive attitude, all that."

She was lean and confident-seeming, with the breezy look and feel and wit of a flapper poetess. She had the slightest accent I could not place—her voice, upland and high, sounded as though it must have rolled through the wheat fields of America for thousands of years, kicking up the soil, filling up on music and Wisconsin grit. An iconic mole, which on my own face would have succeeded nowhere, rested effortlessly just below the western curve of her lower lip like a goddamn jewel.

"Hmm," she purred my way. "Have you tried enjoying it from another angle?"

"I'm sorry?"

"I mean, this party is rubbish, right? It's objectively a bad time. But appreciate it. From another angle. You're a senior, yes? So appreciate it for its novelty—pretty soon, we won't have this level of absurdity in our lives anymore. So you can enjoy this . . . this disaster . . . as, you know, a piece of pre-nostalgia. Something you can hold on to, later, when your life has turned stale."

"I like that—I like 'pre-nostalgia.' That's a solid angle."

Her hair was some new color I wasn't familiar with from twenty-two years on Earth. She spoke with impeccable diction, and stood with perfect posture, and I was pulled quite quickly into her orbit.

"Look," she said, "I know this whole scene is a little much, yeah? I get it. You're too cool for this? Or not cool enough?

One of those options, maybe? But those people—that's your
generation out there, rubbing up on each other."

"My generation."

"It's true!"

"My generation is really getting after it."

"They're excitable," she said, mock-thoughtfully pursing
her entire face and commencing to absently crack each of her
wispy fingers in turn.

"Every time I come to one of these, I like to pretend I'm
an anthropologist," I offered after a torturous beat threatened
to end it all before it began.

"Aw. That's super weird, my new friend. A super weird
thing to say to someone you've just met. Are you . . . are you
like, some sort of a kind snob?"

Some sort of a kind snob. That's probably exactly what
I am. Exactly. Fiona had recently finished her thesis too—
*Thirteen Ways of Looking at 'Thirteen Ways of Looking at a Black-
bird:' Modernist Poetry, Modernist Movement*—and the fact that
she was a double major in theater and dance led me inexplicably
to bring up the not-dark but also not-flattering secret of my
ineptitude in the latter discipline.

"You *can*not be that bad," she challenged, but she was
wrong: I certainly could.

"I am indeed that bad. I am the worst."

"Ugh! Okay, that's it; we need to go dance right now."

Fuck no.

"No, thank you."

"No, you have to come dance. It is decided."

Don't do this to yourself. Don't do this to yourself.

"I need to be really clear with you on this, okay?" I pleaded
faux-desperately, but also actually desperately. "I need you to

consider the consequences of your actions: if you make me dance, you won't ever want to talk to me again."

"No?" she mouthed mockingly, wide-eyed, already pulling my sleeve toward its inescapable destiny of bewildered flailing.

"Not just that. *You'll* never dance again."

"I love to dance," she said.

"Not anymore. Not after you go through what you're about to go through if you make me dance. You can't un-see what you're about see. It'll destroy the whole medium for you."

By then I had realized that I never had a chance, that she had checkmated me—when? Not when I brought up my failures as a dancer. Not when she brought up her successes as the same. No, it was much earlier. When she put on that devastating sundress? The day her parents met? Thirteen-point-seven-five billion years ago, when nothing at all erupted knowingly into everything there would be? I thought of what Joni Mitchell said about us being stardust, golden, billion-year-old carbon; calibrating even for the fact that I was now quite drunk, I decided then that it must be true, at least in Fiona's case. She was made up of prehistoric stars—that elegant electric dust—more obviously than anyone I'd ever met.

"Jesus. You weren't kidding," said the stardust.

I looked like a monumental idiot, and the music tore through the sopping room like a frightened bird, and all night long she called me "Neil," which is not my name. Just briefly then, in the humiliating haze, it occurred to me that I'd never cared enough to dance for someone up until this instant, not ever, and certainly not so suddenly. I am not a sudden person.

By chance, we met again the next day: Bettany Skiles, my natty and occasionally brilliant dorm-mate, was screening her thesis film—*The Nervous System: A Very Deep Film by Bettany Skiles*—in which aspiring actress Fiona portrayed someone's unlovable daughter, a gaunt and ghostly teenager stricken terminally by ennui.

"Leo," I corrected her warmly when we nearly bumped into each other in the clinical-white foyer of the campus theater.

"If I sit with you, do you promise not to talk about the film or about me?"

This would prove to be the first of maybe ten thousand instances in which Fiona spoke to me as though we had been smack in the middle of some longer conversation, and I sensed this, I guess, and smiled.

"Of course you can sit with me. You're in the movie?"

"You're the only person I know here who maybe won't talk about the film or about me," she explained as her eyes darted frenetically between the smattering of assembled students, looking for recognizable faces from which she could shrink.

"We don't have to talk about anything," I answered with my still eyes on hers: twin hazel atoms, agitated, whizzing suspiciously around the room.

"Because we don't know each other, I mean."

"I'm sorry?" I inquired, suddenly and strangely and intriguingly hurt.

"We don't really know each other, so we can talk about anything else. We can talk about the Giants, for example, because I don't know how you feel about them yet."

"Right, I—"

"And you don't know how I feel about them either."

"Right, so I don't really—"

"I hate them. I hate the Giants."

"Alright. Do you mean the New York Giants, or—"

"So we shouldn't talk about that, probably, but what I'm saying is that we can basically talk about anything, just please not the film and not me. Not me in the film, I mean. Not acting."

"Fiona, we don't have to talk about anything. It would actually be . . . rude, to talk, you know? We're at a movie, and everyone will be—"

"We're at a film, Leo," she breathed, almost inaudibly, and in that moment I saw for the first time in my life a whole beautiful future.

I am not a sudden person, but something in her chased that all away. Stardust, maybe, though looking back it's difficult to say what parts of that were real. Even then, Fiona seemed infinitely more alive, and yet less lifelike, than the rest; she was ruled by other impulses, governed by other laws passed down from brighter bodies. And right then and there, in the gaping mouth of the campus theater, she snapped me from my present.

Within a week, it was decided that if we were going to be the perfect little love of the century we were going to have to do everything in double-time. And so it was: days of lunch and dinner, days of breakfast and lunch, afternoons spent hastily Venn diagramming our respective circles of friends, nights spent studying each other for the big quiz that seemed certain to come at the close of the academic year. If our nearest and dearest were shocked by the velocity of it all, Fiona and I neither noticed nor cared. Fast love was a business, and at graduation we took dozens of photographs together, correctly suspecting that our later selves would think us smart anticipators.

• • •

To those who don't know her well at all, Fiona is a dazzling cartoon mouse of a woman. Lithe and full-throated, perpetually bright-eyed and winging, she was impossible to miss, even at those times—and there were many—when she wanted nothing more than to be some icy and long-forgotten planet, rather than the gauzy, centric sun of every eager solar system she happened to flit through.

I learned this and everything else about her that summer and in the three following years. We moved into an apartment together on the first of September—I know, I know, but we did—four days before my first day of law school. The place was, by any metric, stark and sunless, but it provided untold gallons of renewable fuel for Fiona's acting machine; to her (she of the Great Midwest), it felt more like the Eastern Bloc than Brooklyn, a perspective that served to authenticate her entire artistic creaturehood. To me, the apartment brought to mind nothing more than striving, as of two young, squawking lovebirds barnstorming their way through life's challenges, shitting on the windshields of all who dared to question their liberal arts degrees. We were twenty-two when it started.

Becoming an adult is a funny thing in much the same sense that love is a funny thing, which is to say it usually isn't very funny at all. One minute we had been relics—quaint and crumbling New English artifacts quite simply as quaint and crumbling as the Old Man of the Mountain himself—and the next we were the sudden babies of New York City, reeling from the torrential overload of a fresh, strange world. All at once, Fiona and I had gone from feeling the oldest we had ever felt to feeling the youngest we had ever felt, and even though we were right the first time there was a sense that everything we'd done and seen to that point had been somehow prenatal.

The fear made us young, too: I was scared because I had acquired this whole array of adult skills—tandoori cooking, laundromat navigation, knowledge of gyms, relative expertise concerning the Buchanan presidency—but wasn't sure how to convincingly make a complete life out of them, and Fiona was scared because I explained this to her in exactly that way.

"What's it all going to be like?" she asked me with typical moon-eyed wonder, not thirty seconds after we opened our new apartment's thin door for the first time. The frame was splintered; the knob slumped loose from its mooring like a guilty dog.

"The whole thing?"

"Or any part. What will it be like for us?"

"I don't—I think we don't get to know. I think it's good that we don't get to know."

"Yeah, but it's easy for you to say that because you're going to be a lawyer in three years. There are unknowns, but they're completely adorable, like 'what prestigious internship am I going to get,' or 'how well am I going to do on my torps exam?'"

"Torts."

"Torps?"

"It's torts. You really thought—"

"I thought it was short for torpitude. Like crimes that are morally . . ."

"Turpitude."

"Right. Okay, yes—turpitude. That one I should've had. Look, obviously I don't know what torps are, and I'm thrilled that you'll be learning about them, but my point is that your anticipated line of work comes with a certain degree of job security that mine does not."

"Okay, well, absolutely, being a lawyer carries with it a lot less question marks than—"

"Fewer!"

"Nice. Yes. Fewer question marks, but the payoff of being an actress is a lot bigger."

"How?"

"Well, for one thing, you'll be famous."

"Ha!"

"You will. You're that good."

And she was, she really was that good.

"Okay, but even a lot of phenomenally talented actors never break through," she said wistfully, now lying perfectly still, face up, arms splayed, on the hardwood floor.

"You will. I already know that you'll become a star, Fiona. I know that with confidence. What are you doing? Are you making an apartment angel?"

It was hard, then, although that was almost certainly the point of the experience. When law school started, I became predictably overwhelmed by this whole rich and terrible world of ideas and rules, what an old professor once called "those wise restraints that make men free." I dug into the work; it suited something in me, even if I wasn't entirely sure what I was doing there in the first place. My decision to apply to law school had been spurred by the same allergy to suddenness that Fiona later charmed away; why halt my education abruptly when there were so many graduate schools out there to help soften the fall? I had no particular career ambitions, but was frightened of closing doors, and among my several options the least narrow (and therefore most attractive) was the law.

The greatest thing I learned in law school was this, and here you'll want to maybe take notes, because I still find this to be just horribly interesting: if you move onto someone else's property, and if you can stay there long enough without being detected, under certain circumstances it will just *become yours*.

"Shut the fuck up," said Fiona when she heard.

"I'm not kidding. Trespass somewhere for enough time, and eventually you own it."

"That doesn't sound right to me. How is that a thing?"

"It's called adverse possession. It's been around since before America; it's a well-established thing."

"Okay and what are the rules again?"

"Actual, continuous, open, notorious, hostile, and exclusive possession for a statutory period of—"

"English, counselor."

"Well, you need to actually be present on the property, uh, continually, for however long the period of—"

"How long is that?"

"It varies by state, but in New York it's ten years."

"And if you run out of toilet paper or Sriracha . . ."

"You can leave to go to the store. Continuous just means you can't leave for a long time and then come back. You'd have to start the ten years all over again."

"Okay and what else?"

"Open and notorious means you can't actively hide from the owner or pretend you aren't actually squatting there; you need to change the land somehow, which could be by building something, like a fence, or a house—"

"A gazebo!"

". . . Yep. A gazebo would definitely count. You need to be there without permission: that's hostile. The only other thing is exclusive. Exclusive means that the real owner can't be there while you're also there. Otherwise, you know."

"Chaos."

"Exactly."

Maybe she shouldn't know that adverse possession exists, I found myself thinking. Maybe it's too—

"We're doing it!"

"We're really not."

"Why would you tell me about this and think that we wouldn't . . . of course we're doing it!" she practically shouted, now pacing conspiratorially the short circuit of our almost comically small kitchen. "We're gonna do it to a farm upstate somewhere."

"What? Why?"

"Well, you can't camp out in Brooklyn."

"Fair."

"We're gonna do it to a cranberry farm!"

"Is that a real thing?"

"We're gonna do it to . . . a regular farm!"

"There might be cranberry farms. It was a sincere question," I offered, and I still don't know.

"Or an apple orchard! I bet we'd be the greatest farmers, or orchard keepers. You could drop out of law school—"

"Deal."

"And I wouldn't ever have to go to another audition again. We could live off the land," she said serenely, smushing her forehead onto mine for a long moment before clamping her lily teeth around my nose until I agreed to be a trespassing farmer.

Having begrudgingly entered adulthood, we tried to become established quickly as something like naturalized citizens

in our new home—and here is where adverse possession became for us a peculiar sort of manifest destiny, a watchword to
chart our progress as takers of the world. Every restaurant we
ate at twice instantly became Ours, and at every bar we intentionally ordered the same drinks over and over because we
knew that we could build an easy home out of routine. When
we discovered bookstores, we told everyone about them.

"Adverse possession!" she would bellow proudly when we
found something we wanted for our own.

Fiona and I kept taking, kept living in this way, long after
our friends had grown comfortably into their older, smaller
lives. We claimed every experience for only ourselves: the first
snow, the last rays of the day, every star we gazed was ripped
from the public domain—property of Fiona and Leo's New
Life Together, copyright and patent pending and no squatters
allowed. We were celestial thieves; we had no remorse; our
only desire was the annexation of all beautiful things. We adversely possessed things we read about, things we'd never even
seen. The phosphorescent pools out west. Some weathered
stone walls near Galway. Slushy St. Petersburg. *Brooklyn belongs
to us now.*

We almost had the Northern Lights. I found out that if we
rented a car, left in the morning, and drove fifteen hours due
north we could take them for sure:

"I will," Fiona said.

I know.

"I'm serious, I really will," she said.

I will too.

We fought and loved like I imagined the great couples of
history fought and loved. In our worst moments, we whiled
away the time the way some people dice onions: every move

a tiny violent severance, every new layer reached another baf-
fling chemical reason to dam up your eyes, each action so crisp
and so careless that someone is inevitably bound to draw blood.
In our best moments, we were mad for one another, fully pooled
in each other's ideas and aspirations.

She told me once, between sibilant smacks of an apple, that
she could read my thoughts, and I believed that it was true.

"It's good that no one is like you," she told me.

I loved every small thing there was about Fiona. That she
was a bawdy drunk. That she always, always talked to people as
though they could easily intuit cardinal directions ("you're
going to want to head south at the light, ma'am"). The way she
said "Leo," so precisely, every time, as though a rougher enun-
ciation might bruise the word. The way she was warm to no
one but me.

I never loved Fiona so much as I did then, in those first
awe-filled days, because she kept me from having to be born
again, alone. And when we struggled, we did so secure in the
knowledge that this was happening everywhere, and to people
just like us, that it had happened before and would continue to
happen so long as there was college and currency and wine.

• • •

Probably the most important thing to know about me is that
I am a fraud. When I was in second grade, Mrs. Easterling gave
us a spelling test, and because I was good at spelling I finished
it early. We had to sit quietly until everybody finished, though,
so while I waited I decided to doodle on the back of the paper: three-dimensional boxes, those cool letter esses that look
like gothic figure eights, and a small diagram explaining, with
a drunkard's penmanship but accurately enough, the basic
premises of the Pythagorean theorem. I must have seen it in

one of my brother's encyclopedias; I used to sneak into his room at night when I couldn't sleep and read them on the floor by flashlight. We can't know why—I was voracious for worldly knowledge back then, in the way that today I am voracious only for free food.

Teachers, parents: all agreed that my scrawlings had been the unmistakable first gurgles of genius. Within a week I was whisked off to fifth-grade math classes, special little tutor sessions, advanced everything; by the time I was twelve I was essentially in high school, this wunderkind, head down, excelling. Every step forward looked impressive enough on its own to make the next a foregone conclusion, regardless of merit or work ethic or interest, and I can trace that Rube Goldberg device straight from law school all the way back to the moment when I pointlessly regurgitated a little Greek doorstop onto the back of my spelling test in colored pencil.

Mrs. Easterling thought I was the future, but really I was only peaking young. I never cured cancer or split the atom or changed the way anyone thought about anything. I never even wanted to. Rockets were the future, once, and so were drive-in movies, and Lenny Bias, and the Edsel, and Betamax. Bayonets, CD-Roms, Communism. The United States of America. Things get away from you. They get away from you, and it happens so quickly, and all that promise grows obsolete.

Fiona, who was smarter and more curious by nature than I would ever be, never much minded that my super-genius days were long behind me. She didn't much care that I talked in my sleep—she secretly recorded it, in fact, for several weeks, and laid my subliminal maunderings onto a trembling and frankly regrettable "post-dubstep" (?) beat during the fondly-remembered Month She Decided to Be a DJ. She weathered my brimming catalog of neuroses, my soy allergy, the way

I cock my head like a terrier when I get judgmental or confused. My hypochondria.

O, my hypochondria: on occasion, almost totally debili-
tating (or is it, right?), lacking all regard for my otherwise
quite adequate capacity for basic reason. An abridged survey
of the ailments and decrepitudes with which I have honestly
and wrongfully believed myself to have been stricken over the
years would include bone cancer, kidney cancer, lung cancer,
skin cancer, about a thousand brain tumors, calcium deficien-
cies, young adult arthritis, chronic heart attack, various ulcers,
Parkinson's, Huntington's, pneumonia, acid reflux, both types of
diabetes, a torn anterior cruciate ligament, multiple sclerosis,
fibromyalgia, scabies, migraines, carpal tunnel syndrome, ane-
mia, gout, dormant epilepsy, hyper- and hypoglycemia, SARS,
osteoporosis, restless legs syndrome, extremely-early-onset
Alzheimer's, generalized anxiety disorder, very specific anxiety
disorder, and—I kid you not—the avian flu.

Quoth Fiona: "You do not have that." But in the moment—
amid the news reports, the breathless speculations, the hurt
bird I saw that morning on the steps of the law library—in the
moment, I did have that.

Fiona had none of those things, and until her wisdom teeth
were removed on the morning of her twenty-fifth birthday she
had never been a patient in a hospital. She came from Lutheran
stock, and her people were hale and hardy, the starch of the
human species: vigorous and lusty and all other adjectives more
at home describing a gale or a stew than persons. They say
"belly" instead of stomach, and even their littlest (see: five-
four Fiona) seem large, their aspects puffed up and out by their
own magnetism, like folk heroes.

Perhaps it was that indomitable blood that made her so

steady on a stage. Acting came as naturally to Fiona as nothing came to me; she'd wanted to be a movie star since she was eight years old and her older brother let her watch Sigourney Weaver in *Alien* while their parents were away, and it is a rare thing that a child's singular fantasy of adulthood conspires so effortlessly to suit her when the moment comes to choose what she might be.

I wasn't imaginative enough to harbor that kind of desire. When I was little, the concept of movie stardom didn't make a lick of sense to me; I'd see Tom Hanks and be outraged: I know you're not an astronaut, because *I just saw you fight that volcano.* It's the same person! Always the same person, just pretending to be a cop or a baseball manager or an adult kid. If the movie people really wanted us to become engrossed in their stories, why wouldn't they cast entirely new actors for each one? At least then I could imagine that you are who you say that you are. Why should I participate in the universal hallucination of agreeing that you're William Wallace? You're blatantly Mel Gibson, and I see you on television all the fucking time. I don't know when in life I finally caved to the world on this point, but I'm glad that I permanently succumbed to the charade in time to enjoy watching Fiona over and over again. I'm glad.

She worked consistently during Our First Year—in nearly credible black-box art pieces, mostly, and once in a national commercial for auto insurance alongside multiple computer-generated co-stars of the animalic variety, co-stars whose heavy accents bore no relationship whatsoever to the natural habitats of their respective genera.

Even in lesser fare, she cut a brilliant ingénue or fender bender-er, conveying with the merest morsel of a look whichever ineffable feeling was required. Fiona was blessed with easy access to the full bright constellation of human emotions. She was wasted on the too-clever playwrights of New York, wasted on the horn-rimmed directors, wasted on her peers, those parched minds packed unstably into beautiful bodies. I never liked any of her acting friends—not one. Mackenzie Walters, loudmouthed and positively Amazonian, whom Fiona had met at an arts camp in seventh grade. Alice Gerson, a sweet but shivering bundle of unearned insecurities with whom Fiona frequently competed for parts. Joel Enson, Mackenzie's even-louder-mouthed boyfriend who never once came to our apartment without cooking something elaborate out of our freshest ingredients that clearly didn't belong to him. The parade of smirking autolatrists from Fiona's acting class, boring men and boring women, each of whom had long ago convinced themselves that it was their intricate talent alone which daily attuned the spheres of Heaven and Earth.

Fiona wasn't one of them—she had character of the sort for which you cannot simply substitute in hair product—but it made me nervous that these were her friends. I found myself eyeing her for residue every time they came around, the way you might check your partner for ticks after hiking through a stretch of long grass. Could they infect my complicated darling with their swooning idiocy? Is lack of depth contagious? Of course not, I decided each night, as she curled herself once more onto my arm. She writes notes in the margins of poetry books in pencil; she listens to people when they speak.

Her first true break arrived the summer before my third and final year of law school. *Mercy General* was one of the few television shows that still shot in New York; like me, it had been running for twenty-five years, and was a moderately successful soap opera featuring a number of suspicious doctors.

Millions of laundromat employees, inpatients, cat-sitters, and children home sick tuned in each week to watch the uniformly attractive denizens of Titular Hospital make bad writing worse. Fiona won the part of nurse Jeanette, spunky-yet-sensitive medical neophyte and reluctant love interest to the Adonic Dr. Adam Strickland, who was portrayed by the actor Mark Renard: an Olympic-level brooder with no other discernable modes or abilities. Before doctor and nurse were killed off in a boating accident to end the season (but really the harbormaster did it), Fiona would appear in nineteen episodes—enough to quit waitressing, pay off her student loans, and gain a certain amount of traction within the industry.

And when success arrived, she handled the change the way I knew she would, like a guarded but grateful weirdo. Most young actors never come anywhere near even the farthest out-crops of Fame Mountain, but suddenly we were—she was—being stopped on the street. It happened at least a dozen times that year, and in each instance she was embarrassed to the point of near-panic. Once, in a truly seminal display of awkwardness, she even went so far as to ask a befuddled autograph-seeker to reciprocate—there was a great deal of confusion, and no paper, and we landed on having the starstruck old lady sign the back of my hand in blue pen ("EILEEN R. STURDIVANT LOVE THE SHOW THANK YOU!").

It seemed very much like the start of something, even if the show itself was no great shakes. She was acting, I was learn-ing, we were cooking and reading and walking and running together, and brunches and wine-bottle candlesticks and the record player playing and then so suddenly it's summer again, and I'm a sudden lawyer now, and if it weren't for that god-damn harbormaster—

• • •

There are things about Fiona you don't get to know. Infrared secrets, pitched beyond the dog whistle, things stored so far to your east you might just as well head west. There are tigers in those parts—the old kind: tygers with a "y"—too far removed from you in place and time, and fogged in by obscurities to find, nacarat and sable in their primal postures. Everyone who has ever lived has harbored their own unseen ciphers; you can call their home a hiding place, or a furnace room enkindling the ways that each of us will be. The point is this: you will never get to know these things about Fiona, but I had seen them all, had charted every inch of her vast topography, had categorized her fauna and danced a thousand times to her classified music, those arcane and dissonant chords, and it was a hard night, the night I let her go.

TWO

"I'd like to have a conversation with someone. Let . . . me . . . see . . . I'd like to have a conversation with—Mr. Rosenbaum, would you like to have a conversation with me?"

"I'd love to."

"I think you're only saying that because you don't really have much of a choice in the matter, Mr. Rosenbaum."

"I suppose we'll never know."

"Fair point. This conversation I'd like to have, it's of a highly sensitive nature. That alright with you, Mr. Rosenbaum?"

"That's no problem."

"Good. Are you opposed to the death penalty, Mr. Rosenbaum?"

"I'm sorry?"

"The death penalty. I'm asking you about capital punishment, Mr. Rosenbaum."

"Oh. Yes. I mean, yes, I am. Opposed."

"Let me put the question a bit more directly: if you were selected as a juror in a capital case, and the question were put to you by the prosecutor, would you answer that you have a conscientious scruple against ever, under any circumstances, applying the death penalty, such that you would not, from a moral standpoint—and I remind you that you are under oath, Mr. Rosenbaum—such that you would not, that you *could* not, again, morally, be able to impose death on a criminal defendant?"

"Would I . . . I mean, yes, I would say, I guess, to the prosecutor, I could say that I have a . . . scruple . . . against—"

"You would say that you had a moral scruple against the application of the death penalty. Okay. So what does that mean to you?"

"A scruple?"

"To have a moral scruple against the death penalty, yes, Mr. Rosenbaum, yes."

"It's, I guess, a principle, or a value, that—it's a . . . hard-dying principle, that I would have—do have, in fact—so much so that, in spite of the established law, I wouldn't put myself in a position to—"

"Okay, you're saying you wouldn't do it. But that opposition, is it based on purely moral principles, or on some sort of vague empirical sense that the death penalty simply doesn't work?"

"Both?"

"But is it—"

"Chiefly moral."

"Chiefly moral. So let's say that I've got some fresh new data here, Mr. Rosenbaum; I've got this data just back from the academy, from the lab, the boffins, whatever, and I can prove to you—to your satisfaction, that is, empirically, Mr. Rosenbaum—I can prove to you that the death penalty does, in fact, work. I've got here some hypothetical data here showing that, for each guilty person executed, you are *in fact* saving the lives of ten completely innocent potential murder victims. What now? Still opposed?"

"I would still have moral reservations that would be . . . incredibly strong. It would take—"

"Everybody should have moral reservations, Mr. Rosenbaum. We're talking about death here. Yay or nay?"

"I would say . . . I would still be opposed."

"How?! How could you prefer the life of one guilty murderer to the life of ten innocent victims? That's utterly preposterous! Explain yourself, Mr. Rosenbaum!"

"I'm opposed to the notion that it's the job of the state—"

"To what?! To save the lives of innocent victims?"

"No! To kill. I don't believe that it's, uh, within the purview of—"

"The state doesn't have a choice in the matter! They could kill ten people by way of inaction, or one person by way of action! Someone has to die, Mr. Rosenbaum, and you've opted for the ten innocent nuns?!"

"They're nuns?"

"They *were* nuns, Mr. Rosenbaum. They've just been murdered by the low-life criminal you could not bring yourself to exterminate."

"That's . . . that's really terrible."

"I think so too. It's quite the dilemma, right? It reminds me of the old railroad hypothetical—you know the one? The train is speeding along down the track, and all of a sudden the brakes fail. If you do nothing, that train is going to go straight ahead and kill ten people, but if you make the decision to switch tracks, you know, at the track-switching . . . you know, when they flip the lines over to make the trains switch? If you do that, the train will only kill one person. What do you do with that one, morally speaking, Mr. Rosenbaum?"

"Well, I understand the argument that you want to do the least amount of harm to the least number of people—"

"It's a pretty good argument, wouldn't you say?"

"It's a great argument, but there's a civic argument that I would make that it's still not the place of the—you know, with criminals, at least, there are a lot of things that the government can do to—"

"They've tried them all! Every single one of them. They've tried investing in rehabilitation, they've tried life imprisonment, they've tried making the prisons better. In the end, it still turns out—don't worry about the details, Mr. Rosenbaum—it still turns out that the criminal is no different from the runaway train: unless you kill this horrible, plainly guilty mass murderer, ten additional innocent people would be dead, who would otherwise not be dead. Are you still—"

"Even if you've given that person a life sentence?"

"Absolutely. Let's assume now that you're persuaded, okay? I don't want to argue with you about the facts, Mr. Rosenbaum; I simply want to have a moral discussion with you. You're persuaded: by executing this guilty criminal, ten innocent people *will* be saved. Are you still opposed to the state executing him? 'Cause if you're not opposed to it, then your opposition isn't moral at all, Mr. Rosenbaum—it is, in fact, empirical. It's just based on facts, and the facts could be right, or the facts could be wrong, and while they may, perhaps, be right in real life, I've made them wrong in my hypothetical. What say you?"

"I'm sticking with the moral defense."

"So with the train problem, you just go down the track? Kill ten people, just because you couldn't bring yourself to take action?"

"No."

"So you switch the track, and kill the one to save the ten?"

"Yes."

"Okay, so you're prepared to kill one innocent person to save ten innocent people. That's great, by the way; I applaud you for that. So let me ask, again, then, let me ask of you with all your good and decent scruples, Mr. Rosenbaum, why you're not then prepared to kill one *guilty criminal*, who's been convicted beyond a reasonable doubt of *a horrible murder*, to save ten innocent lives? Doesn't that seem inconsistent?"

"My moral argument about the death penalty has more to do with the function of the state—"

"Okay. So now let's say the president of the United States is driving the train. Okay? It's a state action now; what would you have them do?"

"Well—"

"How about this: let's say, Mr. Rosenbaum, that you're the chief advisor to Winston Churchill, the year is 1935, and the Germans have violated the Versailles Treaty. Okay? They're arming themselves, and they have this new leader—his name is Hitler. He says that when he comes to power he's going to declare war on the whole of Europe! He's going to conquer Poland, France, England—and you believe him! And Mr. Churchill says, 'Let's kill him! Come on, lads, let's do it! Let's nip this guy in the bud!' And Mr. Chamberlain says, 'Not

so fast, you know, peace in our time; let's just see how everything plays out,' and that's ultimately what you decide to do—
you go with Chamberlain—and all of a sudden fifteen million
people are dead, and you've got yourselves the Second World
War, a war that could've been prevented, perhaps, by killing a
few thousand people in a preemptive strike on what was then
a fledgling German military. Fifteen million people, and they're
gone. That's state action too. Are you on—whose side are you
on, Mr. Rosenbaum? Churchill's, or, you know, are you on—"

"I'm firmly anti-Hitler."

"How nice for you."

"Look, Professor Barnes, of course I would want to kill
Hitler in that scenario. What I'm saying is that regardless of
what *my* anger or *my* hatred compels *me* to do in the heat of
the moment, I don't want the state to be driven by that kind
of emotional—"

"Isn't that precisely why we have capital punishment,
though—to channel your revenge? Isn't that the whole idea?
We, the state, make a deal with you: a civilized deal. We say,
Mr. Rosenbaum, we understand you have a need to see vengeance done. Somebody has just killed someone very close to
you; we understand what you're feeling, emotionally, but
we're making you a deal here—you don't get to kill. We do.
We get to kill because we have things like due process, we have
things like appellate courts, we have something called a right to
effective counsel. So given a choice between acting on your
own—which you seem to prefer—and this state function that
the whole polity has signed off on, you'd rather leave it up to
the individual rogue actor?"

"I'd rather have the state not act on emotional interests that
I may have. I *also* don't want the right to go around like a vigi-
lante."

"But self-defense you're okay with?"

"Sure. Of course. I don't equate self-defense with capital punishment."

"Right, of course not! With self-defense, you're killing somebody in order to save one life—yours, selfishly—and with capital punishment, you're refusing to kill somebody to save the ten nuns. Why are you better than the nuns, Mr. Rosenbaum, because they're nuns, and as far as I can tell you're—"

"I'm not—I'm not better than the nuns—but in a self-defense case I don't have the option of . . . the state has custody of a criminal; they're not acting in self-defense. Capital punishment is *off*ensive."

"Off*ensive?"

"*Off*ensive . . . and off*ensive*. Both, to me."

"Very well. Thank you, Mr. Rosenbaum."

I glanced across the room at Boots as he drew breath for the first time in six minutes; he was shell-shocked, and looked as though he was hoping that the hypothetical train would somehow veer off course and strike *him*, lest he have to field any more questions. Professor Barnes cycled through two more students, both of whom demurely demurred—they had no quarrel with the death penalty (no moral quarrel, at least). And then—

"Mr. Brice?"

Oh shit.

"Yes, Professor," I spurted.

"Mr. Brice, might you perhaps share Mr. Rosenbaum's moral reservations about the death penalty?"

Shit shit shit shit shit—

"I absolutely do."

"And yours are, indeed, moral reservations as well? As opposed to the loose empirical hang-ups we dispensed with a moment ago?"

Katherine Barnes was an intellectual giant whom the *New Yorker* had once called the "undisputed alpha lioness of the legal academy." In the dilated eyes of her students and admirers, she was fearsome, winsome, and awesome in equal measure, a swashbuckling genius blessed with a semi-automatic wit and a deep well of charm. In another age, she could have been a second Cleopatra; in this one, she taught criminal procedure, and stood as a monument to that certain irresistible strain of austerity that elevates great generals and gods. I have never met anyone smarter in my entire life, and never will.

"My reservations," I sputtered, "are . . . moral . . . but I'm not sure I'll be as adept as Boots—sorry, as Mr. Rosenbaum— I'm not sure I'll be able to defend my particular logic quite so well."

I looked back across at Boots, who had four fingers on each temple and his big mouth unlatched, still recovering from the onslaught.

"And why is that, Mr. Brice? Trying to avoid the inevitable interrogation?"

"No. I mean, yes, if that's a possibility, but really it's because I don't have a well-thought-out reason for my moral opposition. It just feels wrong, to me."

Professor Barnes laughed once, sharply—purposefully, it seemed: a stage guffaw, the sort that cues an especially trenchant rebuttal.

"There's a word we don't hear often in law school, class," she retorted, "that word, of course, being 'feels.' Are you quite certain you want to be a lawyer, Mr. Brice?"

"No ma'am," I reflexed, so sincerely I startled myself. "Like I said, it's probably an unreasonable position if you want to spin it out, but for me . . . I just can't get behind it. I just . . . I don't like thinking about the needle."

"You don't like thinking about the needle?"

"That's it. That's my position. I can't—morally—I can't sign off on being a part of that. Strapping someone in, and just . . ."

"The needle."

"I can't."

"It's not an unreasonable position, Mr. Brice. It might be the most reasonable thing a person can do, right? Be governed by their emotional impulses? Now, of course, we don't do that here. Right? Ms. Kim, should lawyers be driven by their emotions?"

"I . . . don't . . . think . . . we should?" chanted Michelle.

"Mr. Parmalee?"

"Definitely not. No," mustered Scott.

"Ms. Torres?"

"It's important for lawyers to be guided by their principles, and maybe those principles can be rooted in an emotional response, um, to experience, maybe . . . but you can't be driven just by your emotions. Not in law," reasoned Katy.

"Okay, how about this: is there anybody here, apart from Mr. Brice, whose opinion about the death penalty was borne of some sort of visceral reaction to the act itself? Is anybody else thinking about the needle?"

One-hundred-and-sixty eyeballs scurried from the questioner like floodlit raccoons; eight hundred fingers dithered. In the back of the room, Amy Valera coughed twice.

"Does anyone know what happens when they put you to death?" continued Professor Barnes. "Anybody?"

We stayed crickets, and she pressed on, steadily, but more quietly than I remember her ever having spoken before.

"Okay, let me tell you what happens. Right here in America, when they decide that they want you to die, what they do is they strap you onto a gurney. They bind your ankles, and they bind your wrists, and a doctor attaches heart monitors to your chest. The first needle goes into your medial epicondyle— that's the inside of your elbow, where the good veins are—but it's only saline solution. The warden gives the all-clear, and they raise up the curtain that separates you from the folks who showed up to watch you die. They're in the next room, and they'll watch through plate glass as the next needle anesthetizes you, paralyzes your muscular system, and finally stops your heart. They fill your blood with a cocktail of pentobarbital, pancuronium bromide, and potassium chloride. They fill your blood."

Here she paused, and nobody coughed.

"We can talk about capital punishment, and we can break it down with hypotheticals, and logic, and statistical findings, and well-reasoned arguments on every side. That is what law school is for, and you'll get plenty of that—you'll get plenty of that from me as much as anyone. This is not a point about procedure, alright? You're all going to be lawyers, and that means you can have a big impact out there in the world, but it is exceedingly, *desperately* critical that you remember to also be human beings. Don't let your instincts get crushed by anybody's intellectual wizardry, alright? Not even mine. Be a person. Think about the needle. Okay? Okay. I'll see you tomorrow."

Professor Barnes spruced her papers and strode out crisply, trailed as always by her stern TA.

"Well, that was sufficiently terrifying," said a weary Boots.

"Stop it," I replied, stashing my notebooks away. "You did great, and you know you did great, and, most importantly, she knows you did great."

"This coming from Captain Needle-Thinker, who some-how manages to cut to the moral core of the issue even when he's just trying to avoid the third degree."

"Yeah, I sort of lucked out there. Who knew she'd pick today to go maudlin on us for the first time ever?"

A voice from behind:

"Hey Bootsie. Hey nun from *Dead Man Walking.*"

"Clever," I said.

Sona Gasparyan was the third fifth of our study group, and the only one of my classmates apart from Boots with whom I would ever voluntarily have a conversation about, say, the Nature of Existence. She was harsh, affected, a year my senior, the sort of person for whom the word "coquettish" was invented ("more like 'cokeheadish,'" she'd dryly retort, apropos of nothing, after I first advanced the theory). Like Billie Holiday's, her voice was dark and thick—positively glutinous in its slow, low, deep-blue streams of brassiness and cheek—so much so that it nearly repudiated her rather charming physical brevity, which was marked by an elastic, feline slenderness, a perpetually wicked expression, and a dense, cascading forest of wild black hair. She was going to be a prosecutor, and had all the requisite opinions and insecurities. I saw her cry, once, walking home after a party, and she told me that I was the only person who had ever seen her cry. She was a liar.

"Mr. Brice, you're *soooooo* emotionally connected to the material."

"Okay."

"So scrupulous."

"Thanks."

"You really *get it*. You know? You . . . just . . . *get it.*"

"Alright, Sona."

"Mr. Brice, will you put a sensitive baby in me?"

"There it is."

"Come on, you crazy kids," interjected Boots, "we gotta go get smart."

The study group, such as it was, met in KF-1 (the William Burnham Woods Room) on the third floor of the law library every Tuesday after Barnes and every Thursday after Boots and Emily could extricate themselves from their clinical office. Prim, cerebral Emily Roca had started dating Boots on or around the fourth night of 1L orientation; she was probably the smartest of us, and almost certainly the most committed to the ostensible aims of the group qua group. Though she was square in all the ways that Boots was not (and literally so: from her fastidious blond bangs to her quadratic face to her ponderous, square-rimmed glasses), they were reliable to each other and, as a unit, to the world. Nobody could, or would ever want to, say an unkind word about Emily—she did everything right, humbly, and without complaint. I liked the way that she mellowed Boots as they grew up together, just as I liked the way that he frayed some of her neatly-hemmed edges. They were just one of those couples.

Gracie Coolahan was our last member. I'd met her in a gender justice reading collective during our second semester— every week, nine women, myself, and a confounded French masters student would sit cross-legged on scratchy zabutons in Professor Talia Zimmerman's cozy, quirky office and discuss male privilege over wine and beer. I'd come to feminism ignobly, sophomore year of college, on the tracks of a hopeless crush named Marlena, but soon graduated to true believer. As for Gracie, she was perpetually elated, always in the market for her next full-bellied laugh; when she found it, she'd go limp, blithely ensnaring her nearest friends for abutment, infecting them with her gladness, draping their shoulders with her winding, woolly dreadlocks. She was my neurotic equal, and our young friendship proved substantial enough to survive the scholastic fracas that, just two months after its inaugural session, tore that reading collective apart.

"Hey y'all," lilted Gracie on our arrival at KF-1.

"Who's in charge of treats?" inquired Sona sharply.

"That's me," said Grace. "Jim Beam, and hard cider for Emily."

"Cups?"

"Swigs."

"I adore you, Gracie," said Sona.

"*Gracias,* Gracie," added Emily.

"*De nada,* darling."

"*Vamos a tomar!*" Emily squealed, lofting her cider to the overhead light. I asked her what it meant, to which she replied, "come on, Leo—I thought you had a Spanish-speaking aunt?"

"Well," I answered tepidly, "I mean, she isn't really my aunt. And even if she was, that wouldn't automatically just equip me with all Spanish."

"Hey ladies," Sona cooed breathlessly, "did you know Boots and Leo nearly—*nearly*—saved the world today?"

"No! How?" asked Gracie, ever the enabler.

"Passionate moral assault on the death penalty. You should've seen it!"

"You're never going to drop this, right?" wondered Boots.

"I can't just drop it. Everyone needs to know what *good guys* you are. Defending rights. Taking a stand. Stickin' on up for justice. Seriously, though, it was just too ethical for words. There wasn't a dry skirt in the house."

"Gross," squeaked Emily.

"I hope you and Fiona realize how lucky you are to have these decent young men, that's all," continued Sona.

"Boots isn't young," Emily pointed out, and—speaking relatively—this was true.

"Could we get started?" I said. "We don't have a lot of time, and there's almost nothing about this I understand."

∙ ∙ ∙

A brief note on death: it haunts me. Ever since I was five years old, I've been terrified by the unknowable abyss, the perpetual destination which I was stunned to discover represented the only certain part of my future. The way I pictured it was this: death was going to feel like being forcibly ejected into space. One minute you'd be here on the ground, the way you usually are, and then death would come and you'd feel light. And you'd lift, not fast, but insistently enough to stay afraid, and soon the very same buildings you used to go into and out of would begin to look like freckles on the face of the Earth, and after that, you'd cross into cold darkness, the lights growing fainter and fainter until there were no lights at all—not even from the stars, which you'd long passed by—and you'd keep drifting like that, untethered from all the things you loved, in a straight line out, forever.

I couldn't comprehend, and I still can't, the idea that I might not be conscious for the experience. In my mind, the screen never actually turns off—there's just nothing being broadcast apart from the wall-to-wall black. I imagine there will be time to think. I imagine that time will be devastating and endless.

It was still winter when Boots and I each got e-mails from

Katherine Barnes asking us to come meet her for lunch at the Faculty Club. Neither of us had been there before, nor had we ever exchanged words with her outside of class—nobody had, as far as we could tell.

"Misters Rosenbaum and Brice," she began, after Boots and I slinked to the table where Barnes and her astringent TA were already stabbing at tiny, identical salads, despite the fact that we had arrived on time. "You each took my criminal procedure class this fall, yes?"

I turned to Boots awkwardly, as if to confirm.

"Y . . . yes, we both did," he answered.

"And you stood out to me in that class?" she queried, seemingly, at least, before allowing the longest-ever six seconds of silence to tick away.

"I'm sorry Professor Barnes," I spoke up at last, "was that a question?"

"No, I'm—*I'm* sorry, Mr. Brice—I'm saying that you did, as a matter of fact, stand out to me in that class. This is what I'm saying. You stood out to me on a particular issue that we covered on a couple of occasions, which happens to be why I've asked you to come here today. Said issue, Mr. Brice, is capital punishment," she announced with another stab. "I'm sure you recall the conversations the three of us had on the subject? You were the unfortunate two who took the bait, as it were—the metaphorical bait, that is, by which I mean you challenged me on the subject of death."

"I remember," said Boots.

"We—yes, we remember," I added meekly.

"Would it surprise you to learn that I am in agreement with you both regarding capital punishment? By which I mean categorically opposed."

It would. Her insistence on thinking about the needle aside, Katherine Barnes had been a celebrated prosecutor, the youngest U.S. Attorney in New York State history, and had the sort of tough-on-crime bona fides usually reserved for Reagan Republicans or Batman.

"I took the liberty of checking in with the Office of Career Services," she continued. "Neither of you are going to firms next year?"

"That's right," I said.

"And neither of you applied for judicial clerkships?"

We shook a no.

"Do you mind, then, if I ask you the rather obvious question of what you plan on doing with yourselves upon graduating?"

Boots and I made eye contact again, warily. As third-year law students, we'd engaged in this ritual dozens of times before—with parents, friends, strangers, even—and it never grew more impressive or less humiliating.

"Well, I'm sort of interested in helping musicians," offered Boots. "You know, independent musicians who need a lawyer to help them navigate the world . . . of music. The music business, I mean. See, I was a musician before law school. So, that's the, uh, genesis story of why I want to maybe do that."

"Legal . . . services . . . I think," I hawed like a guilty child.

Barnes did us the monumental favor of withholding comment, and carried on just as though we'd said nothing at all.

"I'm involved—quietly involved, that is—in an organization in which I thought, perhaps, one or both of you might potentially have interest. This is a small, but I assure you sleek, non-profit organization that works to exonerate wrongfully convicted death row inmates. They do fantastic work in that regard, and they need thoughtful lawyers. It's hard; it's direct services on the most consequential level imaginable."

"What are they called?" asked Boots as the curt TA signaled for a check.

"The New Salem Institute," answered Barnes, before puncturing her sole surviving cherry tomato and directing it pointedly across the table at each of us in turn. "Could this be something in which you might be interested?"

ABOUT
THE NEW SALEM
INSTITUTE

I. Our Story; Our Mission

Founded in 2007 by former classmates and colleagues Martha
Bok and Peter Ausberry, the New Salem Institute is a Brooklyn-
based non-profit advocacy organization that provides legal support to death row inmates who maintain their innocence. Clients
served by NSI have generally exhausted all other avenues of legal
recourse, and cannot afford to bear the costs of effective representation.

Ms. Bok and Mr. Ausberry first met in 1989 as second-year law
students at Yale, where they served together in the school's na-
tionally renowned Capital Punishment Clinic. After successful
stints in the private and public sectors, respectively, Martha and
Peter conceived of the idea for an innocence advocacy organization in 2005, and spent the next two years making their
dream a reality.

The New Salem Institute was created to advance the cause of
justice in America by ensuring that unfairly incarcerated inmates
are given the opportunity to prove their innocence. The NSI advocates for those who have been denied the chance to advocate
effectively for themselves, with the firm belief that no prisoner
should be put to death for a crime they did not commit.

II. Our Attorneys

Working with our dedicated support staff and interns, our team of attorneys uses their elite research and litigation skills to provide desperately-needed legal assistance to prisoners who have been condemned to death.

MARTHA BOK, CO-FOUNDER AND EXECUTIVE DIRECTOR

Martha Bok was born and raised in Rochester, New York, and earned her B.A. in English from Smith College in 1988 before entering Yale Law School as a member of the class of 1991. From 1991 to 2006, Ms. Bok performed complex litigation at Cravath, Swaine & Moore, first as an associate, and later as the youngest female partner in the firm's history. Since co-founding the New Salem Institute in 2007, Ms. Bok has been recognized as one of the nation's leading capital punishment reform advocates, and was the recipient of Amnesty International's 2010 Blackmun Award. She married fellow attorney Tom Nixon in 1997, and the couple has two daughters, Kerry and Elise. Ms. Bok is admitted to the state bar of New York.

PETER AUSBERRY, CO-FOUNDER AND EXECUTIVE DIRECTOR

Peter Ausberry is the New Salem Institute's co-founder and executive director alongside his former Yale Law School classmate, Martha Bok. Before co-founding the NSI in 2007, Mr. Ausberry clerked for Judge Ray Westley of the Second Circuit Court of Appeals, served as a fellow in the Department of Justice's Honors Program, worked as a senior attorney in the Office of the Solicitor General, and was appointed to the President's

Advisory Council on Prison Reform. A native of Seattle, Mr. Ausberry received his B.A. in Political Science from Yale University in 1987 and his J.D. from Yale Law School in 1991. He has been married to Christine Lanchik since 2003, and is a member of the state bars of New York and Washington. He appears at first glance to be gruff, but he is also kindly in his way.

JESSIE SUNDBY, MANAGING ATTORNEY

Jessie Sundby has been the New Salem Institute's managing attorney since its inception in 2007, and was a member of its original team. Before coming to NSI, Ms. Sundby served as a clerk to Judge Dale Centers of the Ninth Circuit Court of Appeals, and worked as an associate in the San Francisco offices of Morrison Foerster. Originally from Los Angeles, she received her B.A. in Political Science from Pomona College in 1999 and her J.D. from Stanford Law School in 2004. Ms. Sundby is a touch frenetic, and is a member of the state bars of New York and California.

KEVIN BLEDSOE, SENIOR STAFF ATTORNEY

Kevin Bledsoe joined the New Salem Institute as a staff attorney in 2007, and specializes in litigating post-conviction DNA cases as well as talking to Mr. Brice about college football based on one conversation they had on Mr. Brice's first day of work that led Mr. Bledsoe to the mistaken belief that Mr. Brice was at all interested in college football. After graduating from law school, Mr. Bledsoe spent two years as a litigation fellow with the NAACP Legal Defense and Educational Fund before returning to his hometown of Boston to join Ropes & Gray as an associate. Mr. Bledsoe received a B.A. in History from Harvard College in

1997, an M.A. in Political Science from Northeastern University in 1999, and a J.D. from Harvard Law School in 2002. He is admitted to the state bar of New York.

SALIM MCCULLOUGH, STAFF ATTORNEY

Salim McCullough is a proud Texan, and has been a staff attorney with the New Salem Institute since 2011. He's pretty rah-rah about the whole Texas thing—maybe too much, given the line of work he's in. Mr. McCullough received his B.A. in Texan Studies or something from the University of Texas in 2004, and his J.D., also from Texas, in 2010. He spent 2010 clerking for a judge in Texas, and is admitted to the state bar of New York.

SAMANTHA KIDEARE, STAFF ATTORNEY

Sam Kideare joined the New Salem Institute as a staff attorney in 2011 after clerking on the Second Circuit. The two most obvious things about her are that she is tall and joyful. Ms. Kideare always has a sweet thing to say, and always says it earnestly; there is no one with whom she cannot get along. Mr. Brice thinks that she might be interested in him, romantically, he means, but there have definitely been a great number of times when Mr. Brice has thought that and been sort of comically wrong. Once back in high school, Lucy Gafford complimented him on his cool Elvis Costello t-shirt, and Mr. Brice became convinced that the moment stood for something more; she had dyed hair, the color of bad blood, which she always twirled with one thin finger when she talked to him about bands he'd never heard of or art shows he'd never attended. Three weeks after Lucy—who was neither tall nor joyful—broke up with her boyfriend, who at the time would have been several years into college had he cared about that sort of thing, she and Mr. Brice were the last two remaining at a late-night bonfire on the beach. He'd had four or five beers, and, jousting at the embers with a long driftwood stake, he listened as she recounted a dream she'd had of a boat ride: how the black water washed on forever through the dark of her mind, and disappeared at dawn. He tried to kiss her then. He tried to kiss her then, beneath the olive oil moon, but a man has never been so wrong. Ms. Kideare earned her B.A. in Political Science from Harvard College in 2006, and her J.D. from Yale Law School in 2010.

AARON KIA, STAFF ATTORNEY

Aaron Kia has been a staff attorney with the New Salem Institute since 2012, following up a year-long clerkship with Judge Delilah Cobb of the Eastern District of Michigan. Mr. Kia received his B.A. in Political Science from Duke University in 2004 and his J.D. from Harvard Law School in 2011, and is definitely interested in Ms. Kideare, romantically, that is, because he never, ever stops talking to Mr. Brice about it, weirdly. He cares about soccer too much and is a member of the state bar of New York.

RACHEL COSTA, STAFF ATTORNEY

Rachel Costa became a staff attorney at the New Salem Institute in the fall of 2012 after serving as a legal intern during the summer of 2011. She earned her B.A. in Art History from Wellesley College in 2009 and her J.D. from Northwestern University Law School in 2012, and is admitted to the state bar of New York. Ms. Costa is a warm, thoughtful person, and really quite striking, which is a fact that has already touched down, softly, somewhere in Mr. Brice's vasculature.

BOOTS ROSENBAUM, STAFF ATTORNEY

Boots Rosenbaum joined the New Salem Institute in the fall of 2012, and is one of the very few people whom Mr. Brice trusts at this point. He didn't flinch when the walls caved in around Mr. Brice's head; he stuck around to help clear the rubble, and that meant a great deal. Mr. Brice hadn't ever had a friend like that before, one who could be counted on in a crisis. Mr. Rosenbaum received his B.A. in English and Music from New York University in 2004, and also graduated from a prestigious law school in 2012.

LEO BRICE, STAFF ATTORNEY

Leo Brice is some sort of a kind snob. He's been a real mess since Fiona left him for that vacuous prick. He's a lawyer, incidentally, and while he thinks he could become passionately invested in this sort of work, it's difficult for him to concentrate on the deaths of others right now, while his is still so fresh. What went wrong? He runs it back, daily, even now, months later, and will for some time. Just the other night, unsleeping like all others, he reached for a book—something dusty, something dry enough to anesthetize— and carelessly flipped to the inscription she had scrawled inside of the cover not ten months prior: "I love you more and more each day, my Dearest Friend. xoxo, F." This was *The Collected Letters of John and Abigail Adams*, once a birthday present, now another chalky half-column scattered among the ruins of their vast romantic empire. Listen to him prattle on! She wasn't so great, dammit. Once you go, you don't get to be great anymore—she forfeited the right to keep the all-bright things about her. If you run off, you can't be so smart, and you can't be very funny, you cannot be wry or vulnerable. If you don't exist, you can't be anything at all. Listen to this utter garbage! This is at once the end of the world, and not.

How utterly goddamn silly.

THREE

You live your whole life as though it were an ongoing story, but when someone leaves, here is what happens: you wake up the next morning, and all of a sudden you are an epilogue. I dragged myself wrackful through the same environment I'd always known, but absent Fiona those first days seemed to be little more than a ghostly and meaningless afterword, past pluperfect where a present tense ought to be. I remember thinking about God for the first time in ages—I hadn't really bought into growing up (not much, anyway), but I came around to the idea not long after I met her. I just couldn't believe that a rudderless universe would have allowed us to come together like that. I had no doubt, none at all, that our little confluence had been preordained by the Holy Whatever; when I found her, it was so much like finding the lock the key fit—at last, at last. Fiona was gone, and I still believed in God, only now I understood that She is a monster.

Fifty-six days were lost that summer to the New York State Bar Examination, and this thing happened on day fifty-eight, the second-cheapest champagne from the liquor store not yet dry on the loveseat. Boots and I weren't starting work at New Salem until halfway through September, which gave me nearly eight weeks to lie on the floor and dodge phone calls from the people I loved most. I didn't go home to my parents; I didn't go anywhere, and Boots and Sona were the only two people I let into my building during that long dark vacancy—a new house rule. Otherwise, I dealt exclusively with strangers. I started sitting down in the shower, sometimes for an hour or more. I ate and drank alone each day. I stopped wondering about anything, and dimly chased her ghost around the apartment, slouching from bathroom to kitchen to bed like a wounded animal.

Bzzzzzzzz.

"Dude," crackled Boots into the ancient intercom. "The government sent me to make sure you're alive today."

This was the seventeenth of August: three weeks into the new calendar, the one Fiona invented by leaving.

"How we doing today, buddy?" Boots asked, first thing.

"I think I'm dying, Boots."

"Still emo. That's wonderful. You know, I can never tell whether you're actually depressed or whether you're just regular-sad and doing a little commentary about depression."

"Me neither sometimes," I conceded, because it was good to have one sharp ally. I was actually depressed that day.

"So I'll ask again, and maybe you can shoot for an under-the-top response this time: Leo, how are you?"

"I've had better months. All of them, actually," I croaked truthfully, burrowing further into the easy chair.

"And I understand that, but I'm going to keep asking from time to time, just so we can be sure that you're on an upward trajectory."

"I'm fine. I need time, you know? To process. More time."

Boots was a tremendous pal, and perfectly suited to this particular tragedy. He'd had an engagement broken off prior to law school which nearly wrecked him, and that gave him a survivor's view—an aerial perspective on my suffering that I could never hope to comprehend from way down here on the molten ground.

At thirty, he was four years my senior, but his face bore the crags and heavy remembrances of a much older man. He had a face like an old wooden workbench—angular, unshaved, and dusty, and were it not for his hollow cheeks, we could have easily been mistaken for brothers. Before law school he'd been a drummer for a hyper-locally renowned three-piece Brooklyn outfit called Snaggletooth. I joined him on guitar half a dozen times—most often at lushy student organization parties—and together with our bassist acquaintance, Shira Pollard, and Gracie, herself a vivid singer and serviceable pianist, there was much talk of dropping out and making a go of it (what would we call our ragtag band? "Counselor," it was decided). Never happened.

"You gotta clean this place up, man."

"I know," I said.

"These flowers are dying," Boots pointed out, as he plucked an ashen ex-carnation from the vase on the table.

"I know. Fiona got them for me—for the Bar, I guess—and I, uh, appreciate the metaphor."

Boots picked up a bag of grapes from the kitchen counter and began to casually whip them at my chest, one at a time.

"Hey!" he hollered.

"What?"

"Hey!"

"What? Stop that."

"How long are you going to be like this for?" he asked, the next grape striking me squarely on the forehead.

"I don't know. How long did it take you to snap out of it?"

"Almost a year."

"Okay, so, it sounds like I've got a year minus three weeks before you can pass judgment on my mood."

"It's not healthy to be this devastated. Trust me. You've gotta get out there, you know? Out into the open air. Embrace the fresh start! I don't want to have to explain why you're such a sad sack to all of our fancy new colleagues when we get to the New Salem joint. I don't want to have to come up here next week and have you be, you know, dead, or something dramatic like that."

"Ugh."

"It's transition time, man. It's moving day. This is a big, critical moment for you; you just got out of a five-year-old relationship. It's time to grow up and move along and all that."

"Three years," I said.

"I'm sorry?"

"Fiona and I were together for a little over three years."

"I know that."

"You said I just got out of a five-year relationship."

"I said you got out of a five-year-*old* relationship," clari-fied Boots as he launched the final grape and I swatted it away.

"What?"

"I wasn't referring to duration. I meant both of you acted

like five-year-olds. Real relationships are not supposed to be that twee."

"Twee?"

"Yes."

"You think we were twee?"

"Very much so. You two existed in this fantasy romance world that nobody else was privy to. It's not your fault, man—she was a strange one, and you're a little strange too, so I'm sure it was easy to fall into all that. Look, Fiona was great, but Fiona is gone. She does not exist anymore."

"Of this . . . I am . . . aware," I sighed.

"It will end up having been for the best. That's always how it works, and if you could be objective about the situation, you would agree with that."

"That's not necessarily true, at all. You know? What if I'm not okay? What if this is the worst thing that has ever happened or that ever will happen, Boots? I can't even wrap my mind around it. She just . . . unceremoniously broke up with me."

"And what? You wanted it to be ceremonious?"

"I would've liked a ceremony, sure. Candles. Some chanting, you know, Gregorian chants, maybe. Or a live band. A ceremony would've been nice."

"There's that rapier wit. He lives! I gotta run," he said, and started to walk out of my haunted apartment. "Are you going to kill yourself?" he asked me, I think at least half-earnestly, from the doorframe.

"No."

"Is that a promise? Because if I leave here, and you kill yourself, I'm going to be furious."

"I so promise," I said, saluting for no reason.

"Okay, great."

"I will say," I started, "you know, thank God my number one fear is death. Because I'm pretty sure my number two fear is having to live like this, without her. I will say that."

"Okay, Leo? This is pretty much exactly what I'm talking about. That's the sort of thing that people who kill themselves say before they . . . do it."

"I was just making an honest observation."

"Alright. I gotta go pick up Emily at the airport. Sona said she's bringing you food tomorrow. Don't kill yourself!"

"Thanks for stopping by."

"Don't do it!" he shouted from the hallway, leaving the door open, as he always did lately, just so that I would have to distinguish myself from the easy chair for a few seconds in order to fling it shut.

• • •

"Leo, will you teach me about contracts?" Fiona asked me once from behind a pair of her mother's oversized glasses she borrowed from the 1970s.

"Serious or kidding?"

"Serious, I think. I'd like to know something about it, in case, you know, anyone ever asks me to sign one. For acting, I mean."

By the spring of 2010, this wasn't out of the question; Fiona was still a year and several months away from booking *Mercy General*, but did have several small television spots to her credit.

"Well, you know that they're essentially, just, agreements," I began.

"Obviously."

"The terms of which are bargained for."

"Uh-huh."

"By two or more parties acting in good faith."

"*Leooooo.*"

"I'm not sure what you're looking for here, Fiona. In class, we usually only deal with them after somebody has breached their end of the agreement."

"What do you do then?"

"What do *I* do then?"

"I mean, what happens? Wait, no—I know what happens: they sue. It's a lawsuit!" she declared, and she did a little lawsuit dance.

"Well, sure. That's pretty much it."

"Tell me about that. How do they fix a broken contract?"

"Okay, well, the idea is that, usually, at least, the courts will try to restore the party who's been aggrieved to the position they'd be in had the contract not been breached. It's called 'expectation damages.' I mean, there's a lot more to it than that, but the sort of basic, fundamental idea is that you want to make the other person—the non-breacher—the courts will focus on making the other person whole."

"Making the other person whole? That sounds so romantic!"

"I assure you it's not."

"You know what I'm going to say now, right?"

"I assure you I don't."

"Yes you do. Leo . . ."

"Fiona?"

"Leo, darling . . ."

"Mmm-hmm?"

"Leo, my dearest, deepest love . . ."

"Can I help you?"

"Light of my life . . . fire of my loins . . . my sin . . . my song . . ."

"It's 'soul,' not 'song.' Don't come at me with the *Lolita* if you're not going to—"

"It's both for me. Soul, song. You know why?"

"I don't."

"*You . . . make . . . me . . . whole.*"

She pounced upon me like a devilish idea, cackling to herself and pinning my arms against the deep-red spackle of the wall. We were in the waiting area of some Moroccan restaurant; the grim hostess and a blond couple with their blond child glared at the scene we were making, and we glared right back.

"There's also restitution," I hissed into her ear as she nipped away at my neck.

"Restitution doesn't make you whole?" she breathed up to me.

"It puts you back," I muttered, "it puts you back to where you were pre-contract, before you ever exchanged promises."

She clamped down hard now on what I believed to be my jugular vein.

"Sounds like it makes you whole."

"I guess so, in a way," I answered, "it makes you the whole version you used to be. But it doesn't make you the whole that you could have been, in the future, had the other side come through the way they were supposed to."

"That's still mostly whole, though. It's like you never made a contract at all?"

"Uh-huh. Ow! Mostly whole, sure."

"Leo, party of two?" sang the sad-eyed hostess, and we whisked past the disapproving blondies to a table in the back.

• • •

The first time I met the actor, Mark Renard, he complimented me on my handshake.

"That's a great handshake, bro," said he.

Mark had dark features and was inexcusably handsome—Fiona once pointed out aptly that he resembled the evil prince from just about every Disney movie. He was also probably the dumbest human being I have ever met. Not just dumb: he was eagerly dumb, aggressively so. He maintained a stunning capacity for misapprehension and verbal crisis. Every thought his bird brain bred seemed to wriggle its way free from the leash of basic intelligence. Every sentence he deployed was a kamikaze pilot, content to destroy itself and everything around it in the service of stupidity.

Fiona used to rag on him constantly—a sure sign, of course, but only in retrospect—confiding in me each new act of witless wonder her co-star managed to perpetrate on set.

"His favorite book—no kidding—is *Atlas Shrugged*. I don't even think he's political or anything; I think he just genuinely likes the story."

Heh.

"He called me a nerd last night because I used the word 'superfluous.'"

That's hilarious, Fee.

"He wants us to go to the MoMA with him and his new girlfriend, only he pronounces it 'momma.' She's an actual runway model!"

Please tell me we're not doing that with them.

"He told me today that he's 'looking into Scientology.'"

Whoa. Cuh-razy.

"He wears a fucking hemp necklace."

This guy seems pretty absurd.

At that time, Mark could reasonably be called a B-lister: famous enough to play a major character on a long-running television show, but not famous enough to have yet broken into film. As an actor, he was reliably one-note—that tired note, though, was of course the very tonic of commercial success. He could look deeply into anything and think deeply into nothing, and on screen that was enough.

I think he was my opposite. He had the look of a person who slept soundly, every night. I was, and am, completely uninterested in the lives of the well-rested. What is it they're not up thinking about each evening, over there, sealed off from the bountiful haunts and burdens of personhood? It's almost inhuman. And how could a person so self-conscious not also be at least mildly self-aware? I decided that Mark Renard was little more than a born philistine desperately eager for soul. Who really knows, though: maybe it isn't true. But I am allowed to decide things about the person who took Fiona away from me. He really did seem this way; he really did wear a hemp necklace.

I used to hang around the set of *Mercy General* sometimes, and marvel at the operation. Everybody whirring; everybody so damn serious—about what? The show was terrible. Assistant directors flailing wildly about like shot birds; extras gamboling across the lot; craft services people busying themselves with the precise placement of endless tureens of hummus. Mark, with his trapezoid jaw and oafish perma-furrow, running lines with my Fiona—a twelve-dollar kiddie-pool of hair gel splashing pitifully against the ocean of her inborn talent. I used to hang around that set, before the whole of the world got away from me.

The summer that her character was killed off was the same

summer I spent studying for the bar exam. Boots and I were set to begin work at the New Salem Institute that fall, and, for the first time in my life, I had discovered a bona fide professional ambition. I actually *wanted* to be a lawyer; not simply to get smart or fend off the future, I wanted to use this degree of mine for a purpose—the only cause I would ever deem worthy of my sweet, constantly diminishing time. I wanted to advocate against death.

As it happens, they don't pay you to advocate against your own, and so representing people for whom the state had wrongly (or, at least, in a constitutionally suspect manner) invited the monster along early struck me as a decent enough surrogate for the time being. Death couldn't be abolished, not yet, at least, but it could be staved off. And who better to stave it off for than those who were facing the prospect of an artificial ending brought on by a wrongful conviction? If I had to engage daily with this world of stern dictates and high-handed falderal, better that it should be done in this way, with this firm posture—opposed, opposed, opposed to death, and not merely to the penalty, but to the very premise as well.

This newfound fervor—my solitary crusade to halt, for a handful of wretches, the inching glacier of death on a technicality—sparked an unexpected urgency around passing the bar. Summer nights were given over to lamp-lit flashcards and byzantine mnemonics. Summer mornings belonged to interminable lecture videos, which always featured some gray shill holding court in an empty room, waxing breathlessly on third party interpleaders or the exclusion of relevant evidence or the Takings Clause. Fiona rose at seven most mornings to make it over to the set; even on those days when she wasn't on the call sheet, she'd occasionally leave just as early to practice her lines or get breakfast with the cast. Some days, I didn't see her until the evenings, when I'd take a break from studying and she'd return after the shooting had wrapped, and she would be airtight, reserved, humble, and quick to seek sex.

"Is something wrong?" is what I didn't ever say. We were not used to spending full days apart, and I imagined this was simply what that was like. This had to have been it—growing upward and older, like a tree that had been split by lightning: two towering stalks aspiring towards the sun at independent angles, yoked forever by a common stem and braced far under the earth by roots as sturdy and discreet as pythons. Branching out, to be sure, but always conjoining back home on the ground. That was what this was. It had to be. But: I felt a bug in my blood, a small spot of chill coursing through me in quiet moments, and it wouldn't go away.

"I've been talking to my agent about stage names," Fiona called out to me one evening from the kitchen that summer, adding, of two sweet onions, "come chop these for me."

"Why do you need a stage name?" I asked once beside her.

"I don't *need* one," she replied, "but Linda says it could be beneficial. Not sure why, but a lot of actors do it. Probably more than you'd think. And besides, Haeberle is—it's always been—I don't really know. It's a bit cumbersome, I guess. A little bulky."

"Bulky?"

"Mmm."

She absently poked at a simmering pan of eggplant with one hand, and pulled assorted detritus off of the back of my sweater with the other.

"Well, if Linda says so . . ." I started.

"You're not on board?" she asked, and then, wide-eyed and plaintively, "you're not on board!"

"It just feels a little, I don't know, unseemly," I fretted between chops. "It makes me wonder: what else do they want you to change about yourself? Where does it stop?"

"It stops there," she declared hotly.

"Okay, well, if it stops there, and if it's what you want, then you should go for it," I said, sliding a knifeful of diced onion from block to pan. She froze a moment, then started poking me in the shoulder with one finger.

"So?!" she hollered after a few seconds of this.

"So what?"

"So, are you gonna try to help name me, or what?"

"Of course I am. You think I wouldn't try to exert influence here? You think I wouldn't *love* to name you?"

I flicked the last of the onion residue toward its new home, and rinsed the knife.

"So?" she demanded again, tugging at my clothes.

"Oh, you mean right now?"

"Yes! I mean right now!"

"Phyllis Goldberg."

"Here we go."

"Eileen . . . Nissenbaum."

"You're almost *too* hilarious, Leo. Such a card."

"Ruth Bader Lopez. Actress Jones. Oprah Winfrey, Jr."

"This is all just supremely helpful. I'm glad you take my career so seriously," she said, and pushed me away with two palms.

"No one takes your career more seriously than I do, and you know this," I countered, suddenly defensive. And this was true.

"So why are you being such a goon about this name change project?"

"Because changing your name is goony, Fiona. Because you've railed how many times about how shallow and vapid actors are, and here you are artificially altering yourself to please . . . I don't know, the industry, or something."

She tugged me back in, and lifted her eyes to mine.

"Look, I get your opposition here. I get it, Leo. But now that the doctor show is wrapping up and people are becoming available for other projects, things could happen quickly. My name will be out there—"

"Well, *a* name will be out there—"

"And I need to be thinking about making sure I've got my best foot forward, and all that. At least, that's what Linda says."

"I understand."

"Do you?"

"I do. And I recognize that your agent probably knows best in this area."

"Look at that: contrition. Contrition from Mr. Leo Brice!" she squealed, and kissed me, twice, then spun out of my arms.

"Don't get used to it, sugar."

"So you're going to help out for real now?"

"I will do my best. What are you working with so far?"

"A bunch of stuff. Everybody's throwing out ideas. Mark thinks it should be alliterative."

"Does he now?"

"Indeed he does."

"I highly doubt Mark used 'alliterative' in the adjective form like that."

"That's true! Nice work, Detective Brice," she said, returning for one more kiss.

"You really want your new name to be alliterative?"

"It's just a stage name. And—I don't know, maybe. Why not?"

"Only lowbrow losers like alliteration. You see what I did there?"

"Pretty deft, man."

"I do try."

"Hm . . . what's a good name for a star? Fiona Foster? Fee-ohhh-naaa . . . Fisher? No! Fiona Ford? No . . . Fiona . . . Flynn. Fiona Flynn?"

"What about Haeberle?" I said. "I like Fiona Haeberle a lot."

She stuck her tongue out at me, and began to twirl about the room.

"Finnegan? Fff . . . reeman? Fisk? Ooh, what about Fox? Honey, what do you think about Fox?"

• • •

James Buchanan could not have been better prepared for glory. History has reduced him to an impotent, milquetoast, sexually confused footnote, too tragically useless to even find work as a punch line. Being reduced by history is itself an accomplishment, though—you must be gifted enough to stand in the batter's box of greatness, but not so adept as to make any sort of meaningful contact. Historical mediocrity demands both the exceptional rise and the exceptional thud, and James Buchanan was one of the most mediocre public figures ever to have grounded weakly back to the mound.

He was born in an actual log cabin in Franklin County, Pennsylvania, and became a state legislator, congressman, senator, U.S. minister to Russia, U.S. minister to the United

Kingdom, secretary of state, and president of the United States before dying hated. He was dour, and he looked like an old maestro. He was twice offered a seat on the Supreme Court. He failed so miserably, and the whole thing fell apart around his failure. He must have been so desperate for a second chance.

This wasn't very long ago at all. Here's how short American history is: John Tyler, who used to be the president, was born less than a year into George Washington's first term in office; today, which is to say nearly two decades into the twenty-first century, two of Tyler's grandchildren are still alive. That's the whole of the republic—grandfather to father to sons.

You probably remember Buchanan only vaguely from the slowest day in history class. Maybe you know that he was our fifteenth president; certainly you're aware that he was and is unpopular—no, not even unpopular: just forgettable. But did you know that he also had dreams? That he had pain, rich like yours? Did you know how fully he suffered, right here on the same ground we suffer on, under the same pale stars, not so very long ago?

When Buchanan was twenty-eight, his fiancée took her own life, and it ruined him forever. Tragedy anneals great leaders—the horror tends to forge them into soulful and determined visionaries—but it leaves the rest of us broken: Tyler, to take one example, lost his wife in office and never recovered. Lincoln, on the other hand, outlived three of his four sons, and through grave depression extinguished our national fire. On Valentine's Day, 1884, Teddy Roosevelt's wife and mother died in the same house, eleven hours apart, just two days after the birth of his first child. "The light has gone out of my life," he wrote in his diary that night, and by 1901 he was president. To overcome the worst loss you are capable of imagining, to fashion it, somehow, from a seemingly barren future into a character-building speck of past—that is the mark of greatness. It is the skill that separates Lincoln and Roosevelt from Buchanan and Tyler, and, when the time comes, it separates us all.

Buchanan was chosen to save the republic in its hour of fracture and despair because he was capable, and careful, and wise: a serious man with a servant's heart. He couldn't imagine a future that didn't resemble the past, and when South Carolina bolted like a frightened colt from the Union, he announced confidently to friends that he was to be the last American president. He couldn't imagine a future in which he wasn't the future.

"I shall carry to my grave the consciousness that at least I meant well for my country," said Buchanan to the Congress less than eight weeks before the end of his term as president.

Three months later came Fort Sumter. He did the best that he could, and still he broke the world.

• • •

I took the bar exam up in Saratoga on the sixteenth and seventeenth of July. Boots and Emily, Sona, Gracie, and I had made a pact: twenty-four hours would elapse between the moment we arrived back in the city and the moment we would allow ourselves to discuss, commiserate over, or, after knocking all of the wood in Brooklyn, celebrate what had just happened. We each took the eighteenth to rest; I slept late and stonily, took a long walk solo into neighborhoods I hadn't even known were there before—neighborhoods without names—and met Fiona, who was filming that day, for a late lunch. We were all supposed to get drunk together that night, but when the hour came, no one had the resolve. Gracie came over for Thai food, and she and Fiona fell asleep on the couch half an hour into a documentary about big cats. I saw it through to the end, then made myself into a starfish, collapsing alone on our bed.

July 19 was a Friday, and our deferred bash came to be. None of us would have our test results back for several months, but this was secondary to our concerns—the thing was done, the beast bested, and we could all move on with our lives. Sona and Gracie took eager belts from a handle of watery gin. Emily nursed a little jug of hand-crafted cider—something peachy, with a calligraphic name. Boots and I shared a bottle of the darkest liquor the adult versions of ourselves could stomach: a russet rye that sprayed bullets through my throat. Everybody guzzled champagne, and we drained the night away trading stories of heart-stopping computer scares, barbaric multiple choice guesswork, and essay question responses that flew the coop of reason and coherence as our proctors' clocks ticked themselves down towards the exhausting freedom to come.

Fiona was late; it was her last day of filming for *Mercy General*, and she had a wrap party of her own that evening. She slunk through the door just before midnight—by that time, we were all in assorted stages of maniacal repose on the furniture—and her lower eyelids were billowy, cerise gobs. This time, I asked: "Is something wrong?"

"What?!" she called out, startled, and I knew I'd spoken indiscreetly—too loud and too intimate for a late night with company.

"Is—" I started, then shut my mouth and watched her, watching me.

"Fiona," chimed in Emily with sweet concern, "have you been crying? Are you okay?"

She stiffened up, and searched, and I knew that she was searching.

"Oh!" she answered, distantly but with a volume suggestive of nonchalance. "I was just—the show. The show is over, you know?"

"Of course," said Emily.

"Of course," I said.

"The show is over," she continued, "and that's an emotional thing . . . that gets pretty emotional, naturally, and—"

"Of course it does," I said.

"That's all," she said.

"That can't be easy," offered Gracie.

"It's—no," Fiona replied, "it's, you know . . . unemployed again. Ha! And all that."

She smiled her on-camera smile for my inebriated friends, and dabbed at her wet eyes with the hem of her loose T-shirt.

"Well, obviously you're going to be working again soon," Emily responded on behalf of the room, a sentiment echoed by the lot of us.

"Thanks—seriously," Fiona said, adding, "let's just . . . this is your big night to celebrate, you know, take a load off and just—can we . . . let's just all go back to celebrating."

We did, and Fiona kept quiet until everyone had slipped away from the apartment—and even after, when the two of us were alone, she kept quiet still. She had not had much to drink by the time she followed me into the silent bedroom; I was still feeling drunk. Something is wrong, is what I knew then as she wriggled vacantly into the covers. And the bug in my blood made a hole in my heart.

"What's going on?" I whispered right that second. I was staring at where I knew that the ceiling was, but it was much too dark to tell that there was anything up there at all.

"What do you mean?" she answered after fifteen seconds of quiet.

"What do I mean?" I whispered back, incredulous. "I mean, you're being shifty."

"I'm not."

"Awfully shifty, Fiona, and it's weirding me out."

"I'm just tired," she said, sounding every bit like it, and I felt her turn away from me in the darkness, felt the top sheet shift from the berth of my thrumming chest.

"Are you sure?" I asked, still whispering.

"Yes," she said, and there followed consecutive hours of no speaking. And through that time, which felt like infinitely more time than it had to have been, no one slept. Fiona was all twists and whimpers in Our bed, making a big show of being quietly disturbed, pretending to try to hide it, jerking about like a fallen power line. I didn't try to talk, and though I must have been after a certain point completely sober—perhaps more so, I thought, than I'd ever been before—there were times when I couldn't distinguish the pitch black of the room from my eyes being closed. Which was it now: the dark of the bedroom or the dark within my head? I'd catch myself closing them, fling them open wide again, and it wouldn't make a lick of difference. The clock was on her side; I couldn't see it, so I don't know when it was that she shot straight up, but she did, as abruptly as though she'd heard in the stillness a shotgun blast. She produced her phone from the nightstand and typed out something—some message. It must have been sufficiently late to be wholly tomorrow, comfortably Saturday morning, because there was just enough clarity—just enough of the faintest implication of light—for me to watch her rising away. And then she spoke softly from a standing position, but with her arms folded and head down in a way I'd never seen her before.

"Leo," she began, and it sounded alien to me, harsh and charged and quavering, knifing through the black, laden with leaden thoughts, not just anchored to the dirty ground but buried many inches under it with the knotted worms and the unseen loam.

"Leo," she said again, louder, but no more recognizably, "Leo, are you—"

"Yeah, hey," I whispered, feigning, I guess, to wake. "What is it? What's wrong?"

She exhaled for what seemed like a lifetime; a lifetime slipped out of her lips. I felt jungle-hot and wired, but I lay there like an infant in the sheets. She didn't say anything after that—she just let that exhalation spread and settle over everything in the room, fossilizing my deadweight body, freezing the furniture in place, preparing us all for a change in tense. After a few minutes, I gathered the churning lumps from inside my organs and secreted them out as words.

"You have to talk to me," I said, unconvincingly. "You have to talk to me, and tell me what is going on—because I have no idea what is happening here, Fiona. I have no idea what's going on with you right now."

She sighed again, exhaling the last of whatever was in there.

"Fiona," I went on, gaining speed now, and desperation, "talk to me, please. Please tell me what's wrong, if something is wrong. We talk to each other when something is wrong. You can talk to me, if something is wrong, and we can talk about it, okay? We can make it right, Fiona, but you have to talk to me."

In the mustering light, I saw her start to cry before I heard the sound. Her tears became a tempest, and she bent at the

waist, howling madly. I said nothing at all while she rode this
out, but felt tightly-wound tornadoes of my own caucusing inside my stomach and chest. There was a furor ripping through
my brain, sweat gliding out from my fists, the full weight of
the night bearing down on my oaken limbs. I couldn't speed
my breath or slow my heart. So I just waited there, prone, and
sometime later she lulled at last and spoke.

"I don't know how to *tell* you," she cracked, one palm firm
against each of her eyes, "that I have to be gone."

The dam burst, and all the brine inside of me welled up to
my shuddering face, surging for the exits.

"I don't know how to tell you that I have to go," she blurted
out all at once, with a relative calm, before hiccupping violently and convulsing again.

I pawed roughly at my eyes—a lame attempt to stem the
flood—and found myself wanting to speak. But every word
seemed to require a drawn-out and toilsome forging in my
lungs; the work was slow, and the harvest haphazard.

"I don't understand," I sputtered meekly, the very best that
I could do.

"Listen," she said, "listen."

She stood up straight and breathed: the breath of gathering breath, the one I'd seen a thousand times before. It was
the leadoff to her pre-rehearsal vocal warmup routine, making its debut tonight in a new and challenging role.

"Leo," she lit, "there's something I need to say. And I know
this probably will sound like it's coming out of nowhere; and
I know that it . . . will probably be very hard—very difficult
for you, to understand."

She seemed too steady, now—too practiced and performa-
tive, her arms fired down at her sides, her chin up. It seemed
all too much like a recitation. Had she been rehearsing this

for—how long had it been—when could it have—what the fuck, Fiona?

"I don't—" I started, and ebbed back into the quiet of myself.

"There's no television work left in New York," she said.

"There's what?"

"I said there isn't much television work left in New York," she tried again, adding, "Leo, I'm—I have to move on, move on if I'm going to . . ."

This time I had nothing; I gathered up words and spilled them back down, and wound up gulping at the dim air.

"Leo," she went on, "I've been feeling stuck here sometimes, and I haven't really . . . known what to do about it. I've felt stuck with work, with the show, and I've felt stuck with us—like with this feeling of inevitability, if that even makes sense, of like a track that I can't—"

"A track?" I offered dumbly.

"I think that I need to find out who I am independently of us—of, just, what I'm like without . . . without us."

"Without me," I quietly croaked.

"Without us. Sometimes it feels as if we've been together for so long, and not just together, but . . . integrated—an item, one item, that isn't really either of us at all. I feel like the things I like are the things that we like: the music, the . . . food, the—everything, and that never used to be the case before. And that sort of scares me. It scares me that I don't really know myself, or what I would care about if I didn't have someone else there, sort of cultivating all of that. And I need to know what else there is that I can be, just I—and I know that sounds harsh. I do know that, and I'm . . . it's why I need to go, Leo, it's . . . that's why I have to be gone."

I sank deeply into the foam as the words stacked up against

my body. We were still for a while, then—a breather—and then came this.

"And for work—from a work standpoint . . . for my career and this thing that I've wanted to be my whole life, I think me leaving is what's best. And LA is where that all happens; I can't do that, I don't think, if I'm not out there in LA; I just can't do it here."

"Fiona," I eked out between the long, slow heaves of my system, "if you feel like you're being . . . held back . . . by, just, geography—"

"No," she interjected immediately, definitively, soft but stern. "No, Leo, no. That's . . . a part of it, but it isn't all of it. It's more the first part, about defining who I am—really knowing who I am. The LA thing, it's part of the same thing, part of the same whole. This is something that I have to do. I have to go."

"This feels so abrupt," I said. "This comes from nowhere; this is—what are you doing?"

She was throwing open the closet doors, stuffing loose fistfuls of clothing into a suitcase.

"Fiona," I said again, still fastened hard to the bed, "where are you going?"

"Los Angeles," she answered through new tears, sealing up her case and charging for the door.

"But tonight," I said, "Fiona, where are you going right now? Why are you doing this? Why are you leaving right now?"

She stood in the doorway, facing away, frozen for a moment apart from one thin hand sliding down the frame, preserving a last image (an image of leaving; an image of being gone) I could pursue for all time. Something, I thought then, gazing after her, and gazing after tonight—something to re-member her by.

"I have to go," she said, and walked plainly away.

"Fiona, where?" I shouted after her, "Where can I find you? Fiona, where can I find you if I need to find you? Where can—Fiona, we need to talk. We're going to need to . . . I need to know how to find you, and we need to talk. Fiona! What about your things? What about all of our stuff? You just have your clothes, Fiona—what about all of our things here?"

"The rest is yours," she said, and shut behind her the frail door to our home.

I mushed the icy, stupefied dogs of my body into motion, and ran to the open window overlooking the city below. I peered through it, but there was not a trace of light: the dawn hadn't broken after all; I'd only been adjusting to the darkness in the room. I couldn't find her on the street below. And so I called out to her: "Fiona!" Again, nothing: "Fiona!"

I heard a car door open; it didn't pull up, it had already been there, waiting. But what kind of cab would—

"I'm sorry!" she yelled up at me. "Leo, I'm just so sorry."

And everything stopped for me all at once. I hardly heard the words. Headlights burst open the oil-black girdle of the night, and a moment later she was gone.

FOUR

MICHAEL TIEGS WAS BORN IN CAIRO, GEORGIA in the summer of 1976. His father, Barton Tiegs, was an occasional mechanic who killed himself by drinking a fifth of whiskey and driving his Chevelle into a brick wall three weeks after his only child turned four. Michael's mother, Cara Bonner Tiegs, raised him until her own death from lung cancer in 1990, at which point Michael went to live with his father's sister, a state employee named June Jones, two towns over. That same fall, he was arrested for the first time and charged with misdemeanor theft for stealing bicycles; he logged one hundred hours of community service and was placed on six months' juvenile probation.

High school proved, perhaps predictably, to be difficult for Michael. He was undoubtedly one of the most skilled baseball players in the county, and one of its worst students to boot. He failed two courses as a sophomore—the same year he went

15-1 with a 2.06 ERA for the Pelham High Hornets—and was expelled from summer school as a formality after failing to attend a single session. At seventeen, he robbed a convenience store with a kitchen knife, a crime for which he spent the next three years in state prison after pleading guilty as an adult to a lesser offense. He entered a work release program at twenty; he spent his weekends living at a halfway house. On weekdays he mopped floors and bussed dishes at Harmon's Bar & Grill, and every Thursday night he had dinner at June Jones's house with her husband Tom and their three teenage children.

By 1999, Michael had moved into an apartment of his own in the nearby city of Albany, fully emancipated from state custody for the first time in five years. His girlfriend, Therese Calley, was a former teen meth addict whom he had met in the halfway house; she'd been clean for eighteen months, and operated the fryer at a fast-food restaurant inside a terminal of the local Greyhound station. Therese had been arrested on three occasions by the time she was eighteen: twice for possession of a controlled substance, and once for solicitation. She moved in with Michael in March 2000, and the two cohabitated in relative post-custodial bliss for the next seven months.

At 5:35 on the morning of October 21, Therese stepped onto the 86 bus that brought her to work each day. Michael either did or did not wake up to his alarm at 6:30, the hour at which the account of the condemned departs from the ultimate findings of the court. According to the state's narrative, Michael woke as usual, boarded the 65 northbound bus rather than the southbound 46 which typically brought him to his job at Harmon's, and got off three blocks from the home of John Jasper, a thirty-eight-year-old substance abuse counselor formerly employed by the Willow Creek Resource Center, the same halfway house where Michael and Therese had first met four years prior. Suspicious that John and Therese were romantically involved, Michael knocked on the front door of the Jasper residence at or around 7:15. He was let in by John, whom he then shot three times in the chest with an unlicensed Smith & Wesson .22 LR Rimfire handgun, which was later found in John's kitchen trashcan with its serial number scratched off. Michael walked immediately back to the bus stop, switched over to the 46 near his own home, and arrived at work eighty-six minutes late.

According to Michael's narrative, he slept through his alarm that morning, waking at 7:55. He placed a call to Donna Viers, his shift manager at Harmon's, at 8:09, informing her that he had overslept and would be running late; Viers's testimony and the introduction of phone records into evidence confirm this. He took the 46 to work, completed the remaining eight hours and thirty-four minutes of his shift, and remained at Harmon's to drink Bud Lights until 7:30 in the evening. He took the 46 back home, and was not aware of John Jasper's death until two county officers arrived the next day to question him.

Two days later, Michael Tiegs was taken into custody and charged with malice murder. At trial, the richer story comes out in earnest: roguish Jasper therapes his addled patients and sleeps with the junkiest lady-junky from each successive group session. Those early salad days of the Tiegs-Calley romance were marked by admissible jealousies—Michael saw the lech in counselor John, and waxed feverishly about his desire to see him dead on more than one occasion right there in the personal journal provided to him by the administrators of the halfway house for the exact purpose of recording just such feelings (post-discovery, that private journal would be renamed "State Exhibit C"). Teary Therese fields questions in the courtroom on behalf of her lover—the actual word used nine separate times by two attorneys plus the judge: "lover"—but can't account for Michael's whereabouts on the death morning, can't account for his propensity to rage, can't so much as recall whether she'd ever seen her boyfriend of more than four years in the company of a firearm. The appointed defender is unbelievably bad, asking all the wrong questions and planting every fruitless seed. The driver of the northbound bus to Guilty identifies Tiegs as an unequivocally present passenger, while the driver of the southbound bus to Not Guilty doesn't recognize the man at all, despite the fact that Tiegs had ridden the 46 twice per day, six days per week for almost two years. The whole thing—trial to verdict to sentence—takes only two weeks.

From the *Albany Herald*, 6 June 2002:

ALBANY—Convicted murderer Michael Robert Tiegs was sentenced to death on Thursday by a Dougherty County Superior Court jury.

Tiegs, 25, showed little emotion as Judge Paul Cousins read the sentence aloud. He had been convicted by the same twelve-member jury last Friday for killing his former therapist, John Jasper, in Jasper's Lydon Street home nearly two years ago.

Tiegs was sentenced to death on one count of malice murder, and will be transferred to death row pending an automatic appeal to the state Supreme Court required by Georgia law in death penalty cases.

The victim's parents, Hank and Nancy Jasper, as well as his sister,
Corinne Fleming, were greeted with hugs by the many friends and
relatives who filled the courtroom. Tiegs's girlfriend, Therese Calley,
declined to speak with reporters following the verdict. Calley had
testified on behalf of Tiegs during his trial.

Dougherty County District Attorney Janine Huff called the verdict
"fitting, given the clearly premeditated nature of the crime."

"I think what we have here is a good instance of the system working,"
Huff added. "Michael Tiegs committed an act of cold-blooded murder,
and the Jasper family can finally rest knowing that justice will be
done."

Tiegs, who pled not guilty at trial, vigorously contested his role in
Jasper's death. His appeal is likely to be set for this winter at the state
supreme court in Atlanta.

Ten years and three failed appeals go by, and the Georgia
Diagnostic and Classification State Prison visiting area looks
sterile but smells quite like a thousand pre-packaged sand-
wiches.

"Hello, Michael? Good morning, Michael. We're the attorneys from the New Salem Institute who've been assigned
to come . . . meet you, and speak to you about your case.
My name is Rachel, and this—"

"Ms. Costa," said Michael Tiegs. "Mr. Brice."

"That's right. We're your new lawyers, Michael. We're
here to make sure that your claims of innocence are fully and
fairly heard."

He hadn't looked up until just then, and his eyes were

enormous whey spheres—feverish, bold, voltaic eyes, eyes that could only reasonably belong to an addict or a mystic.

"My dear sweet sister in Christ," he said, meticulously wringing two spotted hands against the front of his hoary tangelo jumpsuit. "My dear sweet brother in Christ."

• • •

I spent much of the second half of the year Fiona left me sifting through artifacts. She and I used to write letters to each other— real ones, of the handwritten, licked-envelope variety—and stash them sneakily in our shared mailbox. The rule was: we never mentioned to each other that the letters existed; they were their own, entirely separate discourse, like some mad parallel relationship that was happening between two other versions of our two selves. There was no money then, and on birthdays we always gifted food, wrote poems, or staged elaborate public acts of self-humiliation for the other's entertainment. I put everything in a shoebox, because that's what they did in movies; shuffling through it now was my cruel, private ritual: new shrapnel each and every night—new salt for old wounds.

And here they all were. Affixed to a crudely drawn *T. merula* and dated April 13:

"Thirteen Other Ways of Looking at a Blackbird," written by Fiona Haeberle for Leonard Brice on the Occasion of His Twenty-Fourth Birthday

I   It was evening all afternoon.
        It was snowing
        And it was going to snow.
        I read my copy of Blackbird Enthusiast.

II   When the blackbird returned,
        I had taped a sign to my window:
        Free insects and berries inside.

III   Among the forest trees,
        I dressed up like a different blackbird
        And chilled out near the real black-
        bird's nest.

IV   In the haggard city square,
        I paid a child to draw
        A picture
        Of
        A blackbird for me.

V   Icicles filled the long window
        With barbaric glass.
        I filled the blackbird's nest
        With glue.

VI   O thin men of Haddam,
        Poke a pinhole in a shoebox.
        Point it at the blackbird.

VII   He rode over Connecticut
        In a glass coach,
        Until he reached
        The Junior Varsity Zoo.

VIII   Blackbird singing in the dead of night,
        I left it a ticket to see Wilco
        And then I also showed up.

IX   As the blackbird flew,
I took a picture of it with my cell
phone.

X   In the gloaming light,
I set up
An elaborate series
Of mirrors near the blackbird's tree.

XI   I ordered a Discovery Channel
Special about blackbirds
Off the Internet.

XII   The river flowed.
I challenged the blackbird
To a staring contest.

XIII   Special
Blackbird goggles.

The many dripping letters I kept clipped and sorted by author and date; she took nothing with her when she left, so everything Ours was suddenly all mine. There were several dozen of these sick little ghosts at home in the box, rubber-bound together and meekly decomposing. I poured over them, a heartbroken archaeologist, manhandling each fossil, demanding they squeal.

Dear Leo,

I happened upon this (oh so appropriate) reading in your birthday present from me, which by the way I'm borrowing back from you for a little while. Check it: "I long to hear that you have declared an independency. And, by the way, in the new code of laws which I suppose it will be necessary for you to make, I desire you would remember the ladies and be more generous and favorable to them than your ancestors. Do not put such unlimited power into the hands of the husbands. Remember, all men would be tyrants if they could. If particular care and attention is not paid to the ladies, we are determined to foment a rebellion, and will not hold ourselves bound by any laws in which we have no voice or representation. That your sex are naturally tyrannical is a truth so thoroughly established as to admit of no dispute; but such of you as wish to be happy willingly give up—the harsh tide of master for the more tender and endearing one of friend." That's Abigail Adams writing to John Adams—so third wave! I hope we get to love each other forever the way they did, in a full and difficult way. And if you ever cross me, I will foment the shit out of a rebellion. Won't you be my Dearest Friend?

With all my bursting love,
Fiona

Dear Leo,

I can't stop thinking about the mac & cheese at Declancy's. Now that you're back from class and reading this, will you come upstairs to our home? Will you take me to get that mac & cheese at Declancy's?

Your Dearest Friend,
Fiona

Dear Alvy,

Happy Halloween (almost)! I'm getting into character for tomorrow night. I hope you've been working on your accent, because the

*last time I heard it you sounded like you were from Neptune
instead of Coney Island. Do you remember last Halloween,
when we were John Wilkes Booth and Abe Lincoln? I don't care
what anyone says, that was hilarious. Nobody understands us,
huh? It's okay, because we luff each other! You were SUCH a
great Booth. See you in a couple of hours.*

La-di-da,
Annie

Dear Leo,

*This is a letter to say thank you for holding my hand on the way
to the hospital yesterday, and for making me soup last night and
for picking up ice cream today. I love you.*

YDF,
Fiona

Fee,

*It's been sixteen days since you left home now. Sixteen days:
that's even a little bit longer than Sinéad O'Connor sang about
in "Nothing Compares 2 U," for fuck's sake. I don't know where
you are with any sort of certainty, but I guess, if what you said
was true, then I guess it's Los Angeles. So, I've been thinking
lately about what it's going to be like, these next fifty years
without you. I've been thinking about death again, too, and I'm
shaking like a child—why did it have to be this one? Why were
we born into a world where such big things can go wrong? You
know? We could have been born into anything and not known
any better: same people, no death. Same trees, no fears. No
horses, or maybe everything is a horse. You're there, but I never
was, or the reverse. That's the thing—you can be born into*

anything at all. You just show up on the first day, and those are the rules of the world: proper number of horses and trees, of you and me, various laws concerning gravity, motion, biology, and time, whole preexisting histories involving endless generations of others who have already been here and gone. So why did it have to be this one? I bring this up because what I really need here is a world where I can make it be untrue that you've gone away. How many tries do you suppose that takes, all told? How many billions of planets will I have to wait for you to change your mind? Just please listen: I get that being you wasn't easy; I know how much it took out of you just being the way you were. I know that better than anyone ever will. But also, I know this—I know that the things that came with that difficulty are what made you great, once. You weren't supposed to be simple, Fiona, and you weren't supposed to be easy. You were complicated in a rare and wonderful way. And you may think what you're doing now is something like growing up, but I think you know better. I think you know it's just giving up. I think you gave up on Fiona Haeberle. I believed in her more than you could have known, and there were times when I was the only one. That's what really destroyed me, I think, more than you . . . going away, or whatever. Leaving. I had faith in the thing we made; I had faith in Our thing. And when your faith is, I don't know, predeceased, I guess, by the thing you have faith in, well . . . it is really quite hard to come back from that. Do you understand, Fiona? You were the best person I ever met, and I wanted to spend the entirety of my only life growing up with you. Now you're one of them, one of those other people, and I'm going to grow up alone. And I still—I still—I still believe that I'll always be in love with you in some way, even far down that road, and when the feeling becomes fainter, when I recognize it only as a familiar sweetness in the air

I breathe in and out every day, it will be softer but no less
significant to me. It will linger the way I now realize it has been
lingering there for years, waiting for an explanation that finally
came to me on the night we met. Do you remember that awful
party? For forty short/long months, every portion of me has been
whispering your name and gesturing frantically like a weathervane
toward you. Is that sappy enough to be silly? I cannot believe
you've gone.

> *Your Dearest Friend,*
> *Leo [undelivered of course]*

I was blown open when she left—blown open, and I
couldn't get closed. Everybody knows that, when you're talking about a person, open things can get infected and closed
things cannot. That's basic medical science. And I lay there,
open, taking in all the world's bacteria, all the atomic details,
every microscopic fact let loose to putrefy my self.

It was them, of course; it was they: Fiona and Mark Renard
in horrible concert. It was Theirs and not Ours that, since
spring, had ruled the Earth. *Mercy General* had in fact been
canceled, and the characters played by the two of them had in
fact been killed in that boating accident—that was all true, and
that was all known. But it was no accident, no: Mark wanted
out of his contract; he demanded that they die. He killed her. It
wasn't the harbormaster at all. She must have wanted to go.

She must have wanted to go because they were involved
with each other. An integrated item, to borrow a phrase. I
hadn't seen the signs at the time, so I went back and planted
them in my memory: the frequency of mention, the constant
protestations concerning Mark's intellect and talent, the late

nights on set, and the distance towards the end, while I was, for once, distracted by my legal education. I never received my moment of j'accusatory revelation, my chance to rip away the curtains or the mask. My cathartic confrontation not forthcoming, I had to make do with a set of sputtering assumptions: loose rumors, drips and drabs. I resented Fiona for not having the decency to let me find out, and be the one empowered to tear Our world apart in righteous sadness.

A couple of months after the cold facts set in, I bumped into one of Fiona's actress friends, Alice Gerson, near my building, and she displayed for my benefit the scrunched, cockheaded, treacly-sad rendition of "Hey . . . how're you holding up, man?" that can only truly be served up by a generally (but not specifically) compassionate woman to a man she doesn't know well whom a friend of hers has cheated on.

I'd get my confirmation later on, seeing them born anew, living together in Los Angeles, on a television screen in November. This would be the news: Fiona Fox, the actress—she was rising. Mark Renard was tabbed to be the leading man in some new show.

Four days after Fiona left, I walked across the bridge to Manhattan, an island I'd tried almost religiously to avoid in the course of my Brooklyn years. I wandered that inglorious wen down to new-to-me sectors like a ghost, hip shop to hip shop, the King of Nothing, looking for a feeling in the callous faces of strangers, listening only for her brisk mezzo lilt among the crowd noises. How could I possibly be expected to listen to anything else? What was I supposed to find here when she's gone? Old books. Winter coats. Dishware. A new watch. Walking home, the sky was almost completely black. How many years until I'd be back, hitting on the shopgirls?

• • •

"What's the game?" asked Gracie from behind the echo chamber of her empty wine glass.

It was a winter night—our second year of law school—and the universe was fine.

"No game, sweetie," Sona murmured with moony eyes. "I think Fiona here was asking a serious question. Right?"

"Oh, it's quite serious," chimed Fiona from high atop the kitchen counter. "Quite serious indeed. Should we open another bottle?"

Gracie was perplexed, and also drunk.

"That was the game—should we open another bottle?" she asked.

"It isn't a game," snapped Sona.

"Sorry! I meant: that was the question?"

Fiona slid down to join me on the loveseat, corkscrew in tow.

"The question," she explained furtively, "was this: if you could live at any time in history, when would it be, and why?"

"Oh that old chestnut," groaned Boots.

"It's like summer camp!" Grace added giddily. "You know? Everyone goes around and answers some random deep question before you fall asleep? This is how you really get to know people, you know."

"How much wine did you have at summer camp?" I asked her as I plucked free the cork from our last four dollars' worth of red.

The study group had migrated from the William Burnham Woods Room of the law library to Our apartment, as it was wont to do in thirsty moments. Traditionally, it took just a couple of hours before we came to resemble the aftermath of a particularly devastating carbon monoxide leak—Boots glued to the hardwood, Emily, Sona, and Gracie sprawled out on the couch, Fiona and I sluggishly entwined on the loveseat—and this evening was no exception. Any pretense of legal education always yielded before long to Fiona's insistent whim: what verb is saddest? Would we rather be fish or birds? Which poet would we most like to box?

"Boots, you're first," Fiona declared. "When are you going to live?"

"Good question," he droned back from his spot on the floor. "But seriously folks. I'm going with 1977."

"That's awfully specific," said Emily.

"It's a no-brainer," he replied. "You got *Station to Station*-era Bowie. You got The Clash just starting up. Jimmy Carter's still in the White House. I probably could've played drums for The Pretenders. It's everything you need. Uh, what else? Velcro, I think. Velcro's pretty popular. Pet rocks."

"Bootsie," said Sona, "I think you're supposed to pick a time when you weren't actually alive."

"Good one," he said.

"That was a joke about how old you are," Sona clarified.

"We got it," I assured her. "Boots is super old."

"Emily's turn," announced Fiona.

"If you insist, darling. Let's see . . . I think maybe I'll go to 1977 and make sure this one doesn't overdose on anything."

Boots rolled over to object, then paused.

"That's probably smart," he conceded.

"If not," Emily continued, "then I'll go to Paris in the 1920s."

"What was going on in Paris in the 1920s?" asked Gracie.

"Oh, lots of things. Theater and cinema and jazz. The Folies Bergere. Picasso and Matisse. Fitzgerald and Hemingway. Coco Chanel. It was an incredibly vibrant place and time, and I think, as long as we're free to pick here, I'd like to give it a try."

"Okay," slurred Grace. "That sounds lovely—I'm going to Paris in the 1920s too. Sona, are you coming with us? It's gonna be so . . . freaking vibrant."

Sona's eyes bloomed open, and she craned her leaden arms back behind her head.

"Under no circumstances," she deadpanned. "If I'm going to time travel, I'm going somewhere where I can take over the world, like a slightly thinner version of Cleopatra."

"It isn't time travel!" fumed Fiona.

"Cleopatra didn't take over the world," I pointed out.

"And how do you know how thin Cleopatra was?" asked Emily.

"Yeah!" Gracie shouted, a little too loudly. Startled by her own volume, she added in a self-conscious whisper, "you weren't there."

Sona surveyed us, bewildered, before Fiona took the reins.

"It isn't time travel, Sona. You're just born somewhere new."

"Okay."

"It's an important distinction."

"Okay," Sona said evenly. "I will be a terrifying ruler at any time. Someplace warm, preferably. Has to be at least five centuries ago for it to work."

This satisfied all.

"Your turn, honey," Fiona said, boring a slim index finger into my left ear.

"Ow!" I yelped. "Stop being gross, please."

She retracted, and I gave my answer.

"1857," I announced proudly.

"Jesus Christ," said Boots. "Not this Buchanan shit again."

"A nation stands on the precipice of a bloody fracture."

"Why are you the way you are?" inquired Sona.

"The whole of our American experiment poised either to collapse upon itself or survive by dint of a pyrrhic civil war."

"Shut the fuck up," said Boots. "Shut the fuck up."

"A venerable diplomat of unrivaled credentials is called upon once more by his country to serve. His name—"

"Darryl Strawberry," said Boots.

"James Buchanan! Distinguished, experienced, wise. Alas, devoid of courage and foresight and some other fairly necessary things. In need of an advisor—a trusted voice who could impart upon him the dire consequences of inaction. Together, we could squash slavery and mitigate the losses of war. No Confederacy; no legacy of disunion or treason. I bet I could do it. I could fix it if I were there—if I had the time. That is my answer."

"Are you done?" asked Fiona.

"Indeed I am," I replied.

"Glad to hear it, Professor Dipshit," she said, before planting a loud kiss on the side of my face. "So it's me now. And I choose: the future."

"Well," I said, "you definitely can't do that."

"Of course I can!" she objected.

"Professor Dipshit is right," called out Boots, now resting on his stomach and speaking directly into the floor. "It's against the rules to pick the future."

"But I *made* the rules," Fiona answered indignantly.

"But you said 'history,'" countered Emily. "You said 'at

any time in history'—the future doesn't count. It hasn't happened yet, ergo it isn't history."

"That's ridiculous!" Fiona declared. "Of course the future counts as history. It's part of time! It's on the timeline of, you know, existence. Who cares if we haven't been through it yet? It's on the timeline!"

"I'm not sure you can win this one," I told my agitated love. "You've got five half-lawyers—which is basically two-and-a-half actual lawyers—who are interpreting history as to not include the future. Rebuttal?"

"Screw your legal bullshit; that's my rebuttal," she said. "Tomorrow is just as much a part of history as yesterday. And if you weren't so wrapped up in textual interpretation—yeah, I know that term; I know 'textual interpretation'—you'd all agree with me, because I am so very right about this."

We went on drinking and talking and laughing then, and the night slipped into the past as seamlessly as any other. Later, when the future turned out to be history, just as she'd predicted, I returned to this conversation and got sad. And returning now, I am sad, and I will return again.

· · ·

I've had eight nights I was sure would be the last of my life: two fleeting dementias, one lightning-strike headache, five fevers-you-don't-come-back-from. Eight nights, so I felt relatively relaxed when, on the night after the night that Fiona left, I accidentally swallowed a bay leaf. I thought perhaps that cooking would make me feel better; it was something we'd done together almost every night for several years, and I wanted to maintain whatever consistency I could. I wanted, I guess, to produce and consume the way that people do when they've

not been hollowed out by fresh grief. Or maybe I didn't know
what I wanted; it's possible that I was delirious. Either way, I
cooked and I ate for hours without thinking—but a stray bay
leaf was left behind, and before long I felt those crisp ridges
start to tear at my throat. I thought I'd read it somewhere, but
I wasn't certain—can a person left alone be killed by swallow-
ing a bay leaf? Among herbs, they are the closest to paranoia
or regret: lie down with them at night, and they will cut you
open from the inside.

I called her four times on the day after she left me a nonsensical wreck, baying primal bays, like the very first hominid
evolved enough to comprehend the meaning of his own death.
Four times, and she never picked up, never called back, was
never enough in existence to ping back my last desperate signals.
God only knows what kind of messages I left—I don't remember what was said, and even if I did, I would spare you. The
words didn't matter much anyway; there was nothing I could
do to stop the war. Our breaking up went very badly for me.

In bed I thought about the coming change; I thought about
what my life was going to be like now that she was gone, and
also I thought about the bay leaf swimming within me. I sweat,
and turned, and tracked the little threat as it skulked across my
body. In time I leveled out, and brought the heaving evening
to its logical meridian. I remember the strange dream I had
that night, which was a dream of a family—two parents and
an infant son—running from something awful in the dark.
They swaddled their boy hard in a checkered blanket to keep
him from screaming. They hid in outhouses from Kiev to
Constantinople, and on a ship called the *Braga* I watched them
sail to New York—I watched the whole flight, all in those few
hours of hot and wretched sleep. This was a dream of my his-

tory, and I knew who they were; I knew who that boy would be. This was March 1923, and his daughter is my mother. I have his affection for chipmunks, the paperclip he used as a stickpin. He came into his new world that way: as a treasure, a morsel, a secret prize. I came into mine as an infidel, barking gin-soaked into Fiona's voicemail like a bay leaf, shivving indiscriminately at her insides, and for what? A little desired bitterness. A more thorough stewing. The next day, I woke up.

• • •

My mother's college roommate was a woman named Luz, a Colombian expat of deep intelligence and peerless magpiety. We'd always been close; I called her "aunt" growing up, and she was the only person who got to call me "Lenny." Luz was a businesswoman of some renown—the CFO of a large multinational corporation—and her work took her frequently from her apartment in New York to the most distant centers of commerce for long stretches of time. Ten years widowed, and with her children now in graduate school, she found herself away more and more. Her home on the Upper West Side was opulent, expensive, and empty.

By early October, more than two months after Fiona and I dissolved, my apartment had still stubbornly refused to stop being The Place Where We Used to Live. The premises were littered with toxic artifacts, and crippling relics of her time there were strewn about everywhere like dead leaves. I couldn't stop the infestation of memories; I had to escape. So I called Luz.

"Lenny! *Mi querido!* My little lawyer! Oh, Lenny, it's been far too long! I'd force you to come over for dinner, but—ugh—sweetheart, I am in Houston, Texas, tonight. Oh, and Lenny,

I heard from someone—I'm not going to say who, but it was your mother, and she's very worried about you Lenny, so you need to call your mother more because you know how she worries about you—she told me that your strange little girl-friend ran away with some *idiota*. She didn't say *idiota*—I say that. She said *schmuck*. Lenny! Sweetie! Tell me how you are doing?"

I tried to do just that, making use of the still-evolving vo-cabulary I'd been developing in order to communicate with the outside world: the wistfully encouraging vocabulary of consolation, which was bullshit. Aunt Luz listened expressively, and spoke at length about fleeting love and the fickle nature of women. She insisted that I stay in her apartment, from which she would be absent for seven months at least, and refused my repeated offers of rent. There was a catch, though:

"Oh, Lenny! This is fate—it's *kismet*, your mother would say. We can help each other. Have you met Lita? My mother, Lita? No, you probably haven't, have you—not since you were a little boy. She is eighty-eight years old, but Lenny, she is very much alive, very active, a very sharp lady is my mother. Any-way, she lives there now—she got sick of Florida and she wanted to be close to her daughters and her granddaughters, so she just moved into one of the bedrooms in my place. She doesn't need anybody taking care of her, Lenny, and even if she did that wouldn't be a job for you, and anyway my sisters are all close by. So, no, I will not accept any money from you, *mi querido*—but Lita, my mother, she could use some help with one thing only. She has a dog."

I moved into Luz's penthouse the next week, and sublet my squalid Brooklyn digs to a high school friend of Sona's. My new place was well-kept and womby, and Luz had left no fewer than thirty-five post-it notes clinging to various surfaces and appliances instructing me on everything from towel basics to the creation of ice cubes. A family of six could have lived there comfortably—luxuriously, even—but kismet insisted that the unlikely trio of Lita, the dog, and I suffice.

I actually met the dog before I met Lita: a middle-aged miniature schnauzer named Rafael Uribe Uribe, after the famous Colombian politician and general. He was coy and defensive, with the ragged beard of a graying billy goat and the fusty odor of another, much deader billy goat. The hircine pooch was endowed with a boundless supply of nervous energy; it was clear to me from the outset that he was riddled with the full compendium of dog anxieties, and all day long his skittish paw-nails tapped out their endless retreats on the hardwood floor. Lita was out when I first came in, so my introduction to Rafael was thus: peaceable palms and human words of calm on the one hand, feverish barking and a botched, near-cartoonish scampering away on the other. Could he smell my sadness? I couldn't know. In time we would be friends.

Lita had a majestic little thatch of chromic hair, and a face warmed and thickened by many hot suns. She was sweet, wise, and humble, the very picture of grandmaternity. At least that's what I imagined she was like—for all I knew, she could have been gently flinging curse words at me from behind those kind old earthen eyes. As it happened, she did not appear to speak a single word of English, and my Spanish was likewise limited to an unhelpful handful of clunky, phonetic greetings. For reasons now obscure to me, I'd chosen to take French in school, the result of which was this initial exchange on Lita's return from her morning walk that first day:

Me, unloading cooking supplies from a duffel bag: "Oh!

Hi! You must be Lita. Luz—your daughter, she . . . she must have told you I'd be moving in today. Right?"

Lita, smiling indifferently: "Hola. Sí, sí."

Me, thinking perhaps that she understood: "Oh, great. It's wonderful to meet you—or, I guess, we met a long time ago, when I was very young. I'm Leo. Lenny? Do you . . . uh, we met, I think, once before, when I was very . . . *poquito*."

Lita, creaking downward to rest one ancient, tremulous hand upon the head of Rafael Uribe Uribe: "Sí, sí. Hola, mi perro hermoso. Tranquilo, mi pequeño amor. Tienes hambre, mi dulce?"

Me, beginning to appreciate the situation: "Oh. I don't . . . this is going to be funny, because I don't actually . . . speak any Spanish at all. This is going to be difficult, huh?! Heh. Very . . . diff . . . i . . . cile. *No habla español,* I'm afraid. *De nada*."

Lita, still whispering only to the dog: "Desayunamos, Rafi. Ven conmigo, mi amor."

And she shuffled away with another far off smile, her cantering dog in tow.

FIVE

MITHRIDATES VI BECAME THE RULER OF ARMENIA Minor when his father, Mithridates V, was assassinated one hundred and twenty years before the birth of Christ. The son was only fourteen at the time, a boy king, and for nearly six decades he bedeviled the Roman Empire from his Turkish perch. Deeply and understandably paranoid regarding assassinations, Mithridates the younger began his reign by decamping to the wilderness for seven years—the story goes that the duration of this period was spent gathering and consuming an unholy sampler comprised of every poisonous bit of flora yet known upon the Earth.

Scholars and poets have sung the praises of his antidote, of *Antidotum Mithridaticum*, for more than two millennia. You start with a scintilla, and the venom hardly hurts you. You build from there, quite slowly, and the more you ingest the stronger your resistance becomes. As things move along, you become

sick, but not deadly so. Your resistance blooms into a toler-
ance, which in turn blooms into full immunity; as with anything, you eventually become indifferent to the awful thing
with which you've filled yourself.

The vaccinated king came back to civilization in the wake
of his ordeal, ruling and being and waging battles unafraid of
sly conspirators. He gave his name to the Mithridatic Wars: great
skirmishes with the greatest generals of the old Roman
Republic—Lucullus, Lucius Cornelius Sulla, and the last of
these was Pompey. Mithridates was a graying caudillo by the
time Pompey reached the heart of his kingdom; faced with
capture and the imminent loss of his realm, he opted to kill
himself rather than endure the torture of defeat. Frantically,
he partook of every morsel of poison he could find. He was
foiled, of course, by his own juvenilia: the defenses he so deliberately cultivated as a young man kept him from dying in
the moment he finally wanted all that arsenic, all that wolfs-
bane, all that snakeroot and sumac, all that jimson and jequir-
ity, that columbine, that corn cockle, that foxglove, larkspur,
nightshade, that hellebore and hemlock to take root. He was
required to keep living.

It was early November, and despite my failure to overcome
the things I had been feeling, I too was required to keep living. There were markers resembling progress, of course: my
friends no longer had to actively watch out for me, and the feeling among them—among myself, too—was that my stark
sadness had receded from the existentially dangerous to the
merely pitiful. By then, I'd gone so far as to let Boots set me
up on a series of whiskey-dates with righteous young women
he knew from his past life in the music scene; though none of
them ultimately stuck, several dug my downcast mind enough

to linger for a few nonconsecutive days. They took shifts helping vainly to prop up the rusted little shanty of my love:
Carina, the singer, who wished only to live each hour of each
day rapt with the ceaseless wonder of the universe (terms to
be defined later); Kait, formerly a ticket-girl at The Broken
Promise Rhythm & Blues Club, who could pickle almost
anything and who signed her e-mails "with metta, k"; Marissa,
the bassist-turned-PhD-candidate, who told fascinating stories
at a high and hearty level; Courtney, another bassist, who
mostly wanted to fight about which of us had been more pro-
foundly screwed up by their ex, and who left when I won.
Nobody wasn't sweet in their way—it was I who failed each
time to see them, in a future tense, as something meatier than
Anonymous Woman #7 in the end credits of my life: a bastard
way to conduct one's conduct.

Every Saturday since mid-September, when my slow re-
emergence into civilized society had commenced, Boots,
Emily, Sona, and I would cook dinner together at one of our
apartments—a tradition that began, I discovered later, as just
one stratagem among many that comprised the intricate suicide
watch program my dear friends had created (unnecessarily,
as it turned out) on my behalf. We'd talk about our lives, by
which I mean our jobs, because, in the wild, the latter almost
immediately devours the former. After the bar exam, Gracie
had moved down to Washington to work for a senator—she
sent along regular dispatches of the special madness rooting
around in that place. Because Emily was the only one of us
who had waded into a law firm, with its requisite long hours
and deadening routines, we listened sympathetically to her
prim disapproval of colleagues and senior partners. Sona
had begun clerking for a famous judge in Manhattan back

in September; her stories were more gripping even than those Boots and I—real-life death-row advocates, mind you—brought to the table each week.

"So Tatum," Sona divulged of her illustrious boss one November evening, "he has this thing where he gives all the clerks new nicknames, almost every morning, based around a common theme. Like, we'll go in, and he'll say, 'Good morning, Socrates', to me, and Javon will be Aristotle, and Sammy will be Plato, and that's what he'll call us for the day. So, on Thursday, Javon was Mickey Mantle, Sammy was Yogi Berra, and I was Joe DiMagglio—"

"DiMaggio," corrected Boots.

"Right—DiMaggio. Whatever. So all day Thursday, that's what we are—'Where are we on the summary judgment denial, Mick?' 'Yogi, can you red-line the defense brief?' 'DiMagglio, I need you to—"

"DiMaggio. There is no 'L' anywhere in his name. His name is Joe DiMaggio. How is it possible you don't know that?" Boots inquired.

"Might have something to do with being born in Armenia, jackass," Sona replied. "Now stop being racist and listen. Yesterday, I get to work, and both Javon and Sammy are out sick, so it's just me and Tatum in his wing of the courthouse. And I say, just trying to defuse that being-alone awkwardness, 'How are you going to pick a name for me if I'm the only one here today?' You know, 'cause it's always in threes. And he thinks for a second, and gets this just fantastically creepy look on his face, and sort of eyes me up and down, and says, 'Maybe you should be Marilyn Monroe, and *I* should be Joe DiMagglio.'"

"DiMaggio," said Boots.

"Isn't that wild?" asked Sona, notably more intrigued than disgusted.

"What's wild," nagged Boots, "is that you understand the context of why that's a creepy reference, but still somehow don't know the guy's name. How is that possible?"

"What I think's wild is that you're being sexually harassed at work," added Emily.

"By a famous person, too," I offered.

"Yes, by a famous person," confirmed Emily. "But, for the record, I think my wild thing is sort of the headline here. It'd be great if we could stay focused on that for a second. He was really hitting on you?"

"Hard to say," answered Sona. "But . . . yes. He definitely was. I'm pretty sure he's a huge pervert, too. I hear things. I see things. I mean, the man has been married four times, and—I did the math on this—those four wives were a combined seventy-one years younger than him. Seventy-one years! And his first wife was *his age*. So that's a red flag right there, right? Also: I heard from the woman who does our IT that he has, let's say, very particular tastes when it comes to his Google searches. No joke. 'Young women nude fireplace hearth animal skin rug.' That's verbatim, too—who the hell is into hearth porn? Who uses the word 'hearth'? It's crazy, right? 'Young women nude safari jungle cat.' I don't know what that means, but: gross. I'm just gonna ride this one out, though, see how much dirt I can get on him in case I need it later."

"Jesus," I said, slowly peeling the damp label off of my beer.

"And how are things down at the hippie store?" she asked with a demonic grin.

"Uh, I think we still like it," I responded half-heartedly, and looked to Boots for a second opinion.

"It's as good as a job can be, I guess," he said ruefully, staring off and away. "Of course, I hate all jobs, so there's that."

"You do not hate all jobs," countered Emily.

"Jobs like this, I do. Jobs where you have to go in every day, and wear an arbitrary tie. I don't care how excellent the people are—I'll never stop seeing every office as a kind of prison."

"Well. That's not juvenile or anything," scoffed Sona.

"The people actually are fairly excellent, I'd say," I said, again attempting to speak the language of the well-adjusted. "You really couldn't ask for better bosses than Martha and Peter."

"I heartily concur with that part," conceded Boots. "But still."

As always happened, unfailingly, this conversation of ours ultimately seemed to coil, and then tighten, around the subject of my emotional health. Talk of work begat talk of life begat the game where everyone who is maybe interested in self-harm raises their hand.

"Are you still writing imaginary letters to that stupid hussy?" posed Sona as the night drew on. "What was her name again?"

"Fee-o-na," I intoned. "And no. I've stopped all that." This was less than true.

"You know, I never did like her," she went on.

"Yes you did. All of you loved her, and so did I."

"Not one bit, Mr. Brice. Not one bit. I don't remember that at all."

She smiled broadly; Sona was a dear sometimes.

"I remember her being unreliable," she continued. "Un-predictable, really. You never knew when she was going to attack you for no reason. I always thought of your relationship with her as, like, a lion tamer versus lion type ordeal. You were the lion tamer, by the way. I remember she had this weird mole—"

"That's outrageous," I replied.

"How would you describe your relationship with Fiona, then, in retrospect?" ventured Emily. "Old married couple? Parent-child?"

Everybody giggled the nervous middle school giggle of water-testers.

"What about doctor-patient?" I offered, eager to demonstrate levity.

"What about patient-patient?" shot Boots.

"Hostage," I went on, "and . . . emotional terrorist."

They laughed generously, and I laughed some, too.

"Giving Tree and the Kid from *The Giving Tree*," I concluded. "That's the one."

It worked, and they let the subject drop for another evening. I didn't believe a damn word of it—I wanted to, wanted to be the kind of person who could let a big thing go, but—

Maybe it would come? Maybe it would come and I would believe that we were not supposed to be as we were. Maybe it would come, but it hadn't come yet.

After the plates were cleared away that same night, after the toppled carafes of wine, Boots and Emily left to see a movie, so Sona and I remained. Whenever it was only us, it never took long for Sona to loosen, ever so slightly, the stifling belt of her affections; our conversations had a reliable tendency to dive head-first into the deep end right off the bat.

"Look, this stuff with Fiona," she began as soon as I shut the door behind our friends.

"Yeah."

"I don't mean to be glib about it."

"I know that. I know you don't. It's helpful to joke about it—really, it is."

"It's what I do. I understand you're a sensitive guy, and I appreciate that. I'm not sensitive, so, it's just what I do."

"You don't need to explain yourself to me, Sona."

"No, I want to. You're my friend, and I only have, like, five of those, max. And even though we're very different people—*very* different—I think you know that I care—*blech!*—that I care about how you are. I don't want you to think I don't . . . you know, care, about what you're dealing with."

"I know that you care about me," I said, conclusively.

"And you know how uncomfortable I am with you knowing that."

"Is there a point to this?"

"I think there is, sure. Look. You know how I'm this stone cold bitch who doesn't have feelings?" she asked me, smiling the way she always did, the way she had to let you know that you could never know the earnest, honest truth. And her dark eyes would say: "track my secret," every time.

"I know how you project that, sure. I know it isn't true."

"Well, it isn't true," she confided, and uncrossed her arms.

"I know," I said after a moment.

"I'm familiar with feelings," she said, as though I'd tried to drop an obscure reference, "and I've been, you know, exposed to them at various points in the past."

"Gosh, Sona, that must have been, just, so hard for you," I mocked, knowing she wouldn't bring me any closer unless she was absolutely sure that her escape pods—sarcasm, irony, affect—remained operational and nearby.

"I know how you felt when she left. I mean, I don't know—I've never had a whole . . . *situation* . . . like that. But I . . . I sympathize, even if I can't really empathize, technically. She was your other half, all that shit. I get that. I really do. I'm not indifferent to your shit."

"Sona, this whole therapy bit you're doing? You should really consider turning pro."

"I'm doing my best to be sincere here. This kind of thing doesn't come naturally to me. Look, maybe you don't remember this, but back in the dark ages of, like, a few weeks ago, you told me that you, and I quote, 'couldn't ignore the feeling that your world had ended.' That's some heavy shit, Leo. That stuck with me. Do you know how scary it is to hear that when you're one of the people who cares about you—a club of which I am a dues-paying member?"

"You don't pay dues."

"*Emotional* dues, Leo."

"I get it."

"So, you said you were one hundred percent certain that you would never come back from Fiona. You said that. You were *dead certain* this was the end of the line."

"I was, at the time. I was certain."

"So?" she prodded.

"So what?"

"So, have you noticed that you don't feel that way anymore?"

I twisted in my loveseat.

"I'm still not sure that I'll ever come back from—"

"But the world, Leo! The all-consuming end of the—"

"I don't think the world has ended anymore, if that's what you're asking. Not exactly, anyway."

"And so?" she pressed on.

"And so what?"

"And so it went away, genius. You thought you'd feel that way forever, but you didn't. You were wrong. Can we start by admitting this one truth?"

"That I was wrong?"

"No," she hollered, "that feelings *go away*, and it's never the end of the world. That's the thing about being a person, Leo. Every feeling you've ever had went away."

Not every feeling. She did have a point, though: by that time, I'd begun to think of my time without Fiona as something short of a death. Not quite a life—not the one I'd signed up for—but a kind of afterlife, backward-facing and foggy and still. Devoid of harps and fires alike. Neutral. Post-love.

"We're very much alike," I fired back at her after a full minute of silence. It wouldn't be a conversation—not for us—if I didn't try to provoke Sona too.

"Are we now?"

"We are. We are."

"Well, that's a shame," she said, "because you're an enormous train wreck of a human being right now."

"You kid, but the truth is, we really are very similar."

"Flattering as that is, Mr. Brice, I gotta say I just don't see it."

"I do. You terrify me—you know that? We are *very* much alike, Sona. I bet you've contemplated staying single forever, right?"

"Oh, so this is about that?" she lilted maniacally, gliding her feet up onto the edge of the couch.

"About what?"

"You want me to *date* you. You desperately want for me

to date you. Ugh, this is just pathetic, Leo. You're better than this."

"I don't want to date you," I reminded her truthfully.

"Of course not," she said, adding truthfully, "and I sure as shit don't want to date you."

"Of course not," I replied.

"Because that would be laughably bad for both of us. Two neurotics don't make an . . . erotic . . . hang on. Two neurotics don't make an erotic—"

"I get it," I interrupted.

"Hang on! I'm working on an idiom."

"We're not talking about that right now," I went on, ignoring her.

"So what are we talking about?"

"We're talking about this. We're talking about how you've honestly considered quite seriously just being single for the entire rest of your life. I'm right?"

"So?"

"It's okay. What I'm saying is: I've thought about that too."

"Oh please. How many girls have you been with in the last—"

"Women."

"I actually met some of them, Leo, and they are girls."

"They are—"

"They *act* like girls."

"You're veering the conversation—"

"I *do not like* this conversation," she snapped back, and retracted her feet up beneath her.

"We—I mean you and I—above all else, we don't want to let anyone who is not us inform who, fundamentally, we are," I continued.

"We don't."

"No."

"I don't know what that means. At all."

"Have you ever intentionally let anyone get to know you? I mean more than is socially necessary for them to be a friend, or a person you sometimes sleep with, or anything like that? Have you ever, even one time, divulged any piece of information about your fears, or about what you're really feeling at a given moment?"

"Arrêtez, s'il vous plaît."

"Have you ever voluntarily left yourself open to getting hurt, or changed, or . . . compromised—in any way? And the answer is: no, no of course you haven't, because you don't want to, and you're very good at what you do."

"A great many people are like that," she countered, looking anywhere but my face.

"Yes, but they don't hold up that way for long. But you're smarter than everyone, so you get to keep doing it for as long as you like."

"I'm guarded with myself. You know that. You make me sound selfish."

"We're the same like that! This is what I'm saying. Look, things work out for couples like Emily and Boots, sure. But that's because they're not like us; they're open people, and generous with themselves—with their minds. We are fundamentally not. That's why things like Fiona happen. I let Fiona in; I let her shape who I was in a thousand ways I'd never let anyone else come close to even breathing on me before. I let her into the museum; I let her fuck around with the art. I bought into the fantasy, okay? And that's what it was. A big old fantasy of connection. A bad joke. I bought into the fantasy that someone like me can let someone like that in the door and then come away clean. They all believe in it—everyone out there, but not us. Not you and I, I mean. She wasn't real. She was a fake. A forgery. And look at me now. I swear to God, Sona, I might be ruined."

"You'll get past it, Leo."

"You don't know that," I said.

She huffed at me dismissively, and slipped her feet into her boots.

"Come on, man," she groaned. "You can't possibly think I've been this way forever, right?"

"I just figured you were born into it, or something," I replied.

"You're being willfully ignorant, as per usual," she said. "Of course I've been screwed over, Leo; of course I've been end-of-the-world hurt before. Of course that's why I'm the way I am about these things, *obviously*. Get it? Of course I've been hurt like that. News flash: fucking everybody has!"

"Okay, well," I responded defensively, "I legitimately didn't know that, but, thank you for sharing."

"You're just a monster, you know that?"

"I know," I said. "So how'd you get past the feeling?"

"Which feeling?"

"The feeling that this was the end of the world."

"I don't know. I panicked. I really did, you know—I really did think it was the end of the world. And I believe that you think that, too. I'm sure you're still not sure how you're supposed to be after this, but it's been months now, and Boots is right: you need to start thinking about the rest of your life as, you know, the rest of your life. So back when I was going through some of this stuff—way, way back—I was thinking about it, trying to snap myself out of it, and here's what I came up with. I said to myself, 'Sona,' I said, 'you're an organism. You're full of the science of human existence; you're full of the magic of human existence—you've got soul, baby! And maybe you've got just this one lifetime . . . just the one opportunity . . . *to exist*! One *shot* at an experience, and you're going to waste it—what? Being tired? Being sad? Mad at the other organisms? Fuck no.' That's what I told myself, anyway, although I'm not sure yet whether any of it has sunk in. For now, it's just an attempted mantra."

"Well," I said, "thanks for that. Really—thank you. I know you don't like to talk about this, and I think—I think maybe I still need time. I'm not back yet—I do know that. I don't feel like I'm . . . I don't know how to get back."

"Okay. Well . . . thanks to you too, I guess. But just so you know, even though I just . . . shared a little, just now, I want you to understand that we are emphatically not alike."

"Of course we are, Sona," I said. "Of course we're alike. We know from loneliness, and we know that it's the price you pay for controlling your own narrative. We accept that. Look, going through this has been basically impossible, but it *has* made me think more about loneliness. I've been thinking about that a lot, really—loneliness of the soul: soul-loneliness. And I just am telling you that I'm here also. And I'm like you. I know you. Do you get that? I know how difficult it is to have to live inside yourself all the time. That's what I'm trying to tell you. I know you. There is another Skywalker. Okay?"

"Okay."

Sona stretched herself wide in every direction, drained the last of the wine, and walked briskly out of the apartment without saying another word.

• • •

I never did fall in love with New York. I wanted to—I wanted to love it the way Woody Allen loved it, the way Gershwin must have—but I never could make it mine. How was it that every law of loneliness could cease to apply at city limits? Eight million people, and it could just as easily have been eight for all the good it did me. I grew to see right through them, to brush every last million away as though they were fronds leaking from the wet and gruesome jungle out onto my trail. My trail, me. The poetry I'd once heard in the arrhythmic bustle, the electricity I'd once seen in the currents of those crowded streets, the grace notes I'd so often detected in the vendor's bark, in the madwoman's cry, in the tonant *screeee* of the halting subway train: all of it now felt irredeemably tossed-off.

New York didn't care whether I lived or died, nor, for that matter, did eight million minus maybe-a-dozen of them New Yorkers. There was a time when I found them charming as a breed: hectic, yes, and aggressive, but ultimately harmless; not icy but hot-hearted, and there was something commendable in that. I'd once found it quaint that they believed Central Park was nature—maybe because I grew up in the sylvestral paradise of Northern New England. I envied their unfailing pride of place. Now, of course, at the very moment my world chose so cruelly to revolve around me, their solipsism and their brusqueness made me ill.

A couple of years ago, Sona told me something about New York City that I'll never forget: within the confines of the five boroughs, she'd read, more than eight hundred different languages are regularly spoken. Just sort of offhand, I told her that eight hundred was about twice as many languages as I would've guessed still existed in the entire world, and she coyly raised up her chatoyant eyes and smiled.

"*Inchqan lezoo imanas, aynqan mart es*, homeboy," she intoned.

"What's that? Is that Armenian? I don't know what that means."

"Oh, but don't you understand, Leo?" she trilled, pressing her small hand defiantly against my shoulder. "You don't get to know what everything means."

• • •

It used to be that there was always an age you could look forward to as the age at which everything was finally going to happen. When I was nine, eleven was the top of the mountain—a million large-font novellas said so, and I was told there would be girls and sports. When I was fourteen, sixteen was it; when I was seventeen, I knew it had to be twenty-one, and so it went until it stopped. There comes a time when the person you aspire most to be is a person you were, some old edition that either lived up to the hype or more likely didn't, and the things you have coming seem: not unwelcome, but not nearly so warm as the old batches of newness to which you were long accustomed—prosy stacks of multi-grain bread standing in for the epic cake of youth.

This isn't such a bad thing. At twenty-seven, when taking a break from my moping about, I really do look forward to the things I am supposed to. I always wanted to be a husband and a father, and it's a small comfort to me, at least, that those are the very things that humankind more or less reckons I ought to consider next. I'm glad I am content with the challenges and expectations of the world: they are fine challenges and worthy expectations. Given two hundred thousand years of humanity, it was wildly unlikely that something so gauzy as romantic sadness would ever come close to registering as my chief hurdle—probability suggests that I could very well have been running from lions at this age, or slogging across barren continents, or getting murdered by any of various popular hordes. All told, it's a terribly interesting time on Earth, and I can acquire a little necessary happiness from the fact that I was dropped off here and not elsewhere.

I thought about this—about the quirks of cosmic timing—when Martha Bok called me and Rachel Costa into her office to tell us that we had been chosen to run point on the Michael Tiegs case ("first chair," she called it, although staff attorneys like me never saw the inside of a courtroom). In the three months I'd been at the New Salem Institute, I worked consistently for multiple clients at once, but always as support counsel in the New York office. I'd never spoken to an inmate before, nor had I ever seen the interior of a proper prison; now I was being handed a thick gray binder stamped GA-DOC 1138 PERSONAL AND CONFIDENTIAL, and an itinerary detailing my Monday flight to Hartsfield, the rental car reservation code, accommodations at the Days Inn, and directions to death row.

"What's his story?" asked Rachel with heartfelt concern, drawing a sweep of loose black bangs off her forehead with three fingers.

Rachel was polished, and conjured up images of autumn: scratchy knit sweaters and warm mugs of cider, the silver wisps of apple steam forming a perfect ess above the lip. She struck me as noble—elegant even, but perhaps too elegant for the barking, frequently futile sort of work that we did. She may have been . . . I don't know. Uptight. It was difficult to say.

"Halfway house employee gets murdered—a therapist, slept

around with his patients, one of whom is the girlfriend of our
guy; state says our guy did it," Martha rattled back. "Our guy—
that's Tiegs—maintains his innocence from the beginning and
throughout the appeals process. No witnesses to the crime, and
our guy doesn't make for the most presentable defendant. Surprise, surprise, not much of a defense is mounted. Sounds familiar, right? Right. Okay. Thing is, the prosecutors thought for
a while that the girlfriend did it, this . . . Calley. Therese Calley.
Cops did too—they pushed on our guy, on Tiegs, but they got
nothing out of him on her, so, predictably, they went after
him. Counsel is less than worthless; a couple of local advocacy
groups pick it up on appeal, but the word on the street is they
have to convince him—you with me?—actually *convince* him to
keep fighting the charges, even though he still claims he's innocent. I don't know what it . . . he found religion, made peace,
I don't know. He's hot and cold, according to the folks I talked
to. Too big a strain on their resources, so they called us, and
Tiegs agreed to meet with us—with you. *Begrudgingly* agreed, I
might add, although he was more than happy to dispose of his
prior counsel. Still with me here?"

"Uh-huh," I said.

"Hang on," responded Rachel quizzically. "Just so I'm
clear: you're saying he doesn't necessarily want a reprieve?"

"I'm saying," Martha replied, leaning back at a borderline
fatal angle in her desk chair, "this will be an intriguing case
for a couple of first-time gumshoes such as yourselves. It'll be a
challenge, okay? And you know I have faith in the both of you."

"Well . . . thank you," said Rachel, sitting tidily and
smiling.

"Martha, I think gumshoes are detectives," I added.

"Gumshoe; shyster—what difference does it make?" she

tittered back. "Just go be the lawyers I know you can be. This guy may need to have his hand held a little bit to see the light, but he's letting us in the door, and your job is to go advocate for him zealously. You're gonna go do that. Okay?"

Rachel looked first at me, with searching eyes, then back at Martha.

"Okay," she said brightly, and I nodded in turn.

"Okay," said Martha.

As we rose to leave, she called me back into the room for another moment.

"Leo, before you go down there, I just want to make sure you're ready for this."

"Of course I'm ready," I answered. "Why would you—"

"Please. I know what's up, Leo. I know what's up with my lawyers. Hey Leo? Look at me," said Martha, furiously snapping her fingers at my quiet head as I leafed through the dossier, avoiding her present avenue. "You got this."

"No, I—thank you," I muttered, tilting up.

Martha was a glorious person, all energy and class and elfin, silvery brilliance. She cared about us as lawyers, yes, but more fiercely as people; so profound was her care, in fact, that she frequently took it upon herself to meddle in our personal affairs. This was done with heroic intent, always, but nevertheless this was done. And on this day, this was being done hard.

"Leo, you know exactly what to do. Rachel knows exactly what to do. You're gonna go to Jackson, Georgia, and you're gonna see Tiegs and you're gonna talk to him. You're gonna take the weekend—you have any plans this weekend?"

"I do not."

"That's what I like to hear! You're gonna take the weekend and you're gonna learn absolutely everything there is to know about this guy. Okay? You're gonna immerse yourself in his life and in his case history. Got it? I want you to know every motion raised at trial and on appeal. Okay? Every objection in the record. And—Leo, are you listening?"

"Of course. Yes."

"Leo, it occurs to me that a really effective way to do all of this would be to ask Rachel out to dinner."

"Uh, Martha."

"Not *out* to dinner, of course—no time for that. But! You order Chinese food or something, you go through the court transcripts together—"

"Martha—"

"It might be good for you, Leo."

"Martha, I'm not sure what gave you the impression that I'm looking—"

"I'm telling you, this might be the right thing for you right now. None of my business, of course, but this is how the sparks fly."

"Nope—what am I saying? I know *exactly* what gave you the impression that I'm—"

"Boots said you're sad, Leo. He said you're monumentally sad."

". . . feels like there's a line—"

"He said you were, quote, 'kind of a piece of shit right now,' Leo. That's what *your* friend said about *you*. And that makes *me* sad."

"Colorful phrasing."

"I'm not talking about your work, here—we love your work. Everybody just wants you to be happy! Boots said you used to be a generally happy guy."

"Everybody? Is this really something that gets talked about?"

"Yes. Okay? You're part of our family now, Leo. We care about how you're doing, and I for one think that you and Rachel—"

"Just to be clear—"

"Two bright young kids—"

"Just to be clear, you—my boss—are encouraging me to participate in some interoffice . . . um . . ."

"I'm encouraging happiness."

"Got it."

"Come on, Leo. She's kind, she's gorgeous, she's smarter than you, you're attracted to her—what more could you want?"

"How would you know if I was attracted to her?"

A beat of silence.

"Boots—"

"Boots told you. Of course."

"He's looking out for you, man! So you'll think about it?"

I shuffled the forest of papers in the case binder, nicking my thumb on a glossy close-up photograph of the murder weapon.

"I'll think about *this*," I replied, tapping on the dossier, and stepped back demurely to the doorframe of her office.

"You're a sharp guy, Leo. I'm confident you can think about both at once."

"You know, Martha, I could probably sue you for creating a hostile work environment or something."

"I'll take my chances."

"That right?"

"You're not a very good lawyer!" she whispered, then broke into a warm and raucous fit of laughter.

"Thanks boss," I said, and slipped around the corner into the hall.

"Fly safe, gumshoe!" she called after me.

As it happened, I didn't phone Rachel—although I did order Chinese. Michael Tiegs's case was more or less typical as these things go: grossly out of step with human experience writ large, of course, but fairly typical within the select population of those who have been accused of killing a person in a southern United State in the initial bit of the twenty-first century. I knew enough to know that, guilty or not, the endless chips of the system were stacked against him; I knew enough to know that he would almost certainly fry. Not fry, no—he would just be given that brief new blood. Pentobarbital, pancuronium bromide, and potassium chloride. The "cocktail."

I met Rachel in the airport terminal after a marathon weekend of study. Cramming for the Tiegs case had reminded me of cramming for a law school exam, only the test was: can you save this man's life, and (for extra credit) should you? Now we were in transit to the big show.

"Are you nervous?" was the first thing Rachel said when she found me on the safe side of the security check. For a second, I thought she was talking about the flight.

"I'm always nervous," I answered, and she laughed, though I wasn't kidding. There is nowhere on Earth I am less comfortable than thirty thousand feet above it; I have a fear of flying of the precise middling magnitude where I can still manage to board, but cannot make it past takeoff without near-complete internal panic. This has been true since childhood, when en route to family vacations it would invariably occur to me, somewhere over Ohio or Kansas or the Atlantic Ocean, that cavernous hunks of metal simply were not meant to remain aloft.

"I'm 26F," she said, flopping her ticket skyward. "You?"

"I am . . . oh. 26E. We're neighbors."

"What are the odds?" she purred, and gave the nod which means: follow me, now, to our gate. In the moment, I groped for the exact right word with which to describe her to myself in my head, but it didn't come to me for hours: *gamine.*

When the call came to board, I walked the antiseptic white mile of the jetway a pace behind her, quaking like an aspen tree in the brisk, recycled air. I knew what would happen to me next: suddenly I'd be strapped down, bracing for that first lurch forward. It always goes the same way. Anxiety gestates in my brain, but it's never long before it matures and metastasizes, vacationing in my tropical gut, colonizing my outer digits. It's raw, and I might black out. I forget how to breathe, then remember at the last possible moment. The plane dips and flutters—we're just servants, at this point, to the whims of the violent sky. Head down, ice cold beads of sweat the size of marbles leap desperately from the ledges of my brow. I imagine they are panicking stockbrokers, panicking over the coming crash: Sell! Sell! Sell this flight! My heart can be heard and felt from any part of my body now. It will ease a bit, and only a bit, at the first merciful ding.

The truth is, technology will never overcome the rollercoaster-physical necessity of takeoff, nor, apparently, the ragged-blue cloth and associated 1970s trappings. Any airplane will always, always feel to me like a rickety Buick daring the giant sky.

My primary concern on this plane was preventing all aboard from growing wise to the mounting dread inside me, in the following order of priority: Rachel, Taryn the joyful flight attendant, 26D, the pilot (somehow), our across-the-aisle row 26 cousins, the other attendants, the other passengers. I recognized the absurdity of my fear—even in its grip I recognized the logical failures that brought me dry-mouthed and pulsing to the edge of despair. It is primitive to fear that way, in the face of all reason. Statistics indicate that you are dramatically more likely to die in the cab on your way to the airport than you are in a fiery plane crash, but try telling that to my paper-white knuckles.

Once at cruising altitude, Rachel and I ordered twin whiskey gingers for very different purposes: hers was for regular human consumption, whereas mine was a carbonated antipsychotic. She ordered another one, because what the hell; I ordered another one because damn the torpedoes. I paid for her third so that it wouldn't seem odd that I needed a third, which I did, due to the fact that aluminum was still heavier than fucking air. This is how we ended up drunk over the Carolinas.

"How come you never come out with us, Leo?" Rachel asked cautiously, long after we'd abandoned all pretense of huddling about the case. "We go out—Salim, Sam, Aaron, your boy Boots. Kevin comes out; Jessie too, sometimes. Even Martha came to karaoke one time. How come you never want to hang out? We're fun, and I'm not just saying that. We're fun. Fun crew," and she hiccupped, blushed, and opened her eyes as wide as a person can before bursting into a cavalcade of giggles.

"I know you're all fun," I said, sounding not at all fun myself.

"But you don't come out with us. Is it—are you too cool for us? Is that it, Brice? Too cool for school?"

"I am decidedly not too cool for school," I replied, left hand fastened like an epileptic remora to the armrest I shared with comatose 26D.

"So what is it? Is it—oh."

"What?"

"No, it's just . . ."

"Rachel?"

"It's private," she said apologetically.

"Okay, but it sounds like it might be . . . my . . . private. As opposed to your private. Sounds like it's a private thing about me, is what I mean. So you should feel free to share."

She dislodged the last ice cube from her cup with lissome fingers and crunched it between her teeth before turning all she could of her belted body to face me.

"Boots said you had a really bad breakup, and that's why you're so glum all the time. He said you were a positive, high-functioning good guy, and then someone you loved kind of . . . ripped your heart out, and now you're kind of a piece of shit."

"He's really harping on that phrase, huh?"

"It's none of my business. But just so you know, we've all had some version of that—a lot of us, at least, have been hurt badly, and it's hard to come all the way back from that, sometimes. It's not unusual, I guess is what I mean. It's really not. It's okay; it's normal. Is it the sort of thing where you don't want to talk about it? Or is it good to talk about it?"

My hand stopped shaking for the first time since the engines fired up; here was something worse than a crashing plane. Of course, she had me dead to rights—I remembered having been functional at one time; I remembered a time when I could more readily think about small things, fun things, even.

"I'm pretty sure it's the first one. Not that I don't want to—I can't," I heaved, and each new word grew thornier in my throat. "I can't talk about it, I don't think."

Jesus Christ, man.

She crumpled her plastic cup, and turned back to face forward.

"Oh," she said softly. "Oh, well that's alright."

"Sorry," I said back, stoned by shame.

"No!" she replied, too quickly. "But, for sure, if you ever want to—"

"Uh," I said, just to stop her, "it's just difficult to explain. That's all. I can try, if you . . . it's difficult to explain because I don't quite know what it did to me. What it's done. It's just, it's one of those things where my whole world felt like it ended, but *the* world kept going for everyone else. Can you understand that? Like if the plane crashed—but only for me. Everybody else's plane is just . . . sailing . . . along . . ."

I had lost my train of thought.

"Dude, you're drunk," she said.

"That didn't make any sense, huh?"

"No, that was weird!" she laughed, and I laughed too, to show I knew how.

And we touched down.

SIX

THE TELEVISION WHIRRED AND FLICKERED AND POPPED with rich blue light: the stars were out. Entertainment awards ceremonies were not something I'd given a thought to in my life until the day I had it planted in my head that the actor Mark Renard, whom I at one point knew, would be presenting the award for Best Sound Mixing to this year's person or people who mixed sound best, presumably. Mark was by now a regular on America's number-one new drama, *Briefs*, which, because the world can be so cruel, was an overwrought, underwritten show about fit-and-frisky lawyers. With two movies in the works, his broader fame was impending. He was set to arrive shortly on the Red Carpet, and—in defiance of a whole lifetime of not doing this sort of thing—I was tuning in to see.

"And now we have Mark Renard, who's presenting tonight! Great to finally meet you, Mark!"

"*Great to meet you, Terri.*"

"*Mark, you've had quite a year!*" bellowed a dazzling twit.

"*Yeah, it's been great, Terri. So, so great. It's been, like, unreal.*"

"*Has your life just completely blown up, Mark? You've just blown up this year, huh?!*"

"*Yeah, I guess so.*"

"*Hit show, got some movies coming out—tell us about the movies! When are they coming out, Mark?!*"

"*Uh, one is called* The Drying of the Rain, *and it's a very serious dramatic . . . piece, and, uh, it's coming out in June, and one is called* Timesport, *and that's more like a suspense thriller type-action-thing, and that's coming out early this summer.*"

"*Now, for* The Drying of the Rain, *you filmed that over in Europe, huh Mark?!*"

"*Yeah, we were in Firenze, in Italy, for the filming.*"

The twit was excited. "*Exciting!*" she said.

"*Yeah.*"

"*And you were working with Marcus Wimms on that one. What was that like?*"

"*Marcus is just a great director, you know? It's a real honor to be able to work with a great director like that.*"

"*I'll bet! What was the best part about filming in Italy, Mark?*"

"*Uh, it's really just pretty over there, you know? And the food's good. They have really good olives. I hadn't ever really been a big olives guy. Ha! Right? So, olives, I guess.*"

Mark's date was wrapped in a seafoam gown and loitering, silent, behind him, strung up with a dancer's posture. I was on the wrong side of the television; she refused to look me in the eye. Goodbyes were exchanged, and the sprauncy couple drifted away to live someplace else, off-screen.

In my mind there was a sleek car quietly trembling on the

street below me. I hardly touched the fire escape on the way down, my suddenly divine limbs collaborating with a fearless syzygy they'd never known. I raced across the country and it was night the whole way; "I've never made such good time!" I mused to the Nevada desert as it cleaved effortlessly before me. Outside the nameless theatre, I ditched the car and tidied the cuffs of my tuxedo. Inside, I was flashy, stellified, at home among the beautiful. All I have to do is find her, and then I could explain.

"And the winner for technical editing of an animated foreign short," started some ingénue, "Wladislaw Budziszewski!"

I weaved through the thunderous crowd toward the front, beyond the yachty masses, beyond the orchestra pit. I kept a searching eye on the rows of my audience, but I couldn't find her; the famous faces were somehow unfamiliar. Once on stage, I snatched the trophy and began:

"Thank you! Thank you, Academy! Please! I want—"

"No!" shouted Wladislaw, loping up the steps. "He's not real!"

"Please!" I went on. "I want to tell you—"

"Hey!" barked Wladislaw, and he was irate, grabbing at my lapels, lunging for the statue. I stared out, searching, into the assemblage of stars.

"I want to tell—"

"He is not real!" blasted the superlative technical editor into the podium microphone. "I am Wladislaw Budziszewski!"

I struggled to reclaim my position, and overcame the smaller Wlad.

"You don't know that!" I bellowed to the crowd. "None of you know the animated technical whatever—"

"I am the real Wladislaw Budziszewski," he yelped, his voice cracking.

"No!" I countered. "*I am the real* Vladishaw . . . Budin . . . owski."

"Please! Stop this!" he called up from the ground. "You aren't real!"

"I am! I *am* real! I want—"

"No!"

"I'm looking for someone."

"He's not real!"

"I'm looking for the actress, Fiona Fox—"

"You cannot do this!"

"Listen, everyone: I want to tell you a story."

• • •

The trip from the Jackson Days Inn to the Georgia Department of Corrections death row facility goes like this: Rachel Costa knocks so quietly on the door to your room that you're not certain if anybody is there at all; you drive two-point-eight miles in a rented Nissan Sentra to the easterly end of town, and park in a gated lot designated for visitors to the Georgia Diagnostic and Classification State Prison; you walk nearly two hundred yards from the lot to the guest entrance, where one of you marvels aloud at the fact, learned earlier, back in the car, that it is sixty-two degrees today in Georgia even though this is allegedly December; you hand photographic identification to a sturdy woman with a large gun, then proceed through a metal detector after placing your phone and keys into a gray plastic bin; you give your names and the name of the inmate you are visiting to a stern man in a brown suit, then also provide him with the same photographic identification you just displayed a moment ago; Rachel Costa hands her purse to a gray woman, grayer even than the plastic bin, who spirits it away into another room; everybody signs their name to a sheet of paper and dates it, and everybody gets a visitor badge to be displayed at all times; the two of you and a solitary guard walk together in silence down an impossibly long hallway and through two security doors; you enter a neon-lit room that has no need to be as large as it is—the only thing in it, apart from six folding chairs and one folding table, is the convicted murderer Michael Tiegs.

"How many are here?" Rachel asked the man in the brown suit on the occasion of our first visit.

"Sorry, ma'am?" he grumbled, hands folded palm-to-anti-palm behind his back like a sentinel.

"Inmates. How many inmates do you have in this facility?" she asked again. I figured she was only making small talk; we both knew the answer already.

"Ninety-eight men here, ma'am," he replied, and pushed his lower lip up against the full length of his drooping Zapata mustache.

"They're all men?" I asked, frowning. I guess I felt like making small talk, too.

"The women are kept up at Metro State Prison," he answered stiffly, "in Atlanta."

We trundled past the man in the brown suit, past endless flecked ceiling tiles and caged lights, down the hall to meet Michael Tiegs.

"Hello, Michael? Good morning, Michael. We're the attorneys from the New Salem Institute who've been assigned to come . . . meet you, and speak to you about your case. My name is Rachel, and this—"

"Ms. Costa," said Tiegs. "Mr. Brice."

He was thirty-six when we met him, and just impossibly gaunt. It was difficult to believe that this same man—now monkish and pale—was at one time in possession of a low-nineties fastball, the most feared arm in southern Georgia. His face was fixed in a state of lassitude, but those eyes: Christ, how they darted and swelled. He had the same hushful drawl as the man in the brown suit; words seemed to drip out of him like candle wax. Serene in his movements, he reminded me at once of a place I'd only read about: the Sea of Tranquility, on the moon. It's not a sea, per se, but rather a lunar mare—reflective, mysterious, salty, and completely placid, a basin beyond the reach of human interference.

What we learned that day in the neon-lit room: Tiegs had spent the past decade reading every book in the prison library save for the legal texts and contemporary American fiction. He found Jesus in 2008, and became what he called "a latinitaster—just basically, sorta like a petty scholar of church Latin." Every night, he engaged in three hours of elaborate liturgical prayer. He had an eerie command of religious history, from Stonehenge and the life of Krishna to the Second Vatican Council. He demonstrated no special interest in the outcome of his case or the future of his life on Earth.

"You Jewish?" he asked me, less than twenty minutes after we'd met for the first time.

Here we go.

"In fact, I am," I said, braced curtly for my initiation into some lost strand of truly medieval prejudice.

"I guessed that from your name," said Tiegs, now grinning. "I should've said more like, 'my brother in the Vast Abrahamic Tradition,' I suppose. Leo is Leonard?"

"Yes. Leo is Leonard."

"I knew a Leonard, back in grade school," he went on. "That Leonard, though—he wasn't a Jew. But a lot of them are. Y'all know Leonard Cohen? Leonard Bernstein?"

"*You* know Leonard Bernstein?" asked Rachel, clearly incredulous but somehow not rude-sounding. I couldn't get over the way he said 'Bernstein.' BURR-uhn-stay-uhn, the *uhns* brief, but there, the plosive *stay* ejected from his mouth like a wayward mosquito.

"I do, young sister. I even know Lenny Bruce—he was a Leonard too. And he was a Jew too, I'm pretty sure. I'm not entirely certain about that, now, but I'm pretty sure. I'm wondering now if either of y'all know the story of Mosheh ben Maimon."

I looked over at Rachel, who said mostly everything with her eyes.

"I think that we don't," I said.

"I'm surprised you don't. Mosheh ben Maimon was called Maimonides, and he was pretty much basically like the most important Jewish philosopher in history. He was a jurist, of sorts. A man of unmatched wisdom in his own time. Maimonides, well, he created the thirteen principles of faith—basically, it's pretty much like everything you need to be a Jew. He'd be a lawyer, like y'all are, if he lived today . . . course, he don't."

"I'm afraid you're stuck with us," said Rachel gently.

"You Catholic?" Tiegs asked her, grinning again.

"Agnostic," she replied, adding quickly: "but, yes, Michael, I was raised Catholic for a little while."

"I thought that from your name, too—from your last name—and from your complexion. But you ain't even Catholic after all, are you now? So I guess it'd be more appropriate for me to say, 'my sister in Healthy Skepticism.'"

Rachel allowed a warm smile, and Tiegs chuckled in turn.

"Michael," she began, "you seem to be extraordinarily well-educated—"

"You mean for a Christian?"

"No, of course—"

"For a convicted killer?"

"No—"

"Oh, you mean just for a Georgia boy, then?"

"I meant for a person who dropped out of high school," said Rachel, her whole body stiffened by the still-smiling Tiegs. I swore he liked us already.

"Well, that's certainly a fair enough description. I wasn't ever much for school. I like to read here, though—lucky enough, too, in'smuch as there ain't a thing else to do. In school, they never really taught the sorts of things that grab my interest."

"And what is it that grabs your interest?" I asked. "Religious studies?"

"Not as such, I'd say, but the heap of ecumenical literature is part and parcel. I'm interested in death."

"Death?" I echoed back.

"Death, like the row you're on, ma'am and sir. Death, like the inevitable ceasing of all you've ever known or cared for in this world. I suppose I started to think about it, oh, 'bout the time when it became the next big thing for me. 'Bout then."

"Well," Rachel added, "we're here to see if we can stop that from being the case."

"Yep, yep, yep; the case, the case," mumbled Tiegs. "That's why y'all've come here, after all."

"It's . . ." Rachel started, "it's why we're here, yes. We've been over your case history—all of the appeals, the conviction—

everything. And, Michael, we have reason to believe that we might be able to mount a successful effort that could spare your life. But we need to know—"

"Y'all need to know!" he shouted abruptly. "Y'all need to know . . . I know what y'all need to know, Sister Rachel, despite my apparently discomfiting dearth of higher education— you like that? My discomfiting dearth!—despite all that, I am wisened up enough to understand that y'all can't mount so much as a dead horse, never mind a court appeal, if I ain't cooperating in the efforts. Ain't that right?"

Michael's lips peeled back into a ludicrous grin before quavering into a grim chortle.

"So are you?" Rachel asked, unsteadied by the gruesome enigma before us.

"We can talk," he acquiesced, in a way that sounded as though talking was the very most that we could do.

"Talk about the case?" queried a skeptical Rachel.

"'Bout the case, sure," he responded. "'Bout death. 'Bout anything you'd like."

"Okay," I said, "so let's talk."

"Just to be clear," Rachel pressed, "Michael, if we're going to get anywhere, we need to talk about the case—only the case, and the history behind it, about Therese and John Jasper, and everything like that. Death is . . . of interest to you, I understand, but we're going to need to put that aside for now. Death is what we're trying to avoid here."

"Stave it off though you might," he said, adding, under his breath, "and I do appreciate the gesture," before going on. "But it'll find us—death'll find us, all three—in time. All people agree on this, throughout the ages. Ain't no mystery there. Mystery comes later."

We spoke with Tiegs for an hour that day, and let him know that we'd be back the next morning to run through the trial history of his case. Walking out, I asked him if he had any further questions for us.

"Sure, I got a question. Are y'all as good at being lawyers as Maimonides?"

"No sir," I replied.

"That's where you're wrong, Brother Leo. You're better than Maimonides," he said, snickering to himself quietly. Two guards came in and began their fussy preparations for the short walk back to his cell.

"How's that, Michael?"

"Maimonides ain't here."

•   •   •

Leonardo da Vinci was born out of wedlock to a lawyer and a peasant in the spring of 1452, and everything that came later was just the obvious fruit of that bastard seed. That's if you believe Dr. Freud, of course; the old pervert held up Leonardo as the paragon of sublimation (the most enviable of defense mechanisms, the one that lets you transform your damaged psyche into a machine that pumps out pristine works of art). Whether Leonardo was bent quite so fortuitously by the circumstances surrounding his birth is a debatable matter. What we know for certain is that he dreamed things so infinite that, more than five centuries later, he is remembered by the whole of the world.

Vasari, the Florentine painter and father of art history, wrote of a curious routine of Leonardo's: he used to purchase caged birds for the sole purpose of setting them free. Now, you don't have to be Dr. Freud to discern some of the psychological ramifications of this particular habit (hell, you don't have to be Dr. Phil): each of us faces moments when we cannot free ourselves—and perhaps because it's the best we can do, some among us will move, then, to crack the cell of whatever captive animal is nearest.

Michael Tiegs was a peculiar stray, and his neck was craned so high into the world of spiritual conjecture it was hard to know whether he was even capable of reeling his frantic brain back down to Earth. Our early meetings revealed a decided lack of interest in the more immediate of his two fates (the one to be administered by what he called "the 'lowercase-J' judge," as opposed to "the 'big-J' Judge-on-High"); every question we posed on procedure, memory, or fact was met with a treatise on faith or an arcane historical parable. This exasperated us—Rachel most of all—on the first of our three trips to Georgia, as the final days leading up to the decision on his last-ditch appeal were already falling steadily away.

"Can we talk about Therese today, Michael?" I implored him at the top of our third conversation. There was no dent in his composure, no registration of longing or remorse.

"Well," he proclaimed, "we can talk about anything y'all like, Brother Leo."

"Thank you," I said. "I appreciate that. And today I'm hoping that the three of us can talk a little bit about Therese."

"Alright, fine then!" he chuckled. "Where'd you like me to start? Therese, she's gotta be about five-foot-seven. She's got dark brown hair and she's bowlegged. She's a good soul, too. A real good soul. That a good place to start?"

"Michael," Rachel gently interjected, "we spoke with the officers—the ones who originally arrested you—to verify the reports they'd written up and testified to at trial."

"I hope you gave 'em my regards," he sang back dryly.

"They've maintained from the beginning that when they first came to the house, they weren't coming to question you."

"That right?"

"They were coming to question her."

Michael didn't flinch, but leaned slowly back in his folding chair, revolving his neck to stare straight up into the neon bulbs. I detected a struggle in him: the source, I was sure, of his orphic sleight of hand. He had managed to place into perfect balance his two worlds—one of metal bars and cold concrete, the other of sublime, unknowable mist—and the struggle was to maintain that perfect equilibrium, that perfect serenity of never having to be anywhere full-time. As escape artistry went, it was something approaching genius. Rachel went on, delicately.

"So I guess the first question is: how was it that they ended up arresting you and not Therese? Because the officers made it sound like you were not their first suspect."

"Well," he uttered solemnly, "I was their last suspect. Ain't that what matters?"

"Michael—"

"They came to have a word with her, sure," he went on, still looking up to the lights. "They came, and they asked her some questions about the fella who got killed—that'd be John Jasper—they asked her some . . . questions, and . . . well, after a spell they asked me some questions, too."

For all of the natural ease with which he spoke of old philosophies, Michael bristled when asked to revisit memories of his own. When he did, he tightened, and instead of exhaling as usual, he blew out his breaths manually, like a child trying in vain to whistle. It was like a letting off of steam—the only crack in his tranquility I'd noticed.

"And?" asked Rachel.

"And. Well, I suppose they liked her answers more'n they liked mine."

"Why do you say that?"

"They arrested me that morning, Sister Rachel. They took me away right then and there. Walked me on out. Into the cruiser. We sped off. They brought me down to the jail. Handcuffs, and all that."

"Michael," Rachel prompted, "if you didn't kill John Jasper, like you say, isn't it possible that—I'm not saying this is what happened, Michael; all I'm saying is that isn't it at least possible that—"

"Therese, she's a good soul," Michael blankly interjected. "A real good soul. She never did do nothing wrong. Nope."

I glanced over at Rachel.

"Well," I started gingerly, haplessly drawing out the liquid sonorant 'ell' and the silence that followed long enough for my co-counsel to lose patience and finish the thought.

"She did do some things wrong, Michael."

"Who, Therese? That don't sound like her," he snuffed, lurching his head back down to face us.

"She did," Rachel continued. "I mean, she was a . . . before you met her, Michael, she was a prostitute. She was arrested for solicitation—you know about that."

He blinked twice, then breathed in loudly, but his expression didn't otherwise change.

"Mary Magdalene," he enunciated proudly. "Miss Mary Magda-*leen*."

"What about her?" I asked, though no amount of Hebrew school could have kept me from knowing what came next.

"Well, I'll tell you, Brother Leo—she herself was thought to be a prostitute. Fact is, I'd say she's pretty much basically

the most famous prostitute of all time . . . course, there ain't a
single shred of scripture to back it up. Ugly lies and ugly rumors,
if you ask me. It all goes back to this one homily, see? Back in
maybe the sixth century, Pope Gregory, he declared that—"

"Michael," Rachel broke in.

"Sister Rachel?" he replied innocently.

"Why are you telling us about Mary Magdalene? What
could Mary Magdalene have to do with *your* case, here in the
present, non–Biblical times, Michael?" she asked calmly. These,
it seemed, were fair questions.

Michael only smiled: the civil grin of the prophet. He
planted his elbows onto the folding table and leaned toward us
intently, as though proximity might help make up for the gulfs
in our comprehension.

"Folks thought Mary Magadalene was a prostitute," he explained slowly, oozing forth his personal logic. "And maybe
she was, and maybe she weren't. Point is, Mary Magdalene was
a repentant sinner—a repentant sinner, and she walked with
Jesus Christ."

He nodded at each of us to confirm that we followed, then
went on.

"Okay. Now, Therese . . . some people maybe say that she
was a sinner too. What I'm saying is that, whatever it is she
might've done, she is repentant. She is redeemed. She walks
with Christ now. And that's what it has to do with that. Do
you understand?"

I looked to Rachel in time to catch the finale of a heavy
sigh.

"I understand, Michael," she said. "We understand. But we
need *you* to understand that we are your lawyers. And because
we're lawyers, we live in a world where the things you're talk-

ing about here don't really factor in. If Therese was involved in John Jasper's death, in any way at all, that's something that matters to us a great deal. We talk about crimes here, not sins. We talk about exoneration, not repentance. Acquittal, not redemption. And if there's any chance of us saving you here, you're going to have to—"

Michael and I had perked up on the same word, and he entered into a deep fit of laughter; though it came across as objectively maniacal, I understood immediately the source of his outburst.

"Michael," I said, trying to corral him, "what Rachel means is that our interest is in keeping you alive, and getting you out of prison. And to do that, we need to gather facts and information that could help—"

"Save!" he roared, now beaming at us toothily. "It's the two of y'all who are gonna be saving me? That's just terrific, folks; that's a treasure!"

Rachel and I shifted nervously in our chairs as we waited out his giddy conniption.

"You can throw away them shackles, boys!" he called out gleefully to the expressionless guards. "Lord have mercy; my saviors have arrived!"

• • •

James Buchanan was a goddamn amateur! Picture him, the turgid white old man, kissing greedily the wet hot mouth of pristine Rachel Costa—you can't do it. She emits a little sound in the throes of that kiss, of my kiss, not his, not Buchanan's, and in that sound lies sweetest mystery and purest faith. Because you see, James Buchanan was a failure, but I've not seen my country sliced in two. I've not failed. Not this time.

At a lively chain restaurant on our first Thursday in Georgia, we had too much to drink; we laughed loudly for hours, and stumbled back to the hotel parking lot. Something happened and we were tangled against the warm metal flank of a stranger's white sedan, my heretical hands pawing at her contours, her sleepy lips on mine, our bodies floundering together in the tawny dust of the American South.

"It's about fucking time," she whispered into my chin.

It is?

I didn't know what she'd meant, but the alcohol was emphatically more than enough for me to forget myself. I saw still the large, ghastly bears of memory that for months had preyed upon me, but they had lost their definition in the impenetrable blizzard of my head. For the first time, for a moment, I was free.

We swayed, and stayed together through the night, buoyed by the blissful *ivresse* of eleven total mai tais. I thought of Fiona only twice the entire time. In the fog of the following morning, we surveyed each other like rival gunslingers, stoically sizing up one another's intentions.

"Oh hello," she ventured warily at last, expressionless, still, and beautiful in the spangled glow of the new Georgian sun.

"Hello," I answered neutrally. Our noses were not more than six inches apart.

"How're you feeling?" she asked, brushing truant strands of black hair back behind her ear.

"I think . . . I might be a little hungover."

"I think I might be too."

A long moment passed between us. My saturated eyes limped around the room: flung cloth curtains to moseying ceiling fan to a shockingly decent painting of horses crossing a stream.

"So what now?" she asked.

"We have to go over the appeal motions this afternoon with—"

"No, I mean—"

"Oh."

"We slept together, dude," she said, smiling just slightly. I accidentally let a few seconds go by.

"We sure did," I answered idiotically. A sharp interciliary pain struck me like a lightning bolt, and I groaned.

"That bad?"

"No," I stammered. "No! I just—"

"I'm kidding. Was this so unexpected?"

I wasn't sure. I'd suspected for several long days now that Rachel could be good for me—nearly perfect, even—in a vacuum, in a world in which I was still qualified to entrust critical parts of myself to another's care. Here she was, this warm and touchable future, this living opportunity to end the grim lacuna of my life and begin again. I reached out gracelessly to caress her skyward arm, and attempted to convince myself for at least a little while that it was Fiona who was dead. Not me.

We ended up back in that same chain restaurant the next three nights in a row, and for three nights in a row we ended up back in room 207 of the Jackson Days Inn, enmeshed before the cloth curtains and the ceiling fan and the horses. I'm not proud to say that I was drunk on each of these occasions, but this was true. And it had nothing at all to do with Rachel, who, to her everlasting credit, was easy to be with and easy to know. She lacked nonsense and was largely unpeculiar. She was *there*. She wasn't a capricious, inscrutable sphinx, like *some* people used to be. We spoke freely and enjoyed each other's company, and for a necessary moment nothing was more significant than it was.

And I lay awake those next three nights thinking: why did she go? And when at last I slept, I tried so hard to dream about Fiona again—but you can't control your dreaming any more than you can control your time awake. Rachel was there now, waving and making herself large in that space. In my dreams, she was much too easy to find, this shiny epigone where one had gone before and gone away. I peered around corners in search of Fiona's face, which in my dreams I couldn't quite remember. I lost it, and it faded from my memory in the precise way that you might watch a bright heavy thing sink into the ocean (the instant the last glimmer goes, you find yourself staring at yourself). And the corners revealed nothing, and I woke up beside a pretty woman in the Jackson Days Inn every time.

• • •

After a seemingly endless ten-day stretch of inscrutable dialogues with Michael, of meetings with state officials and interviews with law enforcement personnel and sessions with Rachel comparing our notes over coffees, after consecutive nights of hopefully curative sex, I returned to New York and the lesser prison of my own thoughts. Outdoors, Manhattan remained an indecipherable zoo to me, a sprawling noise machine I lacked the will to appreciate. My domestic life, however, began to grow vaguely charming; as the trilemma of our respective language barriers melted away, a strange normalcy arose between Lita, Rafael Uribe Uribe, and myself. Our routine was simple enough: Lita, fixed to her rocking chair in the corner of the immense living room, would nod sympathetically as I aired professional and existential grievances in what could charitably be described as something just south of a grotesquely mangled Spanglish. After graciously enduring my noun supply, she would nod still, and whisper all the while loving paragraphs I'd never understand to Rafi. We all learned to trust and to nod. Lita spoke frequently, but never to me (except in the form of mellow holas of salutation and response). Rafi stopped barking on my entrances. We became a sort of weird, hieroglyphic brood—unable to communicate, but able to be content with our respective situations.

Things weren't so different with Rachel, actually; in the two weeks that bridged our first and second trips to Georgia, we'd made a cautious effort to further the scope and significance of our romance-like activities, but there was unmissable static in the connection. We managed, somehow, to grow in our distance despite an increasingly close proximity. At times, we seemed like strangers approaching each other from opposite ends of a long hallway. To avoid the collision, one veers left while the other goes right—"excuse me," you say, politely, but then you both correct course. So now one veers right while the other goes left—"whoops, haha," she says, and you smile sheepishly, so eager to defer, and the god-awful dance continues. My left, her right, nearly bumping into the unfamiliar mirror of the one you're approaching, or is it she approaching you? So it goes: the affable incongruity, the smiley failure of your most basic instincts to align, the protection of knowing that you'll never really touch.

I searched every conversation for the key to some higher meaning in our affair, but invariably the thought struck me: was there no celestial spark between us? Was she merely smart, kind, and pretty? I brought this to the attention of Boots and

Emily, whom I supposed knew more about contentment than anybody else in New York.

"You need to give it time," one or both of them told me. "Time to grow; time to develop. It's not magic, Leo. These things don't happen right away."

"It happened right away with Fiona," I countered. "I felt it: that thing, you know, that signifying thing that invades your bloodstream and focuses you like nothing else. It *was* magic, with her. And it's more than a little concerning that I don't feel that with Rachel."

"You are a child," said Boots, one hand on the incorruptible spine of the smart cookie he loved, another drumming absently on the armrest.

"Leo," added Emily, "we've talked about this. That feeling fades away—it isn't the same thing as love. Remember? That Fiona feeling was just a shooting star? And real love is—what was it? A planet. Love is a planet. You said that."

"You stood right here in this kitchen and said, 'Love is a planet,' Leo," recalled Boots. "Felt like a real breakthrough moment."

"I know," I said.

"So it's disheartening to us," Boots went on, "that you still won't let go of this notion—which you *admit* is fantasy—that your life is going to be meaningless without, like, some cosmic connection to ground you through future lives, or whatever the fuck."

"No, I know, but—"

"No buts, Leo. Rachel is awesome, and you're about to blow it before it even begins. Stop soul-searching and live a life."

"Okay," I said.

"Love is a planet, Leo," Emily repeated sweetly.

"I know," I said.

"Not just any planet," added Boots. "It's this one."

They were right—of course they were right, but logic couldn't pierce my stupid heart, so I went to Sona for a contrarian opinion.

"Who even is this broad?" she asked.

"You've met her. A couple of times. Black hair, like yours. Rachel."

"Hm. I don't think I've met her. Anyway, she sounds pretty unmemorable. You should drop her."

"You think—"

"Yo, Leo, if you're not feeling it . . . drop her. She sounds terrible."

"She's great, actually," I responded. "She's thoughtful and generous—I actually really do like her. Or at least I think I could be capable of . . . liking her, of genuinely liking her, when the time is right, and we know each other better, and I have a little more capacity to really get to . . . be a person who could . . ."

"Okay, well, I don't believe you," Sona answered.

"Why's that?"

"Because you're a huge sap, and, if this girl was really it for you, you'd be talking your standard nonsense about riding into the infinite future with her, not about how generous she is."

She had something there. Affectionate feelings for Rachel aside, I didn't know how to love someone in the second way; I didn't want to know how.

Love may be a planet. It may be something ancoral, something firm and steady and muzzled by its own gravity. It may be snug. But what good is love if it isn't also unrestrained? If it isn't supernatural? What good is it if it doesn't course through space and time like a fucking rocket ship, blitzing Heaven and bewildering Earth, not terra firma but terra incognita, raining bright issles down upon the cozy planets below? What good is it if it *isn't* Heaven?

Fiona glowed with purpose on the campus theater's pearlescent screen. This was *The Nervous System: A Very Deep Film by Bettany Skiles*, the second day we met, and down here in the audience, in a memory, her knee grazed mine just barely. The spectators were pooled in her light—in her character's light, I mean—their hearts beating in time with Ours, and I saw her, too, in her own light. We all laughed with her when the moment was right; we all leaned in together when her performance called us near. When I melted back deep enough into the twill cushion of my seat, I could see both versions of her at once: a young woman ticking fatefully by my side for the moment, and a projection of a girl who could stay that way forever.

• • •

"Leo, when we send you off to Georgia, there's an unspoken rule that you come back with peaches," chided Martha as I launched myself onto the cracked leather of her couch.

"Or peanuts," added Peter Ausberry in his graveled baritone.

"Right," said Martha. "Peaches or peanuts. We're disappointed in you."

"I should've known," I responded as sheepishly as one can with one's feet splayed on the coffee table.

"Damn right," she said. "But you're flying back down there on Wednesday; you're gonna remedy this. Okay?"

"Okay."

"You're gonna score us some peaches. Okay? Or peanuts?"

"You bet."

"So Leo," Peter rumbled, "what are you thinking about Michael Tiegs? Any holes in the case? Any angles that might have been missed the first few times around?"

It was nearly December, and our first round of conversations with Michael had yielded nothing of jurisprudential value. Three phone calls placed to his court-appointed lawyer had revealed a certain staggering carelessness, but no likely grounds for a valid claim of ineffective assistance of counsel. Rachel and I had spoken to county officials, amateur abolitionists, and the original arresting officers, all to no avail. The case against Tiegs, though short on witnesses or hard evidence, had been neatly prosecuted. Our only hope of saving him, Rachel and I agreed, was to determine Therese's role in the crime— and convince Michael to stop protecting her.

"He's not terribly forthcoming," I said. "At least not with the kind of thing we're looking for. He seems . . . resigned, I guess, to his fate. No, not that: he seems almost . . . over it. He's easily the most nonchalant condemned person I'd ever expect to meet. I get the sense that Therese Calley is central to everything that happened, but she won't talk to us, and Tiegs refuses to say one bad thing about her. Rachel's sure that she's responsible for everything and that he's—that he went insane, or something, when he found religion, I guess, and that he's just sort of willingly martyred himself by covering for her. We have more digging we need to do, but so far nobody's cooperating. Not Therese, and certainly not Tiegs. And I'm not sure which is the bigger problem between the two of them."

"Okay then," said Peter. "You and Rachel should keep

pushing on him. But you're going to need to figure out a way to connect with Therese Calley soon, uncover something valuable we can show to the court, or we'll have to drop it."

"I know," I said, and quite suddenly I formed a picture in my mind of the consequences if we didn't save him: Michael would be gone.

"Do you trust him?" Peter asked quickly, and, almost as an afterthought, "You and Rachel have been speaking with him for a little while now—do you think he's guilty?"

"I don't know," I answered truthfully, surprised at myself. I hadn't even thought about it—about whether or not Tiegs actually pulled the trigger on John Jasper—not once since the moment I met him four weeks prior. I'd *talked* about it, to be sure, but I hadn't formed an opinion of my own.

"Okay," said Martha, "you've got all your meetings set up for the next trip? You have everything you need from us?"

"I'm all set," I replied.

"Good. You have four days down there, then if we get something new to work with, maybe more, alright? If not, then it's just one more quick trip after that to close out. We have complete faith in you, okay?"

"Yep."

"Go to work."

"I will."

"Uhh, Leo," she stammered. "I almost forgot, before we let you go, I have to ask, and I'm sorry to pry, even though I know you think this isn't appropriate or whatever—has there been any sort of progress with your co-counsel?"

"What, Rachel?"

"I just want to see how you're feeling—how you're recovering, okay?"

"Recovering?" I asked.

"From the . . . bad times. Let your work take your mind off of it, alright? And, like I said, Peter and I think, if you haven't asked Rachel out yet, that you should. Right?"

"I have nothing to do with this," said Peter, solemnly peeling a tangerine in the corner chair. "This is a bad idea."

"Don't be a grouch, Pete, okay?" responded Martha. "We're talking about young love here. Leo, have you put the moves on her, or what?"

"No moves," I told my employers, two opposite poles, perfectly antipodal with respect to my love life. Martha leaning in. Peter in retrograde. "I have no moves to put on her at all."

"Fine," she said, "get out of here. I'm just looking out for your future, Leo, okay? Someday, you'll wise up."

When I flew back to Georgia, I went alone; Rachel had been at her dad's place in Maryland and would meet me the next day for another round of interviews. Thoroughly disabled once more by the flight, I recuperated in my same, now familiar (blessedly low-altitude) twin bed in room 207 of the Jackson Days Inn. I thought about Rachel all night—why did smart people like Martha, Emily, and Boots so insist that we were fools not to pair off?

Yes, she had a rare calming effect on the humming heap of my nerves. She was dignified and generous, and would have made a wonderful queen had the era obliged. Her eyes: tranquil, tranquilizing. On me.

I fell asleep that way, shoes on, Rachel spaniolating my dreams with her black bangs and airy intonations. By the time she knocked, softly, on the door, I'd been out cold for almost twelve hours.

"Leo?" came her muffled song.

"I'm here! I'm up!" I called back. "I'm sorry, I . . . I fell asleep."

"It's morning, Leo," she said. "Everybody fell asleep."

"I meant I didn't mean to fall asleep. Jesus, how are you here already? I'll be ready in a minute. Just—"

"Relax. It's cool. Keep your pants on, man. I just wanted to let you know I got in."

"Okay," I answered, now waking in earnest. "Just give me a minute, okay?"

"Take your time," she said. "We've got a late lunch date we have to leave for in about an hour. Harmon's Bar & Grill. You, me, and the Joneses."

I thanked her through the wall, and rose. The drive down to Harmon's was long and quiet. The whole way, something about Rachel seemed imperceptibly different—not troubling, just different. The feeling it gave me was the same feeling you get just before someone reveals to you, for the first time, that they are Canadian. Did this sensible woman have plans for me? Was a spark of something transcendent erupting from our little friction? Or was she another bit player in my life, a kindly distraction, confined to this Earth and to this moment alone? Whatever it was, this little hitch that could not be placed, it occupied my thoughts as I drove down I-75. It occupied me still as we swung wide the saloon-style doors at Harmon's, where (according to a prominently displayed sign) the drinks are strong but the bartender's stronger.

June and Tom Jones were already seated on the same side of a faded red booth, her glassy left hand resting laxly within his enormous, roughhewn right paw on the table's exact center. In her face, June was nearly as spare as her nephew: angular and forbidding, with pale eyes, and tired. Her jaw was clenched tight, and her shoulders jutted out like bluffs against the sea. Tom was a grizzled jumbo. Woolly gray hair gushed out of him, from bulbous ears and montiform eyebrows and a thick neck and the whole perimeter of his olive drab boonie hat. I wagered that the pair was separated by eighteen inches of height and maybe two hundred pounds, and, sitting together, they gave the distinct impression of a polar bear and his beloved icicle.

"You must be the lawyers," warbled June as we made our acquaintance.

"Rachel and Leo," I answered. "Thank you for taking the time to speak with us about Michael."

"Don't think nothing of it," she said, "though I'm not sure how very helpful we can be to you. We've talked to all kinds of lawyers before—none so young as you, if you'll pardon my taking notice—and we just say the same thing every time. Same thing we said to the police, to the judge, to the reporters back when they were still coming around."

"We're sorry to ask you to go through it again," Rachel offered, primly unfolding a paper napkin and smoothing it on her lap.

"Oh sweetheart!" June exclaimed, extending her skeletal free hand halfway toward us in a gesture, I supposed, of reassurance. "Anything we can do to help Michael, we will do. Anything at all. The thing is, is . . ."

And here she began to quiver.

"The thing is, we've just been such a long time now without hope. The lawyers, they've told us before how hard it was gonna be. How unlikely that things would come around. Of course, if there's anything we can do—but we know that we shouldn't have any expectations anymore," she said, turning to meet her husband's placid eyes. "We've made our peace with it, I mean. I believe that maybe Michael has as well."

We asked June about her knowledge of the crime and the case, and her jagged face lit up discussing Michael's younger days. So thoughtful; so smart. A little rambunctious in spurts. A good kid. They were certain he was going to be a ballplayer.

"And what about his girlfriend, Therese?" Rachel ventured once the better memories ran dry.

June's eyes at once fell cold.

"What about her?"

Each of the four of us tightened and shifted, such was the acid in her tone.

"Well," proceeded Rachel, "she lived with Michael for seven months. They dated for years. She testified on his behalf at the original trial. And she was . . . around, with him, earlier in the morning on the day that John Jasper died."

"Sweetheart," June said sharply, "what do you want to know?"

"I guess I'm just curious why you haven't mentioned her—it seems as though she played such a big role in his life."

June glanced at Tom, who glanced back with calm eyes.

"We don't care for her much," she said with strenuous diplomacy. "She was the root, mind you—the root of all these problems that came upon Michael, you know. None of this would've happened if she hadn't shown up, and messed him all up, and messed all around, all—"

"June," I said, halting her at parboil. She exhaled, cooled, and I asked: "Are you suggesting that you think that Therese was responsible for John Jasper's death?"

"I can't say," she answered. "I just can't say. Well, now, what I can say is that she was absolutely responsible for getting

Michael all wrapped up in it—that's for sure. Michael ain't never fired a gun in his whole life. His whole life; I know that he never did. His parents had guns around when they was around, but we never had guns around. Not in our home, no. But that man Jasper, he was shot with a gun a few times, and they found that gun in the trash can. Michael never even touched a gun—Therese, I know she had a gun before. I don't know what kind, but I know she did because I saw it with my own eyes; Tom saw it too."

"And you brought that up with the police?" inquired Rachel.

"Sure enough, I did," said June. "I brought it up with Michael's old lawyers, too. But Michael—he wouldn't hear of it. Wouldn't allow it. He didn't want no trouble at all for her, though Lord knows why. It was clear as day to the rest of us that she was trouble from the very start."

June sighed, and bobbed her gaze around the restaurant, collecting herself.

"Now, I know I shouldn't be talking that way. I've got to settle myself down, here. What's done is done—please, let's not linger on the sad bits of it."

We ambled back to gentler topics, and the conversation wore on through lunch. The whole time we'd been sitting there, Tom hadn't said a word—he just held the hand next to him and nodded supportively. After forty-five minutes, my curiosity got the best of me.

"Now, Mr. Jones," I began with no ending. Mostly I just wanted to find out what his voice sounded like—a tremendous foghorn, I imagined.

"Tom," he grunted powerfully, not disappointing me in the least. "Tom, or Tom Jones, is fine, son. None of this 'mister.'"

"Tom Jones," I repeated, blankly.

"That's right," he said.

"Oh! Like the singer?" asked a delighted Rachel.

"Yup. Same name as the singer. Pretty strange, I suppose."

"It's not unusual," I replied without thinking. "Sorry, I didn't mean—"

"Was that a crack about Tom Jones?" growled Tom Jones.

"No sir!" I answered stiffly.

Tom and June eased into smiles at the same moment.

"That's a pretty good one, son. But I heard 'em all. And I like him fine. I like the singer version of Tom Jones fine. What's new, pussycat?"

And June chimed in: "Whoa-ooh-whoa-whoa-oh."

We spoke for another minute, the check came and went, and Rachel and I stood to leave the Joneses to their adorable caterwauls.

"Excuse me?" June called after us. "If the judge decides that . . . I mean, if they do decide that they're gonna . . . you know—when does that . . . do you know when?"

"You mean when would the execution be?" I replied without thinking, and she shuddered. "Sorry. I'm sorry. It would happen quickly, though—a few days after the appeal comes down. That's usually how it goes."

"Will you be seeing him soon?" she asked longingly.

"Headed there now," I said.

She gave us a crumb cake packed inside a small cooler that had been stashed beside her. Three hours later, we watched as Michael picked at it delicately in the neon-lit room of the prison.

"Monophysitism," he repeated, pinching another lost speck of cake between his fingers. "Mono. Fizza. Tism. It's basically just the school of thought where Christ, he walks around like any other human, but he's a divine creature. Not some sort of . . . split . . . between a person—a regular person like you or me, that is—and a deity. Then opposite of that there's kenosis, and that's just the idea that Christ emptied himself of his divine side once he took on a human form."

"Uh-huh," we nodded back, flummoxed.

"And never the twain shall meet, and all that," Tiegs went on.

"Right," said Rachel.

"So it's a matter of great debate and uproar amongst all them Christian scholars: what was the nature of Christ when he lived, and when he died?"

"Can I ask," I asked, "why it's so important to you? Or to everyone, I guess? I mean, the end result is the same, right? He's born, and he's either all human, or all deity, or some sort of a hybrid, and then he dies, and then at some point he comes back, right?"

"That's about the long and short of it, Brother Leo," he replied.

"Okay, so, what's the difference if he was completely like us or not?"

"The difference is in the resurrection. It's in the dying and coming back. If you're divine, you can pretty much basically just come and go as you please. It's no big whoop if you arise again after you've departed."

"But if you're human—" started Rachel.

"Yes ma'am. If you're human, the rule has always been that once you're gone, you're gone. And though Heaven may be your ultimate reward," he drawled, slinking his index finger through the last crumbs of the cake, "you don't get to come back here. Not ever."

Tiegs looked even sicklier than usual, his face seemingly

hollow, the gears of his bloodless body churning lamely to hold him upright in his chair. Though he spoke with his standard gusto, I sensed that at any moment he might collapse in front of us. Here was this waif, this wraith, and I couldn't escape his description of kenosis, the human Christ: emptied out of everything divine that was once inside.

Why was his sadness like my sadness? I found myself wondering that. Well, alright, for one thing, we were both locked away with nothing but our questions, heirs to a mystery so remote as to be almost comically untouchable. That was one thing. Of course, I had been sealed off merely by Fiona, whereas he had been sealed off by the thing he called God. But then again: he was probably in prison (in actual prison) because a person had betrayed him, too—because of Therese. And maybe I had been sealed off by something cosmic as well, maybe even something as cosmic as myself, which, if true, would flip our situations in reverse of each other. In any event, I was growing increasingly certain that we shared questions, and that the only person who could deliver us the answers we respectively sought was desperately out of reach. We shared, at the very least, some fundamental mystery; we were dying to understand.

"Now outside Abrahamic tradition," he maundered on, "you've got yourself some options. You can die, and you can pretty much come back as a bug or a bird. That's your reincarnation, of course. You got your Buddhism, your Hinduism, your Jainism, Taoism, the Celts and the Druids, even some strands of Norse mythology. Lotta folks came up with this, across the ages, all over the world. I understand it, too. I mean, it's basically the next best thing to eternal salvation—getting another go around on the Lord's green Earth. Nobody nowhere's real good with endings, as it turns out."

Tiegs let out a series of furious hacking coughs, spit a long sedimentary strand of dark blood and sputum onto the floor beside him, then smiled up at us bashfully.

"What about coming back not in another form, but just as yourself?" I asked, a little too eagerly. I didn't know what possessed me; I was thinking about everything Fiona had once explained regarding the promises of infinity, and this sick man—in the moment, I thought that maybe he'd know. Take the bait, you lunatic, I thought to myself. Share my question.

"What about that?" I continued. "Not reincarnation, but, I guess, recursion, so that it's still you, just . . . coming around again. Reiteration. Does anybody believe in that? I mean, if time is infinite, isn't there a chance that if we just waited long enough for every eventuality to cycle through, the conditions would have to come around again for a place exactly like Earth, and from there, we could . . ."

I heard myself, and trailed off. It occurred to me that I'd crossed the line from merely playing along with Tiegs's cosmic folly to participating in it; Rachel looked at me as though I'd just belched the alphabet.

"Not as much, Brother Leo, though the thought's most definitely an intriguing one. No, I can't recall off the top of my head a civilization that ever landed on that particular idea."

He looked at me as if to apologize for something, and Rachel's bemused expression slacked away.

"So what do you believe, then?" she asked him begrudgingly.

"Well, I believe in the eternal grace and power of Christ, Sister Rachel—be he divine or human. That's more or less where I'm at. I believe I will ascend."

"So, only one trip around the Earth, then?" I prodded, and Rachel shot me another bewildered look.

"Seems more than enough, Brother Leo, though some may disagree. Course mine appears to have come to an end in scandal and disrepute, so I wager once was plenty. I'd rather the heavenly kingdom than another turn as a bug or a bird, or even as a wiser, freer M. R. Tiegs."

He spat again, and leaned back in his chair conclusively. I wasn't ready for the conversation to be over. I knew that he knew what I meant, that he had to have once lurched along the same grim steppe where my life had now left me. Hadn't he been through it all in here at least once?

"Okay, but," I started in, "imagine that, assuming that time is infinite, imagine that—billions of years from now— imagine that the exact circumstances that led to your creation conspire to happen again. I mean, they'd have to, right? Given enough time, a person would have to—"

"Leo," Rachel cut me off, "Leo, we're getting way off target here. Can we go back to the—"

"Let me just ask this," I pleaded, a small frenzy beginning to build in the edges of my skull. "Let me just ask him about—"

"Ecclesiasticus!" he interrupted, and Rachel rolled her eyes in opposition to the unfolding scene.

"I'm sorry?" I said.

"You're talking about coming around again. What'd you call it? Recursion. Well hey, maybe it's a possibility; I'm in no kind of position to say it ain't. Anyway, you won't find out if it's gonna happen until it happens, right? You sure can't bank on it, at least, is all I'm saying. Heck, that's all of religion for you; that's why folks hedge their bets here on Earth. Well, you asked me what my thinking is about that. And if you want my advice on that particular matter—well, I always find a form of an answer in scripture, so here's what I got for advice. Ecclesiasticus. Chapter five. Verse eleven."

And he leaned in again.

" 'Let thy life be sincere.' "

SEVEN

"IT'S THURSDAY, IT'S EIGHT O'CLOCK, SO YOU KNOW that it's GOT to be . . ."

Ba-da-da da-da-doo-dahhhhh! Ba-da-da da-da-doo-dop-doo-dahhhhh!

"Hollywood Update!"

Ba-da-da day-bo-doo-deeeee! Ba-da-da day-bo-doo-dop-doo-deeeee!

"I'm Terri Robbins!"

"And I'm Scott Flukes!"

"Now let's get you caught up with the latest!"

"Hahaha! Let's do it, Terri!"

I slumped into the pinewood of a rattletrap stool, in a Brooklyn bar much too bright for the dim times. There was no one there to see me—just the fat bartender washing steins with a gray rag. The television was on.

"Celebrated director Marcus Wimms has signed on to pilot Op-

eration Mastermind, *the highly anticipated spy thriller due out next summer from DreamScope Atlantis Pictures."*

The fat bartender looked up at me with an impish smirk, rivulets of sweat streaming down the double hemispheres of his low-slung cheeks.

"I don't normally watch this crap, you know," he chirped. "This was just on."

"It's okay."

"If you wanna change it—"

"No," I said. "It's fine."

"Hey Scott?!"

"Yeah Terri?!"

"Can you guess which award-winning singer was seen canoodling with her new beau outside a posh LA nightclub?"

"Haha! I can't, Terri!"

I finished my porter, and the fat bartender poured me another without being asked. The television blathered still, and I sipped intermittently while pulling wiry black dog hairs from the sleeves of my jacket.

"Scott, wedding bells are ringing for one Hollywood power couple this weekend!"

"That's right, Terri! None other than Briefs *leading man Mark Renard will be tying the knot on Saturday with Fiona Fox, star of the upcoming blockbuster* Dreamstalker 2.*"*

"Oh man. Did you see the first *Dreamstalker*? So good."

The fat bartender stretched his back noisily, let out a prolific yawn, and wiped his forehead with the same rag he'd been using to dry the glassware.

"She was good in it, too. When she killed that bald guy with her shoe? Oh man. That was awesome."

"The talented duo will wed in London's fabulous Westcott

Gardens, and our sources tell us that the honeymoon is set for south-
ern Spain!"

"*Well, chip-cheerio to the two of them, Terri!*"

"*Indubitably, Scott! Hahaha!*"

Without peeling his eyes from the screen, the fat bartender
sank both elbows onto the wet countertop and began to shake
his head as prologue to a petty thought.

"You know, it's funny, because the word Renard actually
means—"

"I know," I said.

"I don't know if you know this, but in French, I mean, it
means—"

"I know."

"I just mean what are the odds that—"

"They're terrible."

Ba-da-da da-da-doo-dahhhhh! Ba-da-da da-da-doo-dop-doo-
dahhhhh!

Okay.

Ba-da-da day-bo-doo-deeeee! Ba-da-da day-bo-doo-dop-doo-
deeeee!

This is okay.

I left my porter and stepped out into the failing light. When
things get away from you, and when it happens so quickly, you
begin to lose faith in basic bits of chronology. Fiona couldn't
be a star yet—not this quickly. How many months had passed?
A big-time movie star? When must that have happened? And
married? This had to be the future. On the television, she
looked young, still young, still someone's crisp, unlovable
daughter. But gone was the grateful weirdo, the knotty, tender blackbird who once traced circles on my arm. Her star was
rising. It made me think of a fact I knew about stars—did you

know that most of the ones you see in the night sky have actually been dead for many millions of years? It's only because
they are so far away that you're able to see them as they were
in the past. Distance is like memory in that way—like my
memories, like this one. I ducked back in and looked again;
here was my star. How far from me? Unknown. My star, my
bird, my bug, my snake. The opposite of a snake: she shed her
insides.

· · ·

"Tell us about John Jasper," Rachel urged Tiegs on the morning of our ninth visit to the prison.

It was December, and the time we had left to save Michael
was drawing short. Rachel and I were sharing a bed now, free
from the pretense of the mai tais, and I have to admit that it
brought me comfort to be near her—temporary comfort from
the two ghosts who followed me around, just a step or two
behind me, whenever I was alone. One was Fiona, not dead, but
gone; when I was with Rachel, in all of her pleasant neutrality,
Fiona's memory ebbed steadily away towards an asymptote:
receding towards zero, but never, ever arriving there. The
other was Michael, or rather the ghost he would become if
we couldn't save—not save—stave. If we couldn't stave off
death. Death, my oldest fixation, older even than Fiona—older
than the universe—had come back into my arena, had slipped
through the crevices and set up shop in the neon-lit room.

"How do you mean?" Michael drawled back at Rachel's
inquiry.

"I mean what kind of a person was he. We know you didn't
like him very much, but—a lot of people felt the same way,
right? A lot of the other residents at Willow Creek? Certainly

Therese felt that way—well, eventually, at least. We've read all
of the stuff from the courtroom; we know all that. I'm just curious what you remember about him, maybe why it was that
he inspired such . . . strong feelings."

Michael sat up a bit in his folding chair, gripped with two
dry hands the sides of his heavy head, and painstakingly cracked
his neck in four directions, the frangible bones cuing a choir
of hideous gunshots. Rachel shivered, and I looked quickly
away from the both of them.

"I don't much like to speak ill of the departed," he replied.
"You know what you know from the records and whatnot—
John Jasper, he had his share of trouble with sin."

"He was a bad man?" I prodded, unhelpfully.

"Hardly for me to say," answered Tiegs, "but I can tell you
he was troubled. I can say 'smuch as that."

"What do you remember about what he was like?" Rachel ventured on. "Apart from the negative feelings. What was
he like just in the day-to-day?"

The cloughs below his cheekbones grew chasmal as he
drew in breath, and he held himself there, hollow, for a brief
moment in thought.

"Well, in the beginning," he began, then paused. "In the
beginning, God created the Heaven and the Earth."

"Jesus, Michael," Rachel loosed.

"I'm answering your question," he replied placidly.

"You are not," she quibbled. "You just aren't. The Book
of Genesis is not relevant here."

"Can we hear him out?" I asked as gently as I could.

"Are you serious, Leo?" she countered. "He isn't answering any of our questions."

"I'm answering your question in my own way, Sister

Rachel—in my own way, but I'm answering it just the same."

"Alright," she sighed.

"The Book of Genesis is relevant here indeed, my dear sweet sister in Being a Touch Frustrated with Me Right Now, if you'd be so kind as to listen."

"Alright," she acquiesced.

"Where was I now? That's it, yes ma'am—the beginning. Well, as I mentioned, God created the Heaven and the Earth."

"Yep," I confirmed, "we've . . . we've heard."

"Please go on," Rachel pleaded with him.

"Well, that right there is the start of a story—the first story, in fact—the story of the Garden of Eden, of course is what I mean."

"Of course," I said.

"Of course. Now, that story—I won't bore you with the details of creation, but that story posits a man, name of Adam, formed of the dust of the ground. Can you believe that? Dust of the ground! And God, he went and breathed into Adam's nostrils the breath of life—"

And here Michael blissfully engorged a long, unsteady breath, awash with rhinal whinnies and a look of full joy.

"—Breathed into his nostrils the breath of life, and Adam became alive—a living soul."

"That's fantastic," said Rachel, straining for patience, "but what happens next?"

"Well, naturally, next comes Eve," he responded delightedly, peering directly into her eyes. "Torn from the rib, and the pair of them—man and woman—is all there is for a time, people-wise. Just the two of them, together, naked and unashamed in the garden."

I swung one glance at Rachel, recalling the two of us, to-gether in the Biblical sense, that very morning in the Jackson Days Inn. She didn't seem to register the analogy.

"We were happy, Therese and me, I mean, at Willow Creek and for a time after that. Not perfectly so—ain't no-body is, near as I can tell—but we were happy enough. We were clean, you understand? We were new, and maybe it felt like something of a new start for us."

"And then . . ." I began.

"Like I said: oldest story on Earth," he said, gliding his hands down to rest on the folding table in front of him. "Then comes the serpent."

"John Jasper," added Rachel as a point of clarification.

"In the flesh," Michael replied. "Now, what you have to understand is, the serpent was more subtle than any beast of the field which the Lord had made. The serpent was a beguiler. He was a real smooth operator, he was. Charming; a liar. Every place he went, he slithered. He was a predator, just . . . slink-ing, slinking around the garden."

Michael's thick fists were clenched and laid, like dead stones, on the table. He seemed incapable of anything ap-proaching rage; even in his recasting of slick John Jasper, his enmity was dispassionate—tranquil, even. Fists of remember-ing, of a vestigial fury that had long since been rendered point-less. A frisson of serenity overcame him, and those fists were turned back into hands.

"So Michael," Rachel interceded, groping for meaning, "are you trying to tell us that John and Therese actually—in the story, Michael, in Genesis, the snake leads Eve astray. That's how they lose the garden, right?"

"Correct you are," he said.

"Are you trying to tell us that John . . . forgive me, Michael, but are you trying to tell us that John Jasper . . . seduced Therese? We know about his history with patients. A lot of his patients, they came forward afterwards, and—"

"It don't matter," he declared, defeated. "Don't matter a bit."

"It does, Michael," Rachel reasoned in the face of my silence. "If Therese and John Jasper were involved with each other, it absolutely matters. It's a motive, Michael. It's the motive they used to convict you of his murder—that you believed there was something going on. Therese denied that it was true, but if it *was* true, Michael—if it was true, and it wasn't just something you believed had happened, like the prosecution claimed in court, then it would be her motive too."

"Original sin," he said. "Everybody wants to talk about original sin. I know what it is y'all want to hear from me, Sister Rachel, I really do. The thing of it is, the sin don't matter—it's the fall that matters. I can't know the truth of the sin; she is the only one who knows about that now. But I know the truth of the fall. We had our little paradise for a spell, and then something happened, and we lost it. That's all that truly matters, ain't it?"

"That," said Rachel, "and the punishment."

"Exactly," I added. "God punished humanity—no more paradise, no more innocent days. Maybe Michael is right; maybe it doesn't matter in the end how it came to pass."

"The snake, Leo," she corrected me. "God punished the snake."

• • •

Think of a word that means the opposite of itself—a word that carries two meanings, I mean, that are averse to one another:

a contronym. *Oversight* is one such word; if I conduct oversight, then I am surveying something quite carefully, but if I
commit an oversight, then something has been neglected due
to my carelessness. *Sanction* is another, for I can either approve
of good behavior by sanctioning it or discipline bad behavior
by imposing a harsh sanction. If you wished to escape from
me, you'd be wise to *bolt*—whereas I might bolt the door to
keep you safely inside.

Now think of two people, and all of the damage that words
can do. Contronyms carry their inner tension the same way
that we carry Ours, hunched on the fulcrum of context—and
whatever it is that I might mean to you today, tomorrow I
could mean something else entirely. Take Fiona. She cleaved
to me for many days (and it meant she held me fast), until a day
came when she cleaved us apart (and it meant a separation).
The thing about people is: they can always change what they
mean.

Michael Tiegs was about to change his meaning, maybe.
For the scant months I'd known him, the words of his name
had always been wholly attached to a living person—but here,
now, he was poised at any moment to mean the precise opposite of that. Everything I had ever felt and feared about death
seemed as though it was advancing on my near-precise loca-
tion, adjacent to the condemned. As I found myself drawn
more and more to his web of ideas—nonsensical though I understood them to be—the rift between Rachel and me grew
wider and increasingly unbridgeable.

"He is offering us nothing," she told me sternly over dinner back at the chain restaurant in Jackson.

"It isn't nothing to him," I replied. "In fact, it's pretty obviously everything to him. It's bigger than what we're trying

to do—in his mind, I mean. It's a more important endeavor than just staying alive."

Rachel dabbed a napkin across her lips, then held it there in contemplation.

"I think," she started after a moment, "I think that when we encourage him to live in his head like this . . . when we allow him to dominate the conversation, and steer it into this place where it's all about religion, or philosophy, or the afterlife, or other things that—Leo—that have no legal bearing whatsoever . . ."

I lowered my eyes from hers—in shame or avoidance, I could not say.

"All we're doing," she went on, "is indulging him in giving up."

"Maybe," I said.

"Leo, I need to know that you're with me here. We need to be united here, a united front, because it can't be two against one the other way in there. Do you understand? If he thinks that you're taking him seriously on that stuff, it's only going to . . . it means he won't take *me* seriously—he won't take the real world consequences seriously. Just the magical, existential, whatever consequences. You know he's, like, teetering on the edge of the two. You know that. He can't get the impression that you're out there with him, or we'll have nothing. You're going to have to be a lawyer for a little while. And figure out the other stuff later. Okay?"

Of course, she was right about the fact that we were gaining nothing of legal value from our conversations with Michael; our prospects for saving him grew bleaker by the day. Could he save himself, I wondered, just by thinking it? Just by arriving at a peaceful understanding? I came back from our second trip to Georgia with little to show apart from an impending sense of terror: I didn't want to have to see this man die. This was too big for me to grapple with alone, and so I took it to the person you take it to when you need to devise a plan to keep things just as they are. Nobody did static better than Sona.

Over the precious din of a populous café, I asked her: "Have you ever known a dead person?"

"What are you talking about?" she replied. "What does that mean—'know a dead person?' How do you know a person who's—"

"I meant," I said, "have you ever known a living person who then, later, died. Do you—did you, I guess—did you know anybody who has died?"

"Like, have I ever gone from knowing someone to . . . knewing them, on account of their death?"

"Knewing, yes."

"Well," she reckoned soberly, "hasn't everybody?"

"Known a dead person?" I said. "Maybe. I mean, my grandfather died, for instance, and of course I knew him. But he was of age for it, and he went gradually; that's not really what I'm looking for. I guess what I mean is: have you known anyone who was younger, who went from completely alive to completely not? Someone who just switched, like that."

She fretted and frowned, then sighed at me pityingly.

"Why are you asking me about this, Leo? You're not going to die, you know. Not yet. You don't have stomach cancer, and you don't have an enlarged or shrunken heart, and you don't have whatever else you think you have. Jesus, why are you asking me about this?"

"It's not for me," I protested.

"If you say so."

"Honest. I'm asking . . . for a friend."

"Are you now?" she whimpered.

"Actually, I am. Not really for a friend, though. For a client."

"Ah. I get it now. This the Georgia one?"

"Yes," I responded. "The Georgia one. We have nothing, and he seems . . . okay with it all. And I don't understand—I can't understand that. How can a person be okay with the fact that they're going to just . . . be gone? It's looking very much like they're going to execute him, and it occurred to me that I've never really known someone who's gone out like that."

"By execution?"

"No, I mean . . . unnaturally. Someone who died even though they didn't really . . . have to, I guess. I thought it might be good to talk about it, if you're up for it today."

Sona looked quite insistently into my eyes—she often did this, with everyone—and cradled my whiskered chin with one small hand.

"You're very sensitive," she said.

"Come on; stop it."

"I mean it—you're a very sensitive young man," she went on, wagging my jaw twice to each side before releasing me from her grasp. "It reflects well on your character that you think about these things. That's an honest compliment. Savor that."

"I was just asking," I said, "because I'm not sure, if it happens . . . I'm not sure how I'm going to handle it. I was just asking for a little perspective, if you've got it. I just wanted to know in advance how it feels. How it will feel, I mean."

"It's okay. That's okay."

"So?"

"So what?" she rebutted.

"So you didn't answer me," I said. "Have you ever known a dead person?"

Her body demurred suddenly, and her dark eyes dipped. "Ah," she uttered. "Ah! Uhh . . . yes. Yes, I . . . think I have known one, as a matter of fact."

She began to nod, and almost immediately was nodding so vigorously that I thought that she might be approaching the verge of a panic attack.

"You don't have to—" I began, but:

"No! It's fine," she blurted, steadying herself. "It's okay."

"Okay."

"So," she started, now looking east, now west, now east again, now west again of the apparent tennis net of my face. Now east again. "So," she started once more, "I had this friend back in college—you remember I was an art history major?"

"I actually didn't know that," I said.

"Really?"

"I guess it's never come up? I always figured you studied . . . I don't know, molecular biology, or international diplomacy, or something. Nuclear fission. I have a hard time picturing you as an art history major—it seems like the sort of thing you'd consider to be too frivolous for you."

"Well, I was," she said. "And so was my friend. So was Charlie."

She coiled up into her chair, a posture of defense, and blew daintily for four or five seconds onto the sheeny roof of a coffee that had long grown cold.

"So Charlie, he was a sweet kid; I remember the first time I noticed him he was sitting in front of me in this class—it was called *Rococo to Realism*, or something like that—and he was just sitting there, sketching these immaculate portraits of people in the class onto notebook paper. The likenesses were just incredible. They were perfect. He was a terrific artist—I can't even . . . tell you. This was sophomore year, in the fall. Anyway, he didn't seem to talk much, but I started talking to him a little, and we had other classes together too, and we sort of became friends."

Across the room, a crashing of glasses startled us. Sona lowered her cup to the table with tremendous care, dipped her slender middle finger into the depths of the cool black swill, and, annexing my napkin, swabbed that digit clean.

"He tried to kiss me once, that spring," she continued. "Why do you always have to do that?"

"What?" I asked.

"Men. Guys. You always have to ruin everything that's good, and it's always by kissing."

"We do not."

"You do," she insisted.

"I've never tried to kiss you," I reminded her.

"Only because you're scared that I'd push you away, or, worse, laugh at you. Which by the way is *exactly* what I'd do—laugh at you. But just because you haven't tried yet doesn't mean you haven't thought about it. You've come close. I know you have."

"I have not," I lied.

"Of course you have. All guys have about basically all women. It's fine. Remember when Boots set you up with that chick who used to play bass in his band? And we were all getting drunk at that roof party? Your bass lady was dancing with Emily and Boots, and you and I were talking about—I don't remember, but we were probably talking about Fiona—and for half a minute we were accidentally holding hands—hands of platonic friendship, I might add. You were definitely thinking about kissing me."

"Oh please," I scoffed, though she had me dead to rights.

"It's cool; it's not your fault. You're just an idiot. You know perfectly well—you knew then, even—what a terrible idea it would've been, how rapidly we would've destroyed each other. It isn't your fault; guys have, like, one spiked eggnog and they get so *bold*—so utterly romantic. It happens every time. You're just a moron sometimes. Anyway, it isn't important."

"Can we get back to your friend?" I pleaded, smiling bashfully.

"We can," she granted, smiling back, adding another point to the ledger between us.

"Grand," I said.

"So Charlie tried to kiss me, and because I'm me, I turned away and, you know, played it very coy. He was wonderful—don't get me wrong—but I would've destroyed him too. Trust me."

"I fully do," I said.

"Good. By senior year, we'd gotten much closer, and we used to take long walks through the woods in town—there were these great bike paths and walking paths close to campus. We'd talk: heavy things, sometimes, the way that you and I do occasionally. Only darker, if you can imagine. He wasn't anything like you, or anything, but one thing you had in common with Charlie is that he liked to discuss big things—the biggest things. Life and death and art. He was a phenomenal artist, like I said. That year, he started working on his thesis. His favorite painter was Gustave Courbet. Do you know him?"

"I don't," I said.

"Nineteenth-century French realist. Charlie was writing his thesis on him, and got it in his head that he wanted to accompany the written thesis with a painting—which was all he really cared about. He didn't have to do this, didn't get any credit for it or anything; he just wanted to paint. And Courbet—you don't know him, but he was incredibly successful in France before being exiled to Switzerland, I think. I remember he died there. Drank himself to death in Switzerland, or wherever. Anyway, one of his most well-known works was this self-portrait: it's of a man staring directly out of the canvas at you, the viewer, with these sad, wide eyes, both of his hands clutching at his tousled hair. It's called *The Desperate Man*, and it was Charlie's favorite. He decided to paint himself in the style of that Desperate Man—in the style of Courbet—and pretty soon he was painting more and more and we were walking and talking less and less. He became obsessed with it, really. I tried—a lot of people tried to talk with him, and he just seemed to grow more inside himself, more internal than ever, over the course of that year. He'd sit in his room, touching it up for hours, but he was never satisfied. Never just done with it. And you'd try to get him to come get lunch, or take a walk, or go see a show or whatever, and he'd just say: 'I'm working. I need to work.' I'd go to visit him, and I'd see the painting—it was beautiful, honestly, but it always looked the same to me. In December, in February, in April—it always looked the same. It looked like a completed work to me, so I don't know what he was doing, just touching it up, constantly. We stopped hearing from him for days at a time, but nobody was too worried; he was an intense guy, you know? It wasn't out of character for him to get sucked in, especially when it came to his art. The day we were all supposed to hand in our theses, a group of us went over to his room—we wanted to go celebrate. And he'd—I never know if it's 'hung' or 'hanged'—we found him there. He hanged himself from the pipes on the ceiling."

Sona breathed in and out a few times ("One second," she told me), then sipped from her cold coffee.

"The painting was there, on an easel, and it was beautiful, like I said. It was him—a perfect likeness—in the exact pose of the Desperate Man. There was a piece of notebook paper scotch-taped to the bottom of the painting. And the only thing it said was: 'I'm finished.'"

I waited a while, then weakly said, "Jesus."

"I know," she said, cracking just an ounce. "Pretty heavy, right?"

"I mean, Jesus, Sona."

"I know. It was chilling. I've figured out how to think about it less and less, but sometimes . . ."

"Yeah," I offered.

"Yeah," she breathed, then uncomfortably giggling away the onset of a tear, said louder, "Yeah!"

"I didn't know," I said.

"I didn't tell you."

"'I'm finished?'"

"Yep. Spooky, right? It was like the portrait was, I don't know—"

"It was attached to the painting?"

"Yeah."

"'Cause then it could mean—"

"I know," she said. "I thought about that for a long time after it happened. 'I'm finished' could mean—"

"Two things," I interrupted.

"Yep."

"Perfected . . ." I said.

"Or destroyed," she whispered, finishing the thought.

"Right. God. Right. Maybe it doesn't matter, in the face of everything, but do you ever wonder which he really meant?"

She leaned back, slacking the weight of the conversation off of her narrow shoulders.

"Maybe both? I don't know. I don't like to think about it, but there it is. That was someone I knew, and he died. Like you asked. Does that help? That can't be helpful, right? I don't have any suggestions; there wasn't any lesson. It was only awful. Death is a monster."

"It helps," I said.

"How?"

"It helps me brace for it—I mean, you saw something nobody should have to see, and here you are."

"Yeah," she said, "but I'm pretty screwed up."

"That's true, but I'm willing to bet you were always that way. And anyway, you're a high-functioning person. We should all be so screwed up."

"So your Georgia friend?" she asked, downing the last of her drink.

"Right. Michael—my client—I think he might be, you know, finished, too. He's on death row for murdering his therapist, only there are people who think his girlfriend did it and he's just covering for her."

"Do you think that?" she inquired.

"I haven't met her. She won't talk to us. So it's hard to—but Michael, knowing him, it's hard for me to imagine him doing something like that. He's a man at peace; I just can't see him being vengeful like that. So I don't know. I don't get to know, I suppose is the thing."

"I understand," she said.

"He never confessed, but he never really put up much of a fight, either. When I see him in that prison, he's so serene, it's like he belongs there—like it's his ultimate destination. He doesn't seem to want to get out. That's what I mean when I say I think he might be finished."

"Well, wait," she said. "What *do* you mean? Do you mean finished like 'done for,' or finished like 'completed'? Perfected or destroyed?"

"I don't know," I said.

"Do you have to know?"

"I don't know," I said, adding, "You're right, though. Death is a monster."

"It's okay, Leo," she responded kindly, resting her hands limply on my own. "Life is a monster, too. Don't get me wrong—I wouldn't trade it for the world. It's beautiful, but it's a monster too."

"I wonder how you're supposed to know when you're finished," I thought aloud. "I mean, Christ," I said sadly, "even if you do get to know—how are you supposed to know which one you mean?"

• • •

On the day that Thomas Edison died, his son was tasked with an unusual favor by none other than the tycoon Henry Ford. The two famous inventors had become close in their later years, and Ford wasn't keen on the prospect of a world deprived of his brilliant friend. As Thomas prepared to be gone, his son came through: carefully, Charles Edison held a glass test tube up to his father's waning mouth, and captured for posterity the old man's terminal breath.

This was 1931, and the tube was discovered nineteen years later, after Ford and his wife Clara had each themselves expired. A museum docent found it, sealed with paraffin wax, alongside Edison's hat in a box of the Fords' effects; the breath remains undisturbed to this day. The story goes that Henry believed in the human spirit, a catchable essence that fled the body at the precise instant of death. He was a believer in reincarnation, and held fast to the notion that, by preserving his friend, he might somehow uncover the means through which he could deliver Thomas Edison back to the Earth anew.

More than half a century went by, and my hand rested flatly on the small of Rachel's back as she pleaded with our client to assist in his own salvation. It was our third and final trip to Georgia, and Martha and Peter had sent us back to take one last shot at uncovering whatever truth there was to be had concerning Therese Calley's role in John Jasper's death.

"A week, Michael—maybe less," she explained to him. "That appeal is coming down from Atlanta, and if we don't *do something*—not talk, but *do something*—they are going to kill you. I know that, deep down, that has to matter to you."

"And we ain't doing something here, Sister Rachel?" he replied with that far-off, mystic grin.

Rachel looked at me sharply, quickly, and answered, "Michael, we are not."

I knew she'd been frustrated—our chances of a successful outcome felt as though they'd dwindled to zero, and for a long time now, despite her best efforts, Michael had spoken of nothing but death and its consequences.

"We need to introduce doubt, Michael—reasonable

doubt—and we need to do it quickly enough to ensure a stay of execution," she continued. "Do you understand what that means?"

He looked to me as though I might help stop this, but I stayed silent—which helped no one—and he stayed silent too.

"If you didn't kill John Jasper," Rachel went on, her voice quavering with the room's last rations of rationality, "then it is exceedingly likely that she did. Therese had motive, and she probably had an opportunity—but we can't do anything unless we can talk to her. We need proof."

"So talk to her," Michael muttered. He sounded so low.

"You know she won't answer our calls," said Rachel. "But you—she loves you, Michael. She'd talk to you. The next time she comes to visit you—"

Michael huffed, and rubbed his hands together, and jerked his mottled head from side to side.

"Michael," she continued, "the next time she comes to visit you, you absolutely need to convince her to talk with us. If you don't do that, we cannot save you."

"Save, save," he muttered defiantly.

"Michael, we need you to understand that this is your very last chance. You have no case without her. You have no *life* without her." And turning fully to me, she added: "Leo, tell him it's true."

"Yes, Brother Leo," echoed Michael slyly, still again at last. "Is that the truth of it? Ain't I got no life without her?"

I tracked the whole existence of a single tear, from its birth on the dusky inside corner of Rachel's right eye to its death on the concrete floor. And I thought: you can't save anybody who doesn't want to be saved. You certainly can't save anybody who believes they've already done it themselves. I couldn't pretend, not for one moment more, that I didn't find a certain peace in Michael's well of reason. Those other lives, those planets, this endless future—they had to matter more than earthly acquittal. They simply had to, otherwise—

So I didn't say a word. I stood with Michael, then, in knowing silence. Rachel lost her patience; she breathlessly questioned whether either of us cared if Michael lived or died ("In this life! On this Earth!"), and left me in the prison. Twenty minutes later, I found her sobbing over the hood of our rental car.

"Don't you want to save him?" she asked me calmly.

"Of course I do. But Rachel, we can't—"

"Because he's going to die, Leo. He's going to die, and whatever we're doing in there isn't helping. And I feel like you don't even care—I feel like you're enabling him."

She smoothed her hands over the car's broad hull, and breathed in deeply.

"I think," I said, "we both know how this is going to end. I think all three of us know. Rachel, we've been over this and over this; he's made his peace. Even if he's innocent. Even if she's guilty. He *wants* to go—the things he cares about, at least in his mind, they all come after he's gone from here. What are we going to tell him that will change that? What are we going to tell a judge that will make his next trip through the system any different than the last time, or the time before that? It's always going to end the same way for him."

"So what?" she asked, not crossly but with all sincerity. "Are you really content to just give up?"

"Innocent people die. And sometimes there's nothing we can do to stop that. But if talking about death helps us to—if it helps him, I mean—if it helps him face what's coming, then

I think that we can still provide a service here. And maybe it isn't much, but maybe it's all we can do for him."

"It's not our job to indulge him in his faith, Leo," she said, wiping away the last of her tears. "It just isn't, okay? We're lawyers."

"I know," I said.

Rachel took my hand in hers. I squeezed it, helplessly.

"If we can't save him," she said, "and I mean actually save him, legally, not spiritually, then I can't be here with you anymore. Do what you need to do here. Honestly. Whatever it is. Talk with him about life after death; ask him whatever questions you want answered. Do what you need to do, but please don't wallow down here with him—it's not your prison. I hope you know that. I have to go back to New York. And if you can't come with me . . ."

"I can't come with you," I said. "I need to be here, and I know that sounds—I just need to talk with him a little more."

"Leo, he's insane. The things he talks about—don't you see that he's insane?"

"Death," I said quietly, "makes it very difficult to live sometimes."

She bristled: "Are you making a joke right now?"

"No," I answered. "I just mean—maybe I need to talk about it, too."

"But Leo," she replied, now perfectly steady, "you're not the one who's dying."

I looked around at the cars and the dust, the light, the prison, the hurtling Earth.

"Everyone is dying, Rachel," I said. "That's the end of all our stories—all of us. Okay? All of life, honestly, when you get down to it, is about learning to die, and I think . . . he has something to say about it that I still want to—"

"What?" she asked, incredulous.

"I said that—"

"All of life is *not* about learning to die, Leo," she said. "The fact that you think that . . . of course it isn't, Leo, of course it's not about that. Life is about living, of course—about learning to live. I know you're not that sad, Leo; I know you're not like him."

I stood quietly in the lot, knowing she was right, knowing also that I had to know for sure—that I had to stay, that I had to see Michael go, to see what that would mean to me. Rachel placed a slim hand on my stubbled cheek, and dipped the crown of her head to the center of my chest.

"We can't keep seeing each other, Leo," she said as she rose again to meet my eyes. "I wish that we could—honestly, I do. I like you a lot, but this is just too much for me to abide. I think that you have things to figure out, and I hope that you do."

"Okay," I said, and let her hand slip out of mine as she walked slowly to the passenger side door.

We didn't break things off in a fit of rage. We didn't break things off in a fit of anything; perhaps that was the problem with us. I wanted the fire that Fiona had once kindled in my wooden life, and Rachel lacked the ability to destroy me like that. So I just drifted away from a remarkable woman, and all that promise grew obsolete.

After I dropped her off the next morning, I drove straight from the airport back to death row. I made my way beyond the gated lot and the armed guards, past the ponderous gaze of the man in the brown suit, back down the hallway to the neon-lit room where Tiegs was waiting to speak again about the afterlife.

"And then there was one," he announced grimly, without looking up from the folding table.

"Rachel wanted me to express to you," I began, then trailed off.

"I assure you, Brother Leo, there aren't any sore feelings. She's got work to do; we've got work to do—I understand that. It's good you came back, though. I've been thinking about our last conversation. I'm wondering now: is it possible you might be a Buddhist?"

"Not as far as I know," I told him.

"I got some reading done last night," he went on. "Turns out, the Buddhists believe that you actually can come back as a human after all—doesn't just have to be a bug or a bird or what have you."

"Aha."

"Conditions have to be right. You have to be moral enough in your life to avoid dropping down a level or two, but not so moral that you get bumped up to bo-dee-sat-va or Buddha-Heaven or anything like that. You can come back as a person— not necessarily the *same* person, which I'm pretty sure was your whole recursion thing—but it sounds like it's at least, you know, a possibility for you. If you're a Buddhist, that is. Although you ain't."

"Well . . . that sounds promising, I guess," I told him, and we passed a full minute in silence.

"Brother Leo?" he asked at last.

"Yes, Michael?"

"You seem sorry that she's gone."

I let out one sad chuckle.

"I don't think Rachel really understands the things we talk about in here," I said, although I couldn't be certain that I understood myself. I knew that I wanted something from Tiegs—some proof. I wanted him to validate my parking in the spacious lot of the faithful. I wanted him either to live, or to die and have it be okay. How can it be okay? I had to know for myself just how in the world he would go.

He jerked up suddenly, as though seized by a pain, and spat twice onto the concrete floor.

"Not everybody wants to face their future. Y'all both are smart ones, but I don't know which is smarter: thinking these thoughts about what comes after you die, or pushing them down, not giving them a thought at all."

"It doesn't make a difference, does it?" I responded. "Thinking about it; not thinking about it. We can believe whatever we want—it won't change the truth. Whatever that happens to be."

"You're wrong about that, Brother Leo," he said, grinning weakly. "Faith matters. Belief matters. And we are nothing without it—pure spirit is what we are when the rest has broken away."

I swallowed hard, thinking now of the way that Michael's frail body, which always seemed so close to vanishing, would soon very likely see its own pure spirit forcibly evicted. If there was a soul, it would be pulled out of him at needlepoint, and those electric eyes would empty themselves of light. This would all take place at a scheduled time, this preordained sleep; he'd twitch, and it would be over. And maybe in that instant, he'd know.

"I wouldn't even worry about it," he said after a moment, seeming freshly energized. "About the afterlife, that is. It's pretty much been proven to exist."

"Is that a fact?" I asked him earnestly.

"I know what you're thinking—but I ain't even speaking of faith now. I ain't speaking of truth like the truth of Isaiah or Matthew or Daniel, or the Book of Revelation and the Nicene Creed. I don't mean that kind of truth. I mean the usual kind; the kind a lawyer'd like. Rigorous logical analysis and all that—I'm talking 'bout actual proof."

I shut my eyes.

"Oh, buck up, attorney-of-mine. You'll like this," he exclaimed. "Have we ever talked about *The Phaedo*?"

"Nope," I said, settling in.

"Okay, so it goes like this: the day before Socrates died, see—you know, they sentenced him to death too—the day before that, he starts talking to his student, Phaedo, about the afterlife, sorta like how we've been doing. So the key to the afterlife, according to Socrates, is the immortality of your soul. If you can prove that the soul is everlasting, then there has to be somewhere for it to go once your earthly body hits the bricks. So Socrates supposes that the body and the soul have to be opposites, because every state of being has an opposite one, right, like hot has cold and awake has asleep. Well, you can't have an awake soul without a soul that's been sleeping, neither. The body is brittle, it can be destroyed—but its opposite, the soul, is completely indestructible: when you die, it just goes to sleep for a bit until the next body wakes it on up. Cold things come from hot things; hot things come from cold things; living people come from dead people; dead come from the living. And when you're gone, that soul of yours is just hanging around on the flip side of the coin, as it were. That other side—there's your afterlife. There you are with Socrates and the rest, just waiting around to catch a ride on the next body headed back this way."

Tiegs coughed violently, the folding table executing a noisy spasm in time with his own convulsions.

"Anyway, take that as you will. It's only just another theory. Oh and Phaedo, after he hears about all this, he bears witness to the end of the world. The end of one man's world, at
least—he watches Socrates die."

"Jesus," I muttered vacantly.

"So, Brother Leo," said Tiegs, leaning just slightly across
the table, "are you gonna?"

I shifted in my chair. The persistent hum of the neon flow-
ing above us zapped to an abrupt stop, then surged back to life.

"Am I gonna what?"

Tiegs was looking straight at me—I felt it—but I would
not look at him.

"Appeal's coming down any time now. You think you'll
be there when I drink the hemlock? I'd ask that you do so, if
it's alright with you. You can keep a look out for any . . .
signs . . . any semblance of the coin flipping over."

I'd dreamt about it once already: Tiegs in an ethereal chamber, smoke for a ceiling and darkness for walls, strapped down
and shivering while all about him hordes of strangers watched
in utter silence. They were strangers to him, but not to me;
the cast of my past turned out in staggering numbers—long-
gone acquaintances, old classmates and teachers, my family and
friends. Mrs. Easterling with her colored pencils. Gracie Coolahan, twisting fingers through her woolly hair. Emily, expressionless, with an arm around Boots. A disappointed Katherine
Barnes flanked by her anonymous TA. Everyone had come to
see. But Fiona was not there.

And when the moment arrived, Tiegs froze in his folding
chair. The executioner stepped forward, and I recognized
him from his brown suit. I couldn't get a reaction. I wanted all
of them to speak, but no one would even look at me. "Say

something!" I hollered at them, "Say something before it's too late!"—but their mouths were sealed, and their eyes were fixed on Tiegs. I pushed my way to the front, and lowered my face to meet his. "Christ," I shouted at him. "Won't you say something about this, Michael?"

And he said: "*Olam Haba.*"

And I said: "Michael, I don't know what that means."

And he said: "Don't you understand, Brother Leo? You don't get to know what everything means."

EIGHT

THERESE CALLEY WAS AN UNBRIDLED MESS. AT thirty-three, her skin was cracked and scarred, her hands shook, and the whole of her abessive frame seemed ready to crumble into toxic dust at any moment. Her voice was like a long, slow car accident. Her eyes were so hollow they appeared to be deliberately retreating from the world outside her skull. She had rosorial features, and her tongue, which she bit habitually, was speckled gray.

"I don't know why you came here," she gasped from her depleted front porch, before I'd finished exiting the rental car.

In truth, I didn't either. Michael's appeal would come down the next day, and his fate was unequivocally out of my hands. Rachel and I hadn't spoken in the three days since she requested to be taken off of the Tiegs case, which was the day after we decided to stop trying to date one another. I stayed behind to tie up loose ends and address any of the client's remaining needs—"closing," we called it at NSI. But what I was really doing there: I couldn't say.

For weeks, Rachel and I had asked Therese if she would talk to us about Michael; for weeks she denied our request. It wasn't until December that she relented, citing exasperation with my escalating torrent of phone calls. With the final appeal so close to its resolution, it hardly mattered what she had to say.

"Like I said, I just think it would be helpful for us to talk."

I trod cautiously toward the porch, my palms outstretched, the way you might approach an armed bank robber or a grizzly bear. A pair of vicious-looking Doberman pinschers eyed me lazily from the dying lawn.

"Helpful for who?" she called out.

"Look," I said, now making my way up decaying wooden steps to face her, "I'm not the police. I'm not a journalist. I'm on Michael's side; I'm his lawyer, okay? It's my job to watch out for him. I only want to talk."

Therese lit a cigarette, an act that for her required tremendous effort and concentration.

"What's there to say? They said he killed John Jasper—"

"Did he?" I interrupted.

"No!" she snapped back, glaring at me with sudden contempt. "No he did not. John Jasper was not a good man. You know he fucked all the junkies, right? John Jasper took advantage of weak people. He was a worse sinner than anyone who ever stepped foot in that goddamn house."

"Okay, but—"

"They tried to get me to say I fucked John Jasper! I never fucked John Jasper. And Michael, he knew I never did, and there goes your whole reason they said Michael wanted to kill John Jasper supposedly in the first place. There it goes away."

She fumbled with her cigarette, which the heavy wind first

blew out, then blew out of her trembling hand and onto the porch. She didn't seem to notice.

"Why did Michael write in his journal that he wanted to put a bullet in John?" I asked her, as calmly as I could.

"Nothing to do with me, that's for damn sure. The doctors over at Willow Creek said he had to write down all his feelings, so he wrote down his feelings. Besides, Michael saw right through John Jasper. He saw right through to the heart of him. He knew the truth in everybody. He knew what John Jasper was doing, listening to all them broken-down women tell their stories, and then turning right around and catching them at their lowest, and just hunting them down like they was wounded prey."

"That's exactly what Michael said when I asked him," I said.

She lit another cigarette, and studied me skeptically.

"You talked to him a lot, did you?" she asked.

"Sure," I replied. "We talk a lot. For hours, sometimes, when they'll let us."

Therese emitted a gruesome, snorting laugh.

"Hours," she said. "That's funny."

"Why?"

"I mean, Michael, he don't talk much, does he?"

I scanned her dead, cavernous eyes to gauge her sincerity, and, cursing, she dropped the cigarette again.

"Wait, Therese," I started, "when's the last time you went to visit him?"

Just then, a minor crash came from inside the house. A gruff voice within hollered out: "Who's that?"

"Who's that?" I whispered to Therese.

"Nobody!" she answered defensively, just loudly enough that it could conceivably have been meant for either of her interrogators.

"What the fuck, Therese?" yelled the voice.

"It's nobody!" she shouted. This was for him.

Seconds later, a squirrelly man with no shirt on burst open the screen door. He looked to be mid-fifties, but was dangerously thin; in one hand he held the flapping remains of what appeared to be a meager turkey sandwich, and in the other he held a rifle.

"Get back in the house now, Clay," she scolded him, unimpressed by the display.

"Who the fuck is this?" he raved, pointing the sandwich accusatorily at my torso. A renegade fleck of lettuce jumped ship, touching down on my shoulder.

"I'm nobody," I said.

"He's no one," Therese chimed in. "He's a lawyer."

The man abruptly shoved the sandwich between his teeth, freeing his second hand to cock the rifle.

"Whoa whoa whoa," I started.

"He's Michael's lawyer," Therese clarified. "They're about to make a final decision on frying him or not." I wasn't sure how she knew this; it hadn't come up at all. The man lowered his rifle slowly, and let out a protracted "oh" of recognition.

"I'm Leo Brice," I said, extending my hand.

"This here's Clay," Therese grunted dismissively. We shook, the limp sandwich still protruding from his mouth.

"Nice to meet you, Clay."

"Go back inside, Clay," she chided, and he did, without another word.

Something was dawning that upset me deeply.

"Michael talks all the time," I told her as soon as we were alone again on the porch.

"What'd you say?"

"Before, you said he doesn't talk much. That's not true though—he never stops talking, as far as I can tell. When's the last time you even saw him?"

"None of your goddamn business: that's when."

"You know, it's funny—we'd always assumed that you were still coming to visit him; I guess we never really asked."

I began to feel hot in my neck—betrayed, even, by this stranger.

"But it seems like you don't really know him at all—not the version I know. Not the peaceful man. Not the person who's . . . ready to die. And he's ready, Therese, he's ready. How could you not—"

"You watch yourself," she muttered.

"You stuck by him for years," I went on, starting now to fume uncontrollably. I was shaking on the inside—what was this? "You testified for him. How can a person insist on loving someone and stop? When did you stop?"

"Fuck you."

"How can you just leave him to live and to die on his own when you—"

"Shut the fuck up, lawyer!"

"When you love him? You're not supposed to just disappear like that—don't you know that? Don't you know what happens when you are just . . . gone like that? I know what happens, Therese—let me tell you what happens when you go. When you leave someone behind, he has to keep living. He doesn't just stop, he has to keep—"

Therese shoved me meekly in the chest, and the Dobermans looked up.

"Don't you talk to me like that!" she bellowed.

"Did you kill him?" I asked abruptly, and she melted back.

"You did. What am I saying—of course you did! You killed him."

"Fuck yourself!" she barked, and the Dobermans barked, and she recoiled.

"You killed John Jasper. You shot him, and you let Michael take the fall for it. God fucking dammit, Therese. You killed John Jasper, and now you're killing him. You're killing him! You're killing Michael. Don't you know that? You're killing him."

"I didn't ever do a damn thing wrong!" she hissed up at me. "I never killed anybody, and you're a goddamn liar for thinking it."

"Michael doesn't talk much. Ha!" I huffed. "Michael talks. He talks now—talks to me. He can't kill: the person that *I* know, he has no vengeance in him. He's incapable of it. But you: you can kill. You killed, twice already. Three times! You killed John Jasper with a handgun, and you killed Michael when you let him sacrifice himself for you, and you killed Michael *again* when you gave up on saving him. Three times."

"You don't get to talk to me like that," she said, suddenly deflated. "You got no idea how hard it was with him. You got real nerve coming down here and telling me I gave up."

We stared each other down for a long moment, unspeaking until each of our tempers subsided. She brushed the lettuce off of me—in the presence of the rifle, I'd opted to let it rest.

"I'm sorry," I said, and I was. I was sorry I'd come at all.

"You're letting him go," she went on, subdued. "You gotta let him go. I let him go a while back now; it ain't easy. But he's gone. He's been gone. He was gone the day they locked him up—he was never gonna come back again. There wasn't a damn thing I could do to save him; let him save himself or be done with it. He's in the past, lawyer. He's gone."

I noticed that my heart was racing, and maybe had been for some time.

"He isn't gone," I said, my voice cracking slightly.

"He is," she answered.

"He isn't *dead*," I said back, louder. In the following silence, I composed myself. All at once, it seemed so strange to be there, accosting this defeated woman for no tangible reason on her sad front porch. I smiled grimly and nodded, and walked back to the car.

"Well, he ain't here," she called after me, and this was very true.

"Like Maimonides," I said to no one at all, and I left that place forever.

• • •

The phone in room 207 of the Jackson Days Inn rang at exactly 9:08 on the morning of the fifteenth of December, all alto drones and flashing red bulbs. I'd been up, primed, waiting for this moment; I'd shaved for no one, put on a tie that nobody would see. At 8:52 I found a Bible in the bedside drawer, and began to read a story I'd heard about as a kid—a story Michael had also told me in glimpses. It was the story of Daniel, an interpreter of dreams. He went to work for a king with the somehow familiar name of Nebuchadnezzar; after serving as a faithful advisor for a time, trouble came in earnest. Daniel's friends refused to bow down before the king's golden statue, and as punishment for their audacity they were cast into fiery furnaces (only to have their lives spared by God). Nebuchadnezzar went insane, as prophesied, and another king named

Belshazzar took over. This new boss proved no better, drinking wantonly from sacred Jewish vessels and praising every false idol in town. While Belshazzar was busy desecrating the temple, a disembodied hand appeared and inscribed on the wall the words "*Mene, Mene*," meaning: your days are numbered. Now came the birth of an idiom we all know well—Belshazzar's fate was sealed, but only Daniel could read the writing on the wall. That was as far as I'd gotten by 9:08, when the room came alive with the frantic intrusion of an outside call, the one for which I'd been waiting.

"Why is your cell phone off?" asked Boots from across the buzzy line.

"It's not. I don't get very good service down here."

"You know it's almost impossible to call someone in a motel room," he said. "It's archaic. I had to, like, speak to the person at the front desk, and then I didn't have the room number, so she had to look you up—in a book. Not a computer; a book. I heard her flipping through pages. It must be like the land before time down there."

"It has its charms," I said solemnly.

"So Leo," he went on, his voice dropping in tandem with the weight of the discussion, "Martha and Pete—they need you to come back."

"Uh-huh," I said. "Sure—no—I get that."

"The case is over," Boots said matter-of-factly. "It's been over, Leo, and they told me to tell you that they need you to come home. You missed your flight yesterday. They need you back at work—you can't stay down there for this; it isn't good for you."

"I didn't miss it," I said. "That was on purpose. I paid for the room. And I'm paying for the room tonight."

"That's not what—they don't care about the room, Leo. You need to get out of there and you need to come back. You shouldn't be there for what comes next. That's not part of the job; you know this. You need to come back today."

"Okay," I said.

"And if you need to take a little time after that—"

"Okay," I said.

"They said they'd be open to it, if that's what you need. I know this hasn't been easy for you, on top of everything that's been going on."

"Okay," I said. "Thanks."

"Anyway," he said.

"Anyway," I echoed. "That wasn't why you were calling, though, right?"

"No," he conceded.

"Okay. So Boots?"

"You know why I'm calling?"

I swallowed hard, and loosened my pointless tie.

"I have an idea," I said.

Boots sighed heavily over the phone, and then: "Martha wanted me to be the one who . . ."

"When?" I said, after he failed to keep speaking.

"Monday," answered Boots. "They're going to kill him on Monday."

[LIGHTS COME UP on the interior of an ornate courtroom. JIM DASHER, as portrayed by the well-known actor MARK RENARD, fidgets nervously at the defense counsel's table next to his client, the bedraggled

backwoods machinist BEAU WADE DEAN.
Behind the bench sits a stern-looking OLD
JUDGE, and the jury box is filled with a
DIVERSE AND ATTRACTIVE JURY. The court-
room is also full of OTHER PEOPLE.]

OLD JUDGE
Alright, very well then,
Mr. Dasher. Let's hear this
closing argument of yours.

[DASHER pauses to collect himself with a
heavy sigh, then rises to address the
court. He is visibly shaken—a tired, beaten
man who has poured every ounce of himself
into a hopeless case.]

DASHER
Your honor. Ladies and gentlemen of the jury. I stand here
today because . . . well, to
tell you the truth, I really
don't know why I stand here
today. I know that I'm *supposed*
to stand here for my client; I
know that I'm *supposed* to
stand here for justice. And I
know you're probably expecting
to hear some sort of stirring,
heartfelt closing argument. But
I can't do it.

[EVERYONE murmurs and gasps.]

> DASHER (cont.)
> I can't give you what you want.
> I can't change your minds
> about my client, or about any-
> thing else for that matter. So
> I stand here today not for
> him. He's a lowlife, right?
> He's scum? Just another heart-
> less murderer. We're better off
> without him, wouldn't you
> agree? I know I would. So no,
> I don't stand here for him. I
> stand here for America, ladies
> and gentlemen. Because some-
> thing is very wrong in Amer-
> ica. Something in this country
> is broken. Broken like the
> hearts of the victim's family;
> broken like the hearts of the
> family of Beau Wade Dean.

[The ELDERLY MOTHER of BEAU WADE DEAN
bursts into tears in the gallery.]

> DASHER (cont.)
> Broken, yes, like the *criminal
> justice system itself!* And
> what's broken . . . is a prom-
> ise—a simple, sacred promise

our forefathers made to each
other more than two centuries
ago: that this nation would
forever stand for the highest
ideals of justice, for what
Abraham Lincoln called "the
better angels of our nature."

PROSECUTING ATTORNEY 1
[Rising cynically] Your honor,
where is this going?

OLD JUDGE
Yes, I agree. Mr. Dasher, what
is the meaning of all this?

DASHER
Meaning, your honor? Heh. Sometimes I don't even know myself.
I guess I let my emotions get
the best of me. You know, it's a
funny thing, emotions—they can
make you do things you wouldn't
ordinarily do, say things you
wouldn't ordinarily say, even
see or *hear* things that aren't
really there, just because you
want to see or hear them. Just
because you want an explanation
for something that can't be
explained, for something . . .

that has broken your heart.
When we let ourselves be ruled
by our emotions, well, that's
when we crave things like
vengeance. But justice . . .
justice isn't about our emotions. Justice is about mercy;
it's about reason. It's about
looking at a man—a man like
Beau Wade Dean—and saying, I
will listen to your side of the
story. I will listen not with
my heart, but with my head.

OLD JUDGE
Mr. Dasher, if you do not arrive at something resembling a
point very soon, I'm going to
have to—

DASHER
I'm sorry, your honor. In fact,
I'm sorry to everyone here.
Because the truth is I'm not a
very good lawyer.

[EVERYONE murmurs and gasps again.]

DASHER (cont.)
I'm not even a very good man.
In many ways, I guess you

could say I'm a lot like Beau
Wade Dean here. I've lied and
I've cheated. I've let my emotions run wild—I guess you've
seen me do that right here in
this courtroom. But you cannot
hold Beau Wade Dean responsible
for my emotions . . . for my
failings . . . any more than
you can hold him responsible
for the emotions of the witness
who maybe couldn't quite see
through the rain, or the other
witness who maybe couldn't quite
hear over the sound of the
construction noise. That would
not be justice. Because justice
lies in that shadow of a doubt,
in the feeling you're getting
right now, ladies and gentlemen
of the jury, in your heads,
even if it isn't a feeling you
have yet in your hearts. That
feeling . . . is justice.

            PROSECUTING ATTORNEY 2
[Snidely] Objection, your
honor!

                OLD JUDGE
On what grounds?

PROSECUTING ATTORNEY 2
Relevance! What does all this
talk about hearts and heads
have anything to do with . . .
[He struggles for words]

OLD JUDGE
Yes, counselor?

DASHER
With justice, your honor! He
wants to know what it has to
do with justice, and I for one
don't blame him. Because in all
this legalese, well, something
has been lost. And that something . . . is truth—pure,
simple truth. And the truth
is, a man is dead. And the
truth is, he won't be coming
back. And the truth is, executing Beau Wade Dean won't
make a lick of difference. And
you know—*in your heads*—that
you aren't certain what happened on that day. You've got
what we lawyers call a reasonable doubt. And if what I'm
saying is starting to make
sense to you, if you're beginning to feel just that slightest

```
twinge that you're not
sure . . . well, there's only
one thing for you to do. Stop
the bloodshed. Open your hearts
to the family of the victim.
And open your head to the Con-
stitution of the United States
of America. Because justice
deserves more than the brunt
of our emotions. Thank you.


[DASHER sits back down, sweat dripping
from his brow, brooding with an emotion.
Exhausted, he slowly pours himself a glass
of water at the defense table. We cut to
commercial.]
```

There's a science to putting people to death, an actual field of study with concepts and literature and its own name: ktenology. The Austrian-American psychologist Leo Alexander coined the term not long after serving as a medical advisor during the Nuremberg Trials; he'd observed a number of Nazi euthanasia experiments at Dachau, and was well-versed in the means by which a state might execute one of its own. He had a long career at Tufts, broke ground on multiple sclerosis research and the study of various neuropathologies, and even helped police crack the infamous Boston Strangler case. Dr. Alexander died in 1985, and my mother was fascinated enough by his impressive obituary in the local paper that it lingered in her memory for a full year: this is why my name is Leo.

When the state of Georgia decides that they want you to die, here is what happens: the death chamber is a sort of operating theater, and they bind you to a long metal gurney that gets wheeled to the center of the stage; heart monitors are affixed to your chest; you lie in silence while masked attendants pepper you with intravenous hookups, dry for the moment, but not for long; a supervising technician paces the room with purpose, checking at various stations your vital signs and the apparatuses that shortly will kill you; the tubes in your arms coil through small holes in the concrete wall and terminate in another room, where waits a bag of saline solution and a bag of your deadly cocktail; the saline starts to flow; the warden says "alright," and an actual curtain draws back to reveal a third room—this with a plexiglass window for viewing—where a smattering of prison officials, your lawyer, and your uncle by marriage are standing by.

"I will shortly be granted my heavenly manumission," said Michael Tiegs through the window, his voice faint but clear. It wasn't his time to speak, though, and the warden motioned to the supervising technician, who motioned to Tiegs in turn.

"I was thinking," Tom Jones whispered, scratching freely at the thistles of his beard, "maybe this is what needs to happen. I think he's ready. I think it'll bring some peace to some folks; I know it'll bring some peace to poor June."

On stage, they adjusted the gurney so that the onlookers could see. It must have been a one-way window; Michael didn't seem to be aware of us, as close as we were. His face was severely etiolated, and his skin looked slick. The supervising technician seemed unimpressed by the proceedings—neither he, nor the warden, nor the officials huddled to my left, nor even old Tom Jones betrayed any hint of the day's gravity. All was orderly, and the rooms were so much brighter than they'd been in my dreams.

"Brother Leo!" rang out Michael's voice from beyond the plexiglass, and I jolted and gasped. Then again: "Brother Leo!" I was frozen like that: jolt and gasp, paralyzed, mouth gaping, like a fish being hauled up into the suffocating sky for the first time in its life.

"I think he's talking to you, son," whispered Tom Jones; I thought maybe he was whispering because of the prison personnel in the room.

"I know," I said, then, coming to, I turned to the closest official and asked if Michael could hear me through the window.

"No sir," he drawled, and though I hadn't noticed before, I realized now that this was the man in the brown suit. "What you're hearing from in there gets piped in over an intercom. That's why the sound's a little distorted. No, sir, these rooms are all soundproof."

"I see," I said.

"Lotta times, you get the victim's family in here to watch—mommas and grandmommas and orphaned children and all that; brothers with anger in their heart. Can't have them spouting off at the prisoner. Not at a time like this."

The man in the brown suit went back to his cluster of officials, and I turned again to the window in time to hear Michael call out once more, in the throes of some delirium, some clear fever which terrified me to no end.

"Brother Leo! This is a test! This is just a dying body! My sleeping soul, and this is only a test!"

His eyes were wider than they'd ever been, wider than seemed possible. I looked away.

"He's raving," whispered Tom Jones. "He's stark raving mad. Just talking nonsense—what's he even saying, now?"

The warden motioned to the supervising technician, who imparted something quietly to Tiegs. Right on cue, one of the prison officials pulled up alongside me and Tom at the window, a notebook and pen at the ready.

"I've been asked to say words," came Michael's voice through the intercom. He paused a moment, and shut those eyes for the last time, and spoke.

I knew what was coming—he'd recited those words for me just three days prior on my last visit to the neon-lit room. The moment he finished, the warden motioned to the supervising technician again, and a stream of pentobarbital coursed into Michael's arm, anesthetizing him almost immediately. A second signal brought the pancuronium bromide, which petrified his muscular system and stopped his breathing; here he began to seize violently against the gurney. The warden's final motion ushered in the potassium chloride, relieving his spasms and arresting his heart.

"May God have mercy on that boy," whispered Tom Jones as he placed a heavy hand on my shoulder.

We watched the light spill out of him, calm in the going, and this world ended.

• • •

When I left Georgia for the last time, I was drunker than I'd ever been in my entire life. General Sherman burned this state to the ground in 1864; he marched boldly to the coast, ensorcelled by carnage, while James Buchanan waited out the embers of his second life in Pennsylvania. One hundred and fifty years later, I fled Atlanta in the very last row of a walty jet, so

close to the beverage cart I could hardly catch my combusti-
ble breath. We tangoed with every stiff wind the Eastern sea-
board had to offer, dipping and diving and quaking and I swear
making these sounds like breaking metal parts. Each new bit
of turbulence required a corresponding cocktail—such were
my suffering nerves—and I landed in New York a plastered
mess, geminating the Earth with my woozy brain.

As I filed off the plane, it occurred to me that I would not
have to fly again in the near future. And though I felt depleted,
emptied out by the thing that I had seen, for the first time in
months I knew that I was safe from harm. Emily—a terrific
friend, as it turned out, and the only person I knew who owned
a car—had offered to pick me up on the occasion of my final
voyage home. As I crossed briskly from the jetway into the terminal, I was struck by something: it was a motorized baggage
cart. On the way to the ground, a part of my knee that was
not generally permitted to twist in a certain direction did, in
fact, and snapped. The airport spun with the dual force of in-
toxication and searing pain, and I fell silent as an army of
navy-sweatered personnel gathered above me; all I really heard
was soft jazz and a lot of bored folks saying "sir?" One queasy
hour later I found myself in a hospital I'd been to (as a visitor)
once before—when could that have been? There were X-rays
and hushed conversations and I ended up crutching over to a
bright new wing. Medicated and spent, I dozed off in a waiting room until I heard a voice, soft and even, say: "I have a
theory about your knee."

NINE

My eyes bolted open as my mouth parceled together the raw materials of an apology—I was being addressed by a woman in scrubs.

"I said, 'I have a theory about your knee,'" she repeated, adding: "You're not still drunk, are you?"

I had to think about it for the full six seconds it took to prop myself up in the chair.

"Oh," I said. "I mean, no. I'm not. That was for . . . I'm kind of a nervous flier. I mostly just drink on planes. And I had a—I had a difficult week, at work."

"Uh-huh," she mumbled casually, jotting something down on her frayed clipboard. The room was strictly yellow, and beyond the waiting area I could make out sleek machines.

"So I know that this is the sort of question that a drunk person would ask, but . . . is this still the hospital?"

"This is in-patient physical therapy," she replied without looking up.

"And you're my doctor?"

"I'm your physical therapist."

"Oh," I muttered humbly. "Right. You're dressed like a doctor."

"We dress this way here," she answered back coolly, still jotting.

My vision came to rest on the nametag which hung from her cornflower smock: J. Dailey. She was angular and tall, with good posture—or maybe just average, perhaps, for a physical therapist—and a farrago of auburn curls.

"Got it," I said, although she didn't seem to hear.

The ordeal was beginning to come back to me, and I used both hands to prod at the thick black spongy brace wrapped vice-like around my tumid left knee.

"So what's your theory?" I asked, and she looked up quizzically. "You said you had a theory about my knee?"

"I think you sprained your ACL pretty badly," she said, dropping right back down to her clipboard.

"Just a sprain? I felt something snap."

"You were drunk."

This was fair. The therapist finished her notations with a flourish, sighed, then looked me over.

"We won't know anything for certain until a doctor goes over your X-rays," she went on. "But they wouldn't have brought you here if they thought it was something terribly serious. And they definitely wouldn't have left you here, drunk and unsupervised, if they were worried you might cause yourself any long-term damage. I'm going to be assisting you with some things that will help you heal—twice a week, until you're back to normal. Do you go by Leonard?"

"Leo," I said.

"Leo. We're going to get you back on your feet very soon. I'm Jane."

When I hobbled into Aunt Luz's apartment later that afternoon, Lita was in her rocking chair, knitting serenely. Though I'd been gone for nearly two weeks and was now returning injured—luggage jerry-rigged to my crutches— she did not seem to notice my labored arrival in the living room. Rafael Uribe Uribe confronted me uneasily as I poured myself onto the couch. I offered him a hand of peace and fellowship along with a weary "Hola, Rafi," and he skidded away in terror.

"Hola," said Lita at last.

"Hola, Lita," I replied, adding the now requisite, "cómo estás?"

"Bien, bien," she answered back with a far-away smile. She was nearing completion on what looked to be a superlatively warm sweater. "Y tú?" she ventured on after a moment. "Estás herido?" This was rapidly developing into our longest conversation ever, and the Spanish was already threatening to surpass my understanding. *Herido. Herido.*

"Sí," I said, steering the discussion back into the safest harbor of my vocabulary. As a second act, I opted for, "uh, qué?" This seemed to amuse Lita, and she spoke now with sing-song deliberation.

"Te . . . lastimaste . . . a . . . ti . . . mismo?" she incanted, before slowly tapping a long needle against her knee.

"Mismo!" I exclaimed, idiotically. "Sí!" My face had been buried in the cushions of the couch, but I turned to her now in preparation for the coming explanatory effort. "Mismo is 'hurt,' like 'miserable.' And you're asking me if I'm hurt—no! You're asking me how I hurt myself. Well." I gathered myself, and ventured on: "Yo . . . la tengo . . . *mismo* . . . para . . . una . . . motorized baggage cart. Ooh! Aeropuerto. Airport. Yo la tengo mismo para una motorized baggage cart dans la aeropuerto. Sí?"

Lita looked me over sympathetically. She tapped her knee again with the needle, then pointed it at my crutches. Rafael Uribe Uribe had wandered back into the room, and it was difficult to say between the three of us who was most confused by the proceedings.

"Lay-knee," she articulated carefully, "en qué trabajas?"

I had this one. *Trabajas* was work.

"Yo soy una," I began, then faltered. What is a lawyer, anyway? "Yo soy una avocado?"

I didn't have the words to tell her what was wrong, or what I did, or what I'd seen. She nodded quietly, then began again to knit—content, it seemed, to let the conversation drown in the vast and spectacular sea of my linguistic ineptitude. It was a mercy killing.

• • •

I knew a guy back in high school who joined the Army right around the same time the rest of us were heading off to college; his name was Jack, and in my memory he is smart and good-natured. When I heard he was signing up to fight, I couldn't understand it; I hated that I couldn't understand it. How could a person be so willing to give up his life like that, and for what? His country? I felt strongly that I loved my country, but not with anything approaching the same fervor with which I loved being alive. Subjugating that love—subjugating your whole being—struck me as more than merely a gallant sacrifice. It seemed wasteful. A waste of your self, this individual who would not be making a repeat performance. There was a war then, and I know Jack went to fight in it, although I do not know what happened to him there.

Look: maybe I was a coward, and maybe that's the root of it. Maybe Jack knew something I did not about the purpose of our lives. I understood the appeal of heroism and the nobility of valor; I appreciated the supposed romance of war from reading Hemingway. And I admired Jack. But to give everything up? I was never willing to make that sort of sacrifice. For years, I felt awful for having this belief—then, as I got older, it became more difficult to tell the difference between being a soldier and being anything else. Though I never wanted to be anything other than alive, before long, I was subjugating my love to everything.

In Georgia, I piled my body onto the cause of abolition—a war by another name, albeit one which required no bravery whatsoever and which carried scant risk of a sudden death. Rachel thought briefly about throwing herself upon me, but we each recognized the quagmire that lay in store—hence our mutual retreat. Fiona enlisted in fantastical stardom; the casualties included her integrity and the home we'd built together. Emily and Boots surrendered themselves to each other, and forged a lasting peace. Everyone I knew was engaged in some hue of a conflict. We were all at war, even if no one died. But no: somebody died. Michael died.

I've never stopped picturing him as he was in the moment he slipped off of the Earth, and I never will. Candent flesh and utter stillness, his whole self limp, his parched lips home now to unbreakable silence, his eyes trapped forever under the ice of those two heavy lids. When I saw his body in that instant, I understood right away that he would not be back again, not ever, and that all the possibilities we'd opened ourselves up to were false avenues—there was only one future, not infinite but finite, and our trajectory is a single unbending line from light to ash. Michael was gone.

Michael was gone, and Fiona was gone too. Not her body, of course—I could see it still on television whenever I wanted—but the spirit had fled from her. I guess everybody goes after a while. When we die; when we give up what we love. When we let the future become the past, or when we make it so (not with ruthless time but with our own cold wants). And that's just the thing: I can't imagine wanting anything other than to be here forever, even sad, even alone, even after everyone else had gone. I'd gladly be the last one at the party, remembering the party; I'd stay to see them turn off the lights, and even after that, I'd stay.

My favorite poem is "This Solitude of Cataracts," by Wallace Stevens. Fiona read it to me one night not long after we first moved in together; I was hardly listening until I heard her say this: "He wanted to feel the same way over and over." It captured me, this thought, and the poem ends with its narrator desiring nothing more than, among all things, timelessness: that the record might skip on and on forever, petrifying his senses, abolishing "the oscillations of planetary pass-pass," leaving this bronze man free—simply, sempiternally—just to breathe "his bronzen breath at the azury center of time."

When I saw her for the very first time at that awful party, and flailed and failed to dance alongside her fluid form; when we sat together in the self-lit campus theater; when we adversely possessed the whole of the Earth from crusty owners who could never understand our ways; when I lay with her on a hospital bed, and we hatched a plan to find each other long after the world went dark; when each moment made its momentary promise to put an end to the tyrannical regime of calendar and clock—I wanted to feel the same way over and over.

She snatched that feeling away from me, yes she did. She unspooled all of it: future, present, past, all into this jumble I've got now. She took my precious time, and I won't forgive her for that.

In interviews, her voice is different now from the one I know—it's stripped of lilt and quirk, and that slight Wisconsin accent has given way to a universal normalcy. On screen, her body flows in a different way than it once did: more calculated, less burdened. Every place I see her, she is changed, her wonders compromised, her nature tamed, her vulnerabilities scrubbed clean. Her heart—I don't know her heart. Maybe it's this, and maybe this was the problem:

Fiona's heart was a doe: slight, pretty, and fleeting. Fast as hell. You can't approach or it goes.

My heart was a buffalo: old and slow, grotesque and noble in equal measure, and for a long while I was certain that she had used every part of it.

• • •

"When I ask you to do these stretches at home, it isn't a suggestion," Jane Dailey scolded me ten minutes into my second therapy session. I was flat on my back, staring up at a patternless array of ceiling tiles, with my twisted knee raised high in her insistent hands. Every fifteen seconds, she plied that knee into a previously uncharted pose, giving little if any credence to basic ideas about which way legs should bend, or to this particular leg's long, proud history of inertia. She was right, too: I hadn't been doing my stretches.

Jane had a calm demeanor and a curious habit—she never made eye contact when we spoke. Normally, I'd expect myself to mirror this behavior: all my life, I've involuntarily taken on the characteristics and idiosyncrasies of those around me. I slip slightly into the accent of whomever I am speaking with, temporarily abscond with the minor limp of the man I just passed on the street, even mimic the mood of my waitress. My body is an easy host, and yet it could not bring itself to accommodate Jane's aversion. The more she looked away, the more intently I looked at her.

"Jesus, you're stiff," she said, still manipulating my hopeless limb. "I take it you're not a runner?"

"I'm a lawyer," I answered.

"You can be both," she replied matter-of-factly. "Injuries like this one are easier to prevent and recover from if you regularly take the time to stretch, and, you know . . . exercise, from time to time."

"I play basketball, on occasion," I told her defensively, and technically this was true. But only technically.

"Okay," she said. After several rounds of silence, she added, "I wasn't saying that you're out of shape or anything. I just meant—"

"No, I didn't think—"

"Because I'm just talking about flexibility."

"I get it," I said, still trying to meet her eyes, which remained indelibly fixed on my knees. "So you don't think I'm fat, then?"

"Of course not. You're the dictionary definition of lanky.

I just meant you could benefit a lot from increased movement. You'd heal a lot faster."

"I'll keep that in mind," I said, "for next time."

She went on examining me, and I her, for another ten minutes. She prodded; I stared. The both of us were thorough. My preliminary diagnosis was that Jane was studious and dry—she had a level way about her that came out in crisp, unadorned movements and a relentlessly deadpan tone. She spoke calmly and with purpose. She was, as far as I could tell, a top-notch physical therapist. But she was warm in spite of what appeared to be a mostly serious demeanor.

Not warm like Fiona, who was warm like a match: i.e., not warm at all unless you were so close as to be set on fire, at which point she was as warm as one person can be to another, at which point she went out. Not even warm like Rachel, who was warm like a blanket: i.e., statically and steadily generous with herself. No, Jane was warm like alcohol: i.e., working from the inside.

She prodded; I stared, and, as I recall, this went on for a very long time.

• • •

It was 4:45 in the morning on a summer night—I can't remember the year—when a call came in from a number I did not recognize; I was in bed, and Rafael Uribe Uribe was too.

"Hello?" I said, and was met by labored breaths, a pronounced gulp, and words whispered so softly as to render their authorship undetectable: "It's really you."

"Who's calling please?" I asked, and my heart became a sudden rock, my arteries a petrified forest, my throat seized up with eremic want, my hands grew numb, and my face hot, because the moment I asked, I knew.

"It's me, Leo," the whisper revealed. "It's Fiona."

It had been a long, long time since I'd heard her voice, and in my life I would never hear it again—not off-screen, not like this. I rose, and walked in silence to the window. Rafi paced hurriedly away from the room, because dogs know. I wasn't certain what to say. What was there even to say?

"It's 4:45," I enunciated blankly into the phone, sounding, I thought then, like one of those old time and temp recordings. "In the morning." A long few seconds passed by.

"Well, it's only 1:45 where I am," she said, whispering weakly still. I thought that maybe she was drunk.

"In California," I clarified. She might as well have been in outer space; it might as well have been any time at all.

"Yeah," she sighed, "in California." Another half minute elapsed without words.

"Why are you calling?" I asked at last, but I didn't even know if I wanted to know the answer, if there was one. Three thousand miles away and three hours behind me, she began to cry audibly.

"I don't know," she heaved, keeping her heavy sobs low. "I don't know, Leo. I just wanted—*ha-pfffffffft*—sorry; I blew my nose. I just wanted to hear you I thi-hi-hink."

"I didn't even know you were still out there," I said calmly, but the calm came from shock and not from steely nerves.

She hiccupped, and let go of other wet sounds.

"What do you me-he-hean?"

"I mean, I've seen you on television," I replied, trying my damnedest to sound, I don't know, aloof, or at a minimum steady. "I know that you exist still, or some version of you, I guess. I know that you're definitely still alive. But it doesn't really seem like you anymore—you look very staged, out there, not at all how I remember. What happened to you, Fiona? I mean, Jesus, what the hell happened? Can it really be true? Did you really become all the things you always—and so fast— what happened? Why are you calling, Fiona? I'm really asking. What is it that you want?"

And though I wasn't trying to upset her, this made her cry openly for five whole minutes. No words were exchanged; I gave her time to even out. When she spoke again, she was nearly calm. She said:

"There is something I wanted to ask you. I know you don't owe me anything anymore, but is it alright if I just ask you this one thing, because I feel like I really need some help right now?"

"Sure, Fiona," I said. "What is it? Go ahead and ask."

"Was I a good girlfriend?" is the thing she asked.

"Heh," I ejected, reflexively. It took me a moment to: "Wait, is that a serious—no!"

"I wasn't?"

"Fiona, are you being serious? No! Of course not."

I felt it all rising up inside of me, all at once: every bit of that poison I'd stored away.

"Why?" she asked, her voice leveled, every trace of her tears washed clear.

"I can't tell if you're being serious."

"I am."

"That's insane. You're just . . . insane."

"Leo!"

"You were a terrible girlfriend! You can't . . . you have to know that. Right?"

"You're being mean on purpose," she said, and in that moment I wanted nothing from this world but the words that would make her cry forever.

"You left me for another man!" I shouted, and I knew it wasn't what I wanted; I knew it sounded somehow insignificant in the face of all these endless things.

"I meant before that, *obviously.*"

"You left me for another man—that's, like, the top thing you can't do—"

"Leo," she whimpered, "you're being mean right now, and I obviously meant before that." I took a long, deep, breath, but my temper was on the lam now and it would not be coming back.

"There is no 'before that,' Fiona. You're the captain of the Titanic asking if he was a good captain! Sorry, I meant *before* the iceberg! No. I'm sorry, and it's been a long time now, and things have changed, but you still should know that you were bad; you were titanically bad. If you get nothing else out of this conversation—and maybe it's best that you don't—you should know that you were a bad girlfriend. You . . . *cannot* . . . *possibly* think otherwise."

Across the line, she breathed out recklessly.

"Just please—I want you to tell me I'm special," she said, and it sounded so childish.

"How would I even . . . I don't know. I have no way of knowing if you're special or not. You used to be. I know that. Okay? That's the best I can do for you."

I huffed like a monster; I was agitated still.

"I'm the same," she asserted desperately. "I'm telling you I'm still the same."

"You aren't. You just aren't, Fiona. It's fine now—it is—but you aren't the same. Look, Fiona, if you really want to get into it right now, let's get into it. Let's get real, right now, okay? I don't want anyone to hurt anymore, but if you want to talk, we can talk. So I'll say this. The thing I liked most about you, back then, when it was us, was that you weren't like other people, and the deep-down truth, I think, is that being different also happened to be the thing you liked least about yourself. So, in a way, you got what you wanted now, right? You're not different anymore. Which is fine—it's great, I'm sure. I'm really . . . I'm not happy for you—I can't lie about that—but I am, I guess, neutral for you at this point. And I'm sorry, but I think what happened is: you traded in special for normal, because special was too hard."

"What's normal?" she asked me in earnest.

"Normal, I think, is wanting things to be easy. It's getting by, I guess, and being content with getting by. It's not a bad thing. Not at all. I think I'm getting to be more normal too, in another sense. It's being happy with just this one life, maybe, and maybe it's accepting the idea of death, you know, just being okay with it all. Normal is fine. It's okay. It's . . . maybe it's the way we used to talk about other people. Do you remember *other people*? How they weren't like us?"

"I am *not other people*. I am Fiona—"

"Fox-Renard?"

"Haeberle! Fuck you, Leo; I can be both."

"No," I told her, fully awake now at last. Fully calm. "You cannot be both. You only get to be one person, Fiona, and you picked Fox-Renard, the movie star. You picked that, and that's fine. But Fiona Haeberle—she's just the past now, and that's fine too. That's where she belongs: only in the past. Just memories, now. Okay? She's finished. We're finished. And it's fine."

She was quiet on the other side, but for short defiant breaths.

"You don't have to be mean," she told me, more gently than I'd ever heard her speak, and more wearily as well. "I know how badly it stung you when I left. I know this. I know that you don't understand why I had to go, and I didn't give you a very good explanation when I did. And I know—I never said I'm sorry for that. I'm so sorry, Leo. Leo, I'm so sorry."

I let her apology hang there in the silence to ripen or to rot. But to my everlasting surprise—to my everlasting relief— it didn't do anything at all. The moment it came, it went; I nearly gasped at how slight it all felt, how the experience seemed only to glance past me like a curious stranger on a busy street. I'd always believed that, if it came, it would meet me head on, that I'd face it down like prey and peer into its depths and wail against it so zealously that folks would speak of the spectacle I had made for generations to come. It did nothing to me, and at last, *at last*, I wanted to do nothing back to it. And so after a moment I spoke.

"Well . . . alright," is what I said. "But I'm not sure what the point is now. You don't get to make it better, or make it not-have-happened, in this life or in any other, no matter how badly you feel in retrospect, if you actually do feel badly."

"I do," she said.

"And that's great," I told her. "That's really . . . nice . . . to hear. But it doesn't change anything that happened in the past, and it won't change anything that's going to happen in the future. And I guess it doesn't change the present either. And you know what? That's okay. It is. Okay. We don't need to change those things. Not anymore. And I'm sorry, too. I'm sorry for my parts of it too. Really. But it's fine now."

On the other end of the line, she emitted a long, dramatic sigh.

"I don't want you to hate me forever," she said.

And I said, "I don't hate you. I'm not thrilled that I have to remember you sometimes. But I don't hate you. I don't care enough about you anymore for that, and I don't mean that in a mean way—it's just . . . a matter of time. That's just what time does. It makes all of your feelings go away. Every feeling you ever have, has to eventually end up gone. And everything we went through, the good and the bad, it was all just feelings, Fiona. Strong ones, sure, of course, but those go away just like the rest of them. They go away. You shouldn't be surprised when they go."

"I don't believe you," she replied. "I don't believe you for one second, Leo. Some feelings are forever—no matter what I did, you know that the feelings we had were different. They were the forever kind. Eternal. You know that. It was too much for me, sometimes, but . . . I knew that."

We were both quiet then, and for a long while. We breathed at each other. I looked out through the window and down on the street: there were kids out there. It didn't feel like the morning.

"I was in Delhi last month," she said at last, and she spoke so, so carefully. "Mark's filming a movie there. It's really beautiful there, Leo. It's charming. Do you remember how we used to talk about going to India? About taking it—you know," and here she raised her pitch, "adverse possession!" and here she lowered it: "Do you remember?"

"No," I said. I lied. I remembered.

"Yes you do," she breathed. "You do."

"So did you?" I asked her in spite of everything.

"Did I what?"

"Did you take it? Did you make Delhi yours?"

She sighed briefly.

"That wasn't how it worked," she said. "You can't take things alone. That wasn't how it . . . it isn't how it works anymore."

"So," I responded, "you didn't adversely possess Delhi."

"No," she said. "But I was there."

Next came another period of silence, which lasted—it's not possible to know. I knew this was going to be the last time we ever spoke to one another, and I couldn't hang up quite yet.

"I think I might come to New York very soon," she said some time later, "to do a play."

I didn't answer for a while, and then I said, "I bet Mark will be thrilled."

"Why do you say that?" she asked.

"Uh, because he told me on numerous occasions, back when he was not your husband but rather the super-dumb guy we made fun of together, that he couldn't wait to get out of New York."

"Please don't call him dumb, Leo" she said. "It makes you sound so petty."

"I'm joking around, Fiona. Shouldn't we at least be able to do that? To joke around? Actually, if you want to get technical, I'm not *literally* joking around: he told me that New York was 'a real mindfield.' I remember that specifically: he said it was 'a real mindfield,' because it was fraught with all of these obstacles for working actors, and I said, 'are you saying mind-field?' and he said that he was, and when I asked him where that expression came from, he said—and I will never forget this—he said that it was a very popular term, and he was surprised I'd never heard of it, and that it was 'a *metaphor*, ahem, for when something is so dangerous that it's, like, a threat to the whole entire field of your mind.' Mindfield. Your husband told me that."

"Oh come on," she said, lightening, "he's not that dumb."

"Are you positive?" I asked, and she yielded one small giggle.

It was light out now, and I was beginning to notice how tired I'd been feeling. I could hear Fiona shifting around on the other end of the connection, growing serious once more.

"You're never going to forgive me, are you?" she asked, sighing.

"I'd rather just forget," I answered honestly, right away. "It's not about forgiveness, okay? It's about just putting it away where it belongs: in the past. That's where I've put you, and it's where you ought to put me, too. We can do at least that for each other, can't we? I swear to God, it's just as good as forgiving. It's better. It's the cleanest way out. I'd like you to forget me."

"I can't," she countered, "In spite of everything, I just . . . I don't regret leaving, Leo. I'm sorry for how I went away, but I'm not sorry that I did. I'm sorry, just, that I *had* to. Maybe it was wrong, and maybe we would have had something really special together for a long time—infinite Earths, remember?"

"I remember that," I said.

"I'm sorry I called," she said, "but sometimes I get sad, and I thought that maybe it would help . . . help both of us to talk for a minute."

"And did it?" I asked her.

"Not really," she said. "You?"

"Heh," I replied, "no, not really."

"Goodbye now, Leo," she said at last. "I'll catch you next time."

She hung up the phone, and I slipped away from the window, away from the buzz of the floodlights and the boys down below drawing lazy figure eights on the pavement with their bicycles. I drifted into the living room, where Lita and Rafi were awake on the rocking chair.

"Hola," said Lita, smiling, as I entered. She could probably hear the whole thing—not that she could understand the words.

"Hola," I said back, smiling too.

"Dónde está Jane?" she asked.

"Jane está fuera de la cíudad en una conferencia," I answered.

"Eso es bueno. Y tú? Cómo estás?" she asked deliberately, rocking and grinning and stroking the fur under Rafi's loose collar.

"Tres bueno," I answered, confusing my Spanish and French again.

Lita smiled down at Rafi, who smiled up at Lita, who chuckled softly to herself and corrected me: "*Muy bien.*"

"Sí," I said, "bueno y sano."

"Sí, bueno y sano," she murmured back.

• • •

A few weeks after I sprained my knee, one of Aunt Luz's sisters called to ask me if I wouldn't mind babysitting her four-year-old daughter that night. Boots was out of town on a case, but I wrangled Emily and Sona to come revel in the apartment, appease the dog, and help me to entertain little Elise. At twenty-seven, I'd never been asked to take care of a young person before, and I explained to my friends that assembling a broader network of sitters was likely in everyone's best interest. Emily estimated that she'd logged upwards of a thousand billable childcare hours over the course of her life, and eagerly signed on; Sona claimed that all children hated her, but wasn't about to pass up an opportunity to shower in Luz's palatial master bathroom, which made her own look like "a fucking rat trap."

"Are you really dating your physical therapist?" she asked on her arrival.

"Hola," Lita called out from her rocking chair.

"Hola, ma'am," Sona answered without looking over. "Leo, you're dating your physical therapist?"

"I'm sort of trying to, I guess. Yes. We just started."

"Okay," she said, then glanced over at Lita, who was lovingly stroking Rafi's gnarled pelt. "Is that the old lady you live with?"

"Don't be rude, Sona," I admonished her.

"She doesn't speak English, right?" she countered.

"No."

"Then it isn't rude. And she's very old. That's her?"

"Yes; that's her," I said.

"And that's the dog?" she asked, indicating Rafael Uribe Uribe with a swift twitch of her head.

"Of course that's the dog."

"Okay," Sona went on. She was taking the measure of the evening. "And the kid gets here when?"

"She's being dropped off in half an hour," I replied.

"Okay," she said, nodding in begrudging approval. "This will be fine. When Emily gets here, this will be fine."

Emily got there, and the kid did too, and the six of us—Elise, Rafi, Lita, Sona, Emily, and I—promptly took in a buoyant, computer-animated film about a shark who was friendly but misunderstood. We ate a great deal of popcorn, and only two of us cried during the movie. Later, while we were making drawings, Elise asked me if I was her uncle.

"No, sweetheart, I'm not," I told her.

"But my mommy said you were my Uncle Lee-Lo," the little one sang, about as adorably as you might imagine.

"Well," I began to explain, "I'm friends with your mommy, and I'm friends with your Auntie Luz, too. And I'm friends with your Abuelita, and I'm friends with Rafi. And sometimes when people say 'uncle' what they really mean is 'friend.'"

"You're not my uncle?" she clarified.

"Not technically," I answered.

"So who *are* you?" she cooed, then peered up at Sona and added an emphatic: "Who *is* he?"

"Elise, this is Leo," Sona responded. "He's a self-hating egomaniac."

"Stop it," I said.

"He's a very confused young man," she went on. "For example, he's rushing into something with his physical therapist, if you can believe it. I mean, come on, right?"

"Very funny," I said.

"He's hard to pin down, Elise. A real mystery, this one is."

"Thanks for that, Sona," I said.

"No problem, Uncle Lee-Lo," she replied.

When it came time to put Elise to bed, I released Emily and Sona from active duty, freeing them to start in on the evening's wine. I searched for a decent story from among the scant collection of children's books gathering dust in the room that had belonged to Luz's youngest daughter, and chose the only one I recognized.

"This is an old story, Elise. Older than me. Definitely older than your mom and dad; it's probably even older than your Abuelita. It's called *The Velveteen Rabbit, or How Toys Become Real*, and it was written by a woman named Margery Williams."

"Okay," she said sleepily.

"Okay," I said. "Are you ready?"

"Mmm-hmm," she nodded, and I opened the worn front cover.

"Alright. '*There was once a velveteen rabbit,*'" I began, "'*and in the beginning he was really splendid.*'"

Elise burrowed into the side of me like a cub, and lubberly rubbed her eyes. Were we ever that young, my friends and I? No, we were not. Not according to my memory—in my memory, there is nothing at all before the first grade.

"'*For at least two hours the Boy loved him, and then aunts and uncles came to dinner, and there was a great rustling of tissue paper and unwrapping of parcels, and in the excitement of looking at all the new presents the Velveteen Rabbit was forgotten.*'"

There are enormous gaps in my memory; I really only kept the few handfuls I could draw from the ocean of all that's happened, and one day every last drop of it will slip through my fingers. Losing memories is easy, and looking back—there are things I went through that no one can recall. Much of the past is as obscure, now, as the whole of the future.

"'*He was naturally shy, and being made only of velveteen, some of the more expensive toys quite snubbed him. The mechanical toys were very superior, and looked down upon every one else; they were full of modern ideas, and pretended they were real.*'"

A faulty memory could help explain why we don't remember having existed all those many times before. If I went back to the hospital where I was born, I'm sure I'd have no sense that I'd been alive there once: I wouldn't remember the hospital; I wouldn't remember me in the hospital.

"*For nursery magic is very strange and wonderful, and only those playthings that are old and wise and experienced like the Skin Horse understand all about it.*"

Maybe there are things about Fiona I don't remember all that well. I remember lying, side by side, in a hospital.

"*What is real?' asked the Rabbit one day, when they were lying side by side near the nursery fender, before Nana came to tidy the room. 'Does it mean having things that buzz inside you and a stick-out handle?' 'Real isn't how you are made,' said the Skin Horse. 'It's a thing that happens to you.'*"

I hope that I forget all of this—every last moment on Earth, and especially the best ones. I hope I forget my friends. I hope I forget Fiona and her goddamn theories. I hope I forget the way that Jane and I loved each other fully for so many years. I hope I forget Michael in the moment he went away. I hope I forget the past.

I like remembering it now, of course, while the present is still mostly intact. But someday I'd like to forget that I was ever here, because if I can forget all this, it opens up the possibility that I've forgotten it all before—once, or a million times. And that would mean—what? That I can do it all a million times again. That I can repeat myself. That I'll have another chance, an endless series of chances, to dance against my better judgment at some awful college party. That I'll learn to love and loathe the law. That I can wander the earth, an absent-minded fool, not saving Michael on an endless loop. A near-syllogism: if I've forgotten that I've come this way before, there's still a chance I can come this way again. Have I already said all of

this? Have I already let go of Fiona a million times before? Can
I live it all out in endless iterations, and hurt, and forget, and
grow, and forget, and forget, and forget, and forget. If so, I am
confident that I can make death irrelevant. If I can only come
back, and meet her again, and lose her again, and hurt, and
get better, meet Rachel, and lose her, again, meet Jane, and
keep her, and go, come back—I hope I'm repeating myself. I
wanted to feel the same way over and over. In spite of everything, I want to learn it all over again.

   " 'Does it hurt?' asked the Rabbit. 'Sometimes,' said the Skin
Horse, for he was always truthful. 'When you are Real you don't mind
being hurt.' 'Does it happen all at once, like being wound up,' he
asked, 'or bit by bit?' 'It doesn't happen all at once,' said the Skin
Horse. 'You become. It takes a long time. That's why it doesn't happen often to people who break easily, or have sharp edges, or who have
to be carefully kept.' "

   Elise had long since gone to sleep, her small bright body
turned to lead in my weary arms, but I read on, faintly, all the
same. I wanted very badly to remember what came next.

   " 'He thought of those long sunlit hours in the garden—how happy
they were—and a great sadness came over him. He seemed to see them
all pass before him, each more beautiful than the other, the fairy huts
in the flower-bed, the quiet evenings in the wood when he lay in the
bracken and the little ants ran over his paws; the wonderful day when
he first knew that he was Real. He thought of the Skin Horse, so wise
and gentle, and all that he had told him. Of what use was it to be
loved and lose one's beauty and become Real if it all ended like this?
And a tear, a real tear, trickled down his little shabby velvet nose and
fell to the ground. And then a strange thing happened.' "

TEN

Three days before he died, I'd gone to visit Michael for the very last time.

"I wasn't sure if you'd come back down to these parts again," he said as the guards walked him into the neon-lit room. "Brother Leo, let me just ask you: are y'all friends with the Governor?"

"I'm not."

"Is there some soup-ream judge up in our nation's capital who owes you a mighty big favor?"

"There isn't."

"Well, did you happen to bring with you a fast car and some heavy ammunition today?"

"I did not."

"Alright," he said, "so I'm correct in thinking that you're here at last as a brother and not, as you've long maintained, as my alleged attorney?"

I smiled at this, although I knew that below the banter he was just as tense as I was.

"That's right, Brother Michael," I told him.

The guards freed his hands from their restraints, and he swung his brittle wrists around wildly, provoking a flurry of cracks.

"Well I'll be damned," he said flatly, adding seconds later: "Get it? I'll be damned?"

"I get it, Michael."

"I'm told they call that 'gallows humor,'" he chirped with a self-satisfied air.

"Indeed they do," I replied. He seemed more animated than usual, and I cringed at the sight of him, alive but damned, squirming like a child in his folding chair.

"I don't suppose," he said delicately, "I'll have the pleasure of speaking with Sister Rachel again?"

"I'm afraid not," I said—we'd broken things off a few days before.

"Well, that right there is a mighty shame," he declared. And then: "I heard you met my own lost lady?"

"Who, Therese?"

"The one and truly," he said, grinning weakly.

"How did you know about that?"

"I hear things," he said. "You ain't my only source of news and information, Brother Leo."

I smirked at him, but didn't follow up. As was our custom in moments of gravity, we let a long, pregnant pause come to term in lieu of further discussion.

"So Monday's the day," he said with resignation at last. "The bitch of it is, there's so much more I wanted to learn about while I was around. So much more I wanted to think about, and say. No time now."

"Have you thought about it?" I asked, then immediately regretted asking, then continued anyway. "Have you thought about what you'll say at the end?"

Michael laughed a little to himself, a sort of private laugh I knew I wouldn't be able to understand—not yet.

"You mean have I thought about my words," he said, staring off beyond me.

"Your last words," I corrected him.

"There's the rub, I suppose," he said, then looked back to me. "That would be Brother William: 'there's the rub.' I read all that too. Shakespeare. Plato. Not just the liturgy. More to truth than faith, you know."

"I certainly hope so," I replied. "What do you mean, 'there's the rub?'"

"My brother, don't you spot my meaning? There can't be any 'last words' in'smuch as there ain't no 'last.'"

It was my turn to laugh a little to myself.

"Of course, Brother Michael."

"But you still want to ask the question," he continued, and ran a slow paw west-to-east across his stubble.

"If it's alright with you. Have you thought about the words you'll say before the execution?"

He closed his wild eyes so tightly I was certain they'd burst, and began softly to speak:

"I believe in one God, the Father Almighty, maker of Heaven and Earth, and of all things visible and invisible, and in one Lord, Jesus Christ, the only-begotten son of God, begotten of the father before all worlds; God of God, light of light, very God of very God; begotten, not made, being of one substance with the Father, by whom all things were made. Who, for us men and for our salvation, came down from heaven, and was incarnate by the Holy Spirit of the Virgin Mary, and was made man; and was crucified also for us under Pontius Pilate; he suffered and was buried; and the third day he rose again, according to the Scriptures; and ascended into heaven, and sits on the right hand of the Father; and he shall come again, with glory, to judge the quick and the dead; whose kingdom shall have no end. And I believe in the Holy Ghost, the Lord and giver of life; who proceeds from the Father and the Son; who with the Father and the Son together is worshipped and glorified; who spoke by the prophets. And I believe in one holy catholic and apostolic church. I acknowledge one baptism for the remission of sins; and I look for the resurrection of the dead, and the life of the world to come."

A minute passed in stillness, and then:

"Olam Haba," Michael said, opening his eyes at last.

"What's that?" I asked. " 'Olam Haba'—what is that? Is that part of the last words?"

"No," he replied, "that part's just for you, Brother Leo. It's pretty much sort of the Jewish version of the words. It's a heck of a lot shorter in Hebrew."

"But what does it mean?" I pressed him, and a brief glow crept back into his face.

"According to your own tradition—to Jewish tradition, that is—when you die, your soul is brought to judgment. And if you lived a good life, you enter into Olam Haba, which means: the World to Come. Now, that old big-thinker Maimonides, he taught that the soul lives inside the body the way a person lives inside a house."

He paused, and stared directly into my eyes before continuing.

"The way a person lives inside a prison. You die, and the

soul sort of just peels away. And it goes on without the rest of you, living other lives in other worlds."

"I didn't know that," I said.

"It's the closest thing y'all got to a resurrection," he explained apologetically. "That's pretty much it."

I decided later that there was no world to come. Not on some distant planet in utero, at least—not out beyond the things we've come to know. Our tomorrows, I thought, are the ones we've always heard about; our future is here.

And then, later still, I came to think: well, maybe that's not true, and maybe I can count on coming back this way over and over again.

Even later, I will come to understand that we don't get to know. It's good that we don't get to know.

When the time came, I stood to leave the neon-lit room once and for all, and I was shaking.

"Brother Leo," he called out to me, and I froze; I couldn't turn around to face him. "Brother Leo?" he said again, his voice cracking just slightly.

"I have to go now, Michael," I whispered with my back to him still, but it circumnavigated the whole of the Earth and he heard me.

"Leo," he said. "I'm so . . . sorry, Leo. I did it."

• • •

Three Mondays after the Monday that Michael was executed, I made my way back to the sparse, gutty offices of the New Salem Institute. The first person I saw there was Martha, beaming.

"He lives!" she hollered down the hallway and through the still-parting elevator doors, and I winced at the sudden attention.

"Hi, boss," I sheepishly replied.

"Come on; come in, come in," she said, ushering me into her office. "A little bird told me you'd be dropping in today, Leo. I'm beyond glad to see you. Look at you—you shaved!"

"So I did," I said, leaning my crutches up against the doorframe. I flopped my body onto the leather couch, and sighed for the effort.

"You look like a person!"

"Thanks."

"A real person, I mean. A person who is thinking, perhaps, about coming back to work?"

The time I'd spent away after Georgia had been mostly given over to recovery (of a life and, less gravely, of a ligament). This had been fruitful, I'd thought; Lita and Rafi were always there, so I never was left alone. Boots and Sona came around to indulge my lingering questions and wean me off of remorse. Even Rachel was speaking to me again. And now there was Jane. If the future wasn't entirely bright, at the very least, for the first time in ages, it was there. I could see it.

"I was hoping we might talk about that," I said, and Martha whisked a thick gray binder from her desk. "I, uh," I started, and noticed she was paying no attention to me whatsoever— she was rifling through the file. "As you know, Martha, I had a hard time . . . getting over . . ."

She gathered, then lofted, the binder, and it landed heavily on the open seat next to me on the couch. A splotchy stamp on its front read LA-DOC B19411607-2013 PERSONAL AND CONFIDENTIAL.

"Denard W. Cope," she said.

"Martha," I began.

"We got a ripe one here," she continued.

"I'm just not sure I can handle—"

"You talk about your all-time terrible lawyers, Leo—this guy's counsel takes the cake."

"I was hoping—Martha, I was hoping we could maybe talk—"

"Here's what you're gonna do: you're gonna go to Louisiana, okay? You ever been to Louisiana? It's crazy. You're gonna go down there, and you're gonna meet this guy, get the scoop, figure out our best play. You're first chair on this—you and Boots. And Leo—Leo, look at me."

I did.

"Leo, this guy—what'd I say his name was again?"

I took a long breath, and repeated it steadily: "Denard W. Cope."

"Yep. Cope. Leo, you might not save this guy. He might die. I know you understand that now—I know you know what that means—but I need to hear you tell me that it's alright. You know it's alright, right? You're gonna get back on the horse, yes?"

I leaned in from the couch, my left hand absently tracing the edges of the case binder. A smile evolved on my clean face, and Martha smiled right back. Stashing the dossier under my arm, I propped myself up, collected my crutches, and began to move with purpose.

"Good man," she said warmly.

"I almost forgot," I said, and dug into my jacket pocket. "I brought a couple of these back from Georgia like you said, but it took me a while to—look, I'll be honest: they went rotten. This one isn't quite the real thing; I actually bought it on the street on the way over. It isn't what you wanted, but, you know, it's actually even better, because it's what's here."

I tossed the little morsel, and as I started out the door it described a perfect arc from my hand to hers.

"What the hell is this?" she called after me.

It was a New York peach.

. . .

James Buchanan lived to see the world go on without him, and for that reason he died with a wisdom that Lincoln could never grasp. He died like Mithridates, just a moment too far beyond the future, and not like Socrates, on whom the poison worked. I myself lived for a very long time, and that was good. It took me years to mend the broken oarlock of my life—but I did become happy later on in the story, someplace off-screen.

The present carried on, unflinching. It never did get more profound than twenty-two. Jane didn't promise me forever; she didn't promise me an afterlife. Just this one.

We do some things together, but not everything. She is very bad at dancing—maybe even worse than I am—so we took a class, and flailed around, the very worst students there ever were. We made real things Ours: a home, a new city. When Lita passed away a few years later, we took in Rafi, and we also went down to the shelter and got him a friend. There are things about us you don't get to know, but it couldn't matter less.

What's important is: she rehabilitated my leg, and I fell in love with her. I can say this now, in the present tense, because four years after she contorted my stricken hinge, I actually married Jane Dailey. I can speak to her warmth, her grace, the full planet of her love—here in the future, I am free, at last, to remember those things.

And every night when the world ends, I hold her in my

arms. Our dying bodies stick so close together, and it always makes me feel the same way: warm.

A kajillion years later, I wake up.

. . .

"I have a theory about the universe that, if true, will just blow the lid off of everything," Fiona whispered to me from her side of the hospital bed.

"Go on."

She came out of surgery still punch-drunk off of the anesthesia, and as I wheeled her to the taxi stand it started to rain: big hissing drops.

"I was wondering about that theory of yours," I started.

"What?"

"I was wondering about it. About infinity. I was wondering if—I mean, if it's true—I was wondering if it guarantees us a world where it all works out, you know? If it *is* true, and we get to come back as many times as we need, then there should be a version of events where everything's okay."

"Everything is okay," she murmured.

"How will we know?" I continued, though I knew she couldn't understand me now. "How will we know if it's this one?"

In the future, she was gone, and now also in many parts of the past there are whole expanses where she is missing.

I am speaking to you now, Fiona, because this is the end of the world we built up from the soil. We raised it the way you would a child: we taught it to speak our language, spoiled it, steeped it in the stories of our own sacred adventures, watched it grow until it was large, watched it grow until it was larger than both of us, and one day we locked eyes—we watched it die.

You are not supposed to outlive the things you create, but if you do, you have two choices. The first is you can sit at home—elbows on knees, hands clasped and forming a cross with your lips—and stare straight ahead while your mind plays detective, scouring the scene, making wild accusations, planting evidence: a bad cop. The second is you can go for a walk by yourself; that's what you chose. And walk you did, but walk you never did alone.

I saw you in Delhi, picking out new fruits at the dusty bazaar.

I saw you in London, smelling the salt in the gray air.

In Firenze you ate nothing but olives, and in Cadiz you drank nothing but red wine. You dined also in Prospect Heights, on linguini and whole tomatoes.

I saw you in Los Angeles the next time you fell in love, and I saw you years later when that scene came to pieces right before your eyes.

I saw you when the scales tipped, when all the stars turned to so much dust. And for so long, I bled to find those places again; I sweat cold and breathed heavy, kissed you hard on the mouth, wandered the same well-worn streets in my mind. I tried so hard but they were gone, turned to stone by the setting sun, lost to the historical record, captured by the cruel photography of a past that sped mercilessly toward us from behind, that threatened always to catch up with us, to overcome us. Letting go was hard, but it was nothing compared to the letting go that comes next. You know how that goes, don't you? All of our stories begin with the creation of the universe. All of our stories end with its death—when *it* lets go at long last, however many iterations and tenderfooted Leos from now, unmooring itself from the bracing waters of existence. Fiona, if that's true, then I will try my damnedest to stick around for

the extremities of time, and maybe I'll see you there, an ac-
complice in leaving, one hundred trillion years in either direction, before there was light, after there was darkness, my
lips on your forehead when the world seemed right, my hands
in my pockets when came creeping loneliness.

And I'm telling you this because you are the only one who
knows, because I'll never let go of life, or of Jane—I'll forever
love her for not speaking our language. So I refuse to say goodbye to anybody but you, because I know how, now. And I'm
telling you this, maybe, to create some ripple in the still water
we've shared, or to remind you of your place—the large, vacant
room, full of the things you taught me and of words and
silences, which my memory will preserve exactly as you left
it—in the immense, creaking vessel of my private heart. And
though I'm ready to admit that I'm capable of dying, I have a
difficult time believing that I ever actually will. If—*if*—it happens, most likely a hundred years from now or more, we can
call it waiting; I have more faith in time than I do in death,
and the more I think about infinity the more certain I am that
you were right, and that we eventually have to recur. I will be
waiting for that billionth Earth to come along again so I can
find you, the way I have a billion times before, and tell you
about the infinite future, about adverse possession and the
Northern Lights, and about being made whole. And I will be
waiting, again, to let you go. And could we convince the world
to surrender just one more of its countless secrets?

This is not the version where everything is okay. This is
the version where I ask if there is a version where everything
is okay. Fiona, if by whatever coincidence you happen to be
there when I go, explain this whole operation with patience
to anyone who cries. Tell them I'm not yet finished. And if

they need it, do not say that I am in Heaven but rather that I already was. Heaven, ha! It turned out to be a bit of a joke, right? I mean, what good is it now anyway? You wait around there, maybe, for the Earth to break; you wait around to come back and hear, again, the joke about Heaven. Each time, heavenly was how it felt, is how it feels, will be how it will feel. To be gone. To be gone.

ACKNOWLEDGMENTS

I used to be one of those people who, when happening to come across an awards show on TV, and hearing some actor or singer lead off his or her acceptance speech with an ardent "I'd like to thank my agent," would roll his eyes and find it all so cold and trite and ridiculous. I am no longer one of those people. The simple truth is that this book quite simply would not exist but for the talent, faith, wit, and wisdom of Claire Anderson-Wheeler (she of Regal Hoffmann & Associates). For more than three years, Claire has been this novel's principal advocate, editor, and chaperone. She has etched bits of her bright energy on every page, and squired the whole of it safely through every obstacle with characteristic rigor and good humour-with-a-u. In the story of how this book made it from my head to your hands, Claire is the hero. So, yeah, I would like to thank my agent.

Gratitude being a thankfully renewable resource, I turn

next to Laura Chasen of St. Martin's Press. As an editor, her instincts are impeccable; as a literary Sherpa, she is quite simply peerless. Laura is responsible not only for making this a better book, but for making it a book at all—when she brought *The Life of the World to Come* to St. Martin's in November of 2014, Laura ensured that, if you're reading this, it isn't necessarily because you are my mother. I am hugely indebted to her for her keen judgment and ceaseless savvy.

In addition to being the best writer I personally know, Bree Barton is a dynamite correspondent whose timely e-mails from California kept me from deserting this book more than a couple of times. Sergei Tsimberov provided significant guidance. I've never met Dorie Barton or Megan Kurashige, but they were the first people to read the first draft, and their feedback meant a lot to me.

As for Miriam, my family, and all my wicked friends, the acknowledgments section is not nearly enough, except to say that I will acknowledge you deeply for the rest of my days. I'll tell you about it later.